MURDER BY THE BELL

A Murder Mystery

By James H. van Buren

PublishAmerica
Baltimore

ISBN: 1-4137-6762-1
PUBLISHED BY PUBLISHAMERICA, LLLP
www.publishamerica.com
Baltimore

Printed in the United States of America

Dedicated to Nancy,
my best friend and my wife.

CHAPTER ONE

Sunday, June 7th

The bell at the bottom of six feet of water wasn't ringing. It was deathly still. It had drowned.

Cornelius smiled cynically and blinked his eyes several times as he stared at the pool and watched his bell dissolve.

Yes, his magnificent bell was now silent—as silent as a poignant memory—as silent as it undoubtedly had been last night—*before* it had drowned—as silent as it must have been at the moment it was treacherously yanked from its perch. Otherwise—otherwise, surely, someone within earshot would have heard its resonant reverberations protesting the ugly work it was being forced to do.

Curious! Very curious, Cornelius decided as he eased his tired body down onto the hard slab of a cement bench near where he had been standing at the deep end of Jeffrey Endecott's swimming pool. He massaged the pinkie on his left hand and suddenly recalled that this finger always seemed to twitch when he was in the throes of entering into the investigation of a complex new case. My goodness! So long ago and still—a familiar feeling!

Yes, this case would be complex. He could feel it and not only in his pinkie. A drowned man, with a bell's chain around his neck, lying at the bottom of this pool. And— before that, the black hand of the murderer carefully stilling the heavy clapper of a ship's bell in order to—Obviously, not a routine drowning. Strange! Very strange, indeed!

Cornelius shook his head. The bell didn't fit. Already, he could sense this. No, the bell was wrong. Surely, this had to be. That lovely bell—He looked up wistfully at the soft white cumulus clouds floating gently overhead and thought of Emily. How long had it been since he'd sold that ketch? Seventeen years? He counted quickly on his fingers and nodded his head.

Selling that light-of-his-life those many years ago had been a wrenching experience. It certainly had! But alas, there had been no other way. The other Emily in his life, for whom the boat had been named, had a heart that wasn't up to sailing anymore, and so—it was either his boat or his wife which had to go. Absolutely the easiest choice in life he'd ever made.

Cornelius's wistful smile slowly turned into a frown. He should have sold the *whole* boat, maybe—not just part of it. If he hadn't retained, as a momento, that bronze ship's bell which had graced the foredeck of Emily for so many years, then—then sentiment would not have compelled him to give *that* unfortunate treasure to Ethel and Jeffrey as a wedding present eight years ago.

The murder he had been called in to investigate would have still occurred. No doubt. But his beautiful bell would have remained un-profaned and wouldn't now be consigned to the county cache as prime evidence in a first degree murder case.

And just as important, maybe—the peerless retired private investigator,

Cornelius Pire, wouldn't have that queasy feeling now lurking in the pit of his stomach.

Corny shook his head disgustedly as he let his hands gently rub over his disquieted tummy.

He'd solved many puzzling murders in his day, hadn't he. But this one—this one was sadly the first he'd ever even been remotely involved in. He stood up and let his gaze drop down to the pool. He leaned over slightly and studied his reflection in the water. Ugh! His bow tie was askew. Automatically, his hands moved up to correct the unpardonable. With his tie properly positioned, he dropped his hands to his side and inspected the rest of his persona. Ah, good. Yes, otherwise, he was presentable. He looked closely again at his tie and checked its color. Thank goodness! In his hurry to catch that crack-of-dawn plane this morning, he'd still managed to select just the right hue. How many seventy-seven year old men could do that in the dark, do you suppose? Not very many. Navy blue. Yes, just right. Just right for his pale blue seersucker suit.

He ran both hands lightly over his closely cropped curly white hair and noted in the water that nothing up there seemed askew.

Image. Not as important as the gray cells under that white mane of his. Not anywhere near. But—if the image isn't precise, those gray cells won't be either.

Some of his day-gone-by slovenly colleagues obviously hadn't agreed with him on this matter of image. Good men all. But then again—well, their performance hadn't matched his by a long shot either.

Cornelius chuckled.

Ah, yes—the proof is always in the pudding, isn't it.

He straightened up, turned and started pacing slowly back and forth along the side of the pool.

Tony Bleckmore. Dead. Murdered to the silent knell of Emily's bell. Wonder if this deceased gent had any Mafia connections.

Huh! Now, where did that strange notion come from? Might have something to do with the picture of Bleckmore he had seen in the paper this morning. Looks the part, maybe. Piercing black eyes, wasn't it? And a large, drooping mustache. Yes, sometimes people *are* as they seem to be. Suppose it might have been a hit. Probably should ring up some old connections on the East Coast. They might know something about the man. That would help, maybe.

Cornelius paused and rubbed his chin with his right hand.

But then again—maybe it was a bit more complicated than just a hit. Maybe one of the guests here last night had wanted Bleckmore dead. A close group of old friends, Jeffrey had mentioned on the way in from the airport this morning. Old friends? Sometimes *old* friends are *just exactly that*, aren't they.

He leaned over and checked the razor crease in his trousers. Perfect. He then raised first the toe of one shoe and then the other to inspect his spotlessly white leather Johnson & Murphy loafers. Finally, he carefully buttoned the top two buttons of his jacket and turned to leave.

As he walked slowly away from the pool up towards Jeffrey Endecott's imposing manor house, a familiar twinkle appeared in Cornelius's eyes. It was a deceptive twinkle, born many years ago, and one which many malefactors in the past had learned to fear too late for their own good.

Cornelius shoved both hands into his pant's pockets.

Now, let's see. Better take stock. Where was he? He had been asked by Jeffrey last night to fly in here post haste and help authorities find the murderer of Mr.Bleckmore. Well—respect and affection for Jeffrey, and that alone, had gotten him on that insidiously early morning plane, so he had better stop dawdling. Probably the first thing he should do was to return to his room, stuff down two or three pills and see if they wouldn't help his rebellious stomach. Then he'd go to work for the first time in almost four years and attempt to comply with what he'd been asked to do.

Cornelius's pace quickened as he walked up towards the house.

The glint in his eyes brightened.

Ah, yes. It would be kind of fun to get involved again. And for starters, it would be necessary to murder Bleckmore all over again, wouldn't it. But this time, without the bell. Most certainly, without the bell.

CHAPTER TWO

Wednesday, June 3rd

The overhead fan was turning at about the same rpm as the loafing brain of a very large man lying below on a soft leather sofa. Tony Bleckmore had his imposing handlebar mustachio and his cold inky black eyes propped up on a couple of pillows and was surveying the immediate vicinity of his spacious and elegantly appointed third floor condo.

Not bad!

He'd probably said "not bad" to himself under similar circumstances a thousand times. Not bad at all. Comfortable. Fit him to the tee. Starting with the paintings. Abstract Expressionism—that's what this lousy world's all about. Off balance. Wide awake. Wild. Screaming. Everyone on their toes. That's the ticket. Absolutely!

Tony reminded himself again that he liked the way these flaming paintings clashed with the Oriental and Iranian rugs covering the dark hardwood floor in his L-shaped family room. He loved the way the harsh colors and cryptic hieroglyphics seemed to be having a ball fighting one another from wall to wall.

Perfect! He'd decorated this place pretty good. He sure had. Banging heads is what keeps the world alive. For sure!

The piercing intensity of his black eyes softened a little as they rested abstractly on the darkness penetrating a large bay window. The best thing about this joint, he reminded himself again, is that he owned the seven digits here free and clear. Didn't owe a dime, man. Not one thin dime. If that ain't enough to impress the world, what in hell is? Don't make too much difference whether your friends like you or hate you. Naw. What counts—the only thing that counts—is respect. You got respect, you got everything.

"Right?" The silence in the room was broken suddenly by the rhetorical question Tony blurted out to no one in particular.

"Right!" He always enjoyed answering his own questions.

Tony sat up and tossed his legs onto the floor.

Yeah—but that wasn't completely true—almost, but not quite. A man's got to have at least one good friend. Helps if he does. Sure does.

Tony leaned forward, rested his huge forearms on his thighs, and smiled as he thought of Jeffrey Endecott.

Jeff. Good ol' Jeff. The wonder of the man. Jeff was probably the only guy around who had more bread in the bank than he did. Was absolutely, for damn sure, the only guy in the whole bloody world who could screw more dames in one month than he could. And yeah—hard to admit it—but Jeff, baby, was surely the only guy, besides himself, who could manhandle booze all night long and still keep all twelve cylinders purring like a Jag.

Another thing. If Endecott wasn't one of the best known and best loved guys east of the Mississippi, then who the hell was? A venerated, five star VIP. That's what he was. Didn't hurt to have a good buddy like that. And the spillover affect—That didn't hurt his business or himself one bit either.

"Not one damn bit!" Tony's mumbled affirmation interrupted the silence in the room again.

Tony stood up. He decided that the soft Country-Style music flowing out of the stereo at the end of the room was pretty much in sync with his mood. He walked around the couch and then moved lazily a few steps over to the hearth. Turning and placing his arms behind his back, he let the crackling fire warm his hands.

Yeah, thank God for Jeff—a good man—except that he could sure get nutty ideas in his noggin once in a while. Like that crazy party he was hell-bent on throwing at the end of the week. What a lousy crew Jeff was inviting. Dumb-ass idea! Absolutely! Huh—but knowing Jeff, he'd probably manage to make this weekend bash a smasharoo. Sure hope so!

Suddenly, Tony started shivering. What the hell! It's almost summer. There's a fire going. I'm damn near in it and I'm shivering. What's going on?

Tony gave a tug to his warm-up pants. Wrapping his arms around the tawny turtleneck he was wearing, he moved a little closer to the fire and once again let his eyes roam here and there throughout his favorite room.

Not too shabby for a tin-horn cement mixer. Not too shabby. Yeah, but not so good either. Kind of a sad pad, too. Too damn big for one guy to live in alone. Good idea when he bought it and was married to Lena. Ah, Lena—now there's a broad! Never could understand why she wanted a divorce. Couldn't talk her out of it. Oh well, what the hell—she'll be back one of these days. You can make book on that. A temporary cross to bear. But—hey, if he had to make a pick right now, he'd still rather be whoring around with Jeff than to own a broad and a stable full of kids.

Tony moved to the bar. Late. Time for one nightcap before he hit the sack. As he dropped a few ice cubes into a glass, he heard several loud raps on his front door. Startled, Tony's hand jerked and knocked over the glass, sending it onto the floor with a splintering crash.

"Damn!"

He glanced at his watch. Almost midnight. Someone knocking on his door at this hour? What'n hell'd happened to Oscar downstairs? He always phoned before he'd let a stranger by.

Huh! Maybe it was Jeff with a couple of tomatoes. God, he hoped not. Not tonight. He was too damn tired.

"I can't get it up, pal—not tonight," Tony muttered to himself as he moved to the door.

Tony started to open the door. Then he paused.

"Who's there? Jeff, that you?"

No answer. Absolute silence.

Tony stood transfixed. Someone was on the other side of that door. But why didn't they say something?

He turned to move back to the bar when a high-pitched voice came through the door.

"Tony, it's me. Open up."

A broad? Or a guy? Tony couldn't tell. But one thing—it sure as hell wasn't Jeff. Only one way to find out

Tony slid back the dead bolt and flung open the door.

There, standing at his door, was a six foot bucko with a bow tie, porky-pie hat and a nondescript sports coat resting on top of a pair of neatly pressed black gabardines. He was holding onto a large bulky suitcase.

"Hi there!" A knockout smile from under the hat. Also, a soft twangy low tenor voice. "You Bleckmore?"

"I'm Bleckmore. Who'n hell are you?"

"I'm Alfie, pal. May I come in?"

"Alfie?" Tony guffawed. "I don't know any Alfies, thank God, and I'm damn sure I don't wanta start knowing one tonight."

"If you don't know any Alfies, Bleckmore, you're in for a treat. You're going to love me. I'm the pick of the lot."

"I don't care if you're a parrot that farts to the beat of a tom-tom. Now, get lost, OK!"

Tony's arm moved quickly to slam the door shut—but not quickly enough. One size twelve shoe abruptly stopped the door from completing its swing.

"What the hell?"

Tony stared in wonder at the shoe for a moment. Then, he reopened the door and pivoted in anticipation of sinking his balled fist into the superstructure of this annoying foot.

Instead, Tony, along with his fist, froze. The man holding a suitcase and calling himself Alfie was pointing a thirty-eight cannon right at Tony's stomach. The second thing Tony noticed instantly was that this cannon had a silencer attached to it. The sight of that silencer scared Tony more than the gun itself. Instinctively, Tony knew that this punk was no amateur. Amateurs were one thing. He'd handled lots of amateurs—all kinds in his time—but a pro with a suppresser on his rod—this was something Tony had never bargained for—not in his wildest dreams.

"Hi there, again." Alfie's smile had broadened considerably. "May I come in? Second request."

Warily, Tony backed up a few steps where he stood and glowered—obviously waiting for Alfie to make the next move.

"Thank you. Appreciate your invitation, Bleckmore. I kind of thought you might change your mind."

"You shit head! What do you want with me?"

"Reasonable question, Bleckmore. My answer is that I'd appreciate it if you would back up exactly three more steps. This little toy I'm holding doesn't like people too close to it. I'm sure you understand."

"Come in or blow it." Tony's voice was uncharacteristically low and muted. "I'm not moving nowhere."

"Bleckmore, let me tell you something." Alfie's smile had disappeared. "At this distance, this little peashooter I'm holding has an accuracy of plus or minus half a millimeter. It can knock off one of your balls with a sneeze you'll hardly hear. Or it might just as easily shatter one of your kneecaps. Funny thing is—I never know ahead of time which it will be. So, please—one more time, move back precisely three steps—NOW!"

The sudden explosion of Alfie's voice jerked Tony's head back. Simultaneously, he complied as directed.

Alfie moved into the room. He put down his suitcase and used his free hand to close the door and reposition the lock.

"You want to know what I want. I heard you ask, Bleckmore. But before I answer, business first."

Alfie reached into the pocket of his jacket and withdrew a pair of handcuffs.

"Here." He tossed the cuffs over to Tony. At the same time, he kept his gun trained on the Bleckmore belly.

"Nice catch. You notice they're a pair of cuffs. I'm sure you've seen a pair before. You also notice, they're open. So please, put one of your hands in one of the bracelets and close it."

Alfie eased himself down to a sitting position on his upright suitcase and waited for Tony to comply with his request.

The world stopped breathing for several moments while Tony directed his glower alternately between Alfie and the cuffs. Finally, Tony's expression softened. So did his voice.

"Okay, so you're Alfie, and you wanta talk about something. I got your message. I'll listen. But I don't need these damn things on to do that. Let's go over by the fire and sit down, and you can say what you wanta. Okay?"

"Bleckmore—"

Alfie's eyes were boring in on Tony.

"Do you realize that I am sitting in the posh pad of someone who, if he doesn't learn to listen better, is soon going to be either dead or missing part of his anatomy?" Alfie paused for a moment before adding, "Please, the cuffs." Tony slipped his right hand into one of the bracelets.

"Good play, Bleckmore. Now lock it, please."

Tony slapped the bracelet shut and then used his free hand to wipe off his freely sweating brow.

"That-a-boy. Now, let's see how good you are at working in the blind. Put your hands behind your back, please, and cuff your other hand."

Angrily, Tony took a couple of quick steps forward and shook his cuffed fist at Alfie.

"You bastard! What'n hell you trying—"

A dull thump froze Tony's vocal chords and caused him to grab his left forearm. A small trickle of blood began oozing from the scratch on his arm which had been grazed by a thirty-eight slug.

"Jesus, man!"

Tony's face had turned the color of death. He retreated a couple of steps. His eyes caught the pearly white teeth of Alfie's broad smile.

"I'm bleeding, ya god-damned fool!"

"No harm done. Just a little scratch. Here, wipe off that glop with this."

Alfie tossed a handkerchief onto the floor in front of Tony and chuckled as he glanced at his still smoking gun.

"Like I said, not a bad little piece, would you say? It wanted to nick you a little, by golly, and that's exactly what it did."

Tony reached down and picked up the handkerchief. However, instead of using it on his arm, he applied it to his face which by now was bubbling with perspiration.

Alfie stood up and lowered his gun.

"Don't worry, Bleckmore. This baby probably won't go off again. It won't that is, if you continue to be a good boy. Your au-wee better now? Good. Okay, let's try again. Slip that cuff on your other wrist—behind your back—and please, let's MOVE IT."

Again, Tony jumped at the re-explosion of Alfie's usually well-modulated voice. Tony's hands went behind his back, and the handcuffs were snapped into place.

"Super. Another good play. I only wish we didn't have to go through everything twice."

Alfie pulled a soft four inch rubber sponge ball out of his pocket and walked over to within a foot or so of where Tony was standing. The two men stood, squint-eyed, staring at each other.

Alfie broke the silence.

"Bleckmore, I know what you're thinking. You don't like me. You don't like me one little bit. And you're seriously considering just how you might successfully go about kicking me where it hurts. Please don't try. I'm fairly fast, and even if you connected, you'd be dead before I hit the floor. So please, be a sport and turn around."

Slowly, Tony complied.

"Thank you. Now, let's see how wide you can open your mouth— Okay."

Tony remained impassive with his mouth clamped shut—until suddenly, Alfie's left arm clamped itself around Tony's throat and Alfie's right knee rammed into the base of Tony's spine. Tony let out a high-pitched screech. At this same moment, Alfie's right hand jammed the sponge ball into Tony's wide-open mouth. The ball just fit. Tony's mouth partially relaxed on a ball he immediately became very attached to.

Alfie backed away from Tony, who was slumped over in deference to his throbbing back.

"Sorry about that, pal—but as I said—if only we didn't have to go through everything twice."

Alfie pulled a straight chair from a corner of the room and placed it behind Tony. Then he put his hand on Tony's shoulder and pulled him backwards towards the chair.

"Here, sit down and we'll chat. Probably make you feel better if you rest for a couple of minutes before we get on with our little exercise."

Tony sat and tried to use his shoulder to wipe away the profusion of sweat and tears running down his face.

Alfie moved over to his suitcase.

"I've allowed myself only ten minutes in your sumptuous fortress, Bleckmore, and time's a flying. So I'll explain what's cooking while I work, if you don't mind."

Alfie opened the suitcase and extracted from it a cubic foot of block ice. He carefully placed the ice on one of the nearby Persian rugs while he talked.

"I'm an artist. I'm an artist who gets well paid to deal with annoying people. Usually, my clients select mean, nasty characters like yourself to work with. Makes the job kind of fun. Occasionally, however, they give me a guy wearing a white hat. You know who I mean—a good guy. And well, when that happens, it makes my job a lot tougher. You understand what I'm saying, I'm sure."

15

Alfie reached back into the suitcase and pulled out a long half-inch piece of coiled rope.

Tony's eyes had been following Alfie's every move. Suddenly, Tony froze as he spotted the noose fashioned at one end of the rope Alfie was holding loosely in one hand. A muffled groan managed to force its way through the rubber ball.

Alfie moved briskly back to Tony who was slumped over in his chair Alfie glanced up at the overhead beams.

"What do you know. We won't have to move you an inch. You're absolutely where you want to be. Aren't we lucky."

Deftly, Alfie tossed one end of the rope over the beam. As he caught the rope on its way down, he used his other hand to position the noose around Tony's neck.

"Stand up, pal."

Alfie added emphasis to his request by pulling the slack out of the rope and then exerting a little pressure on Tony's neck. Quickly, Tony's back straightened into an upright position in the chair.

"That's a sport. All the way up now."

More pressure. Slowly, Tony rose to his feet.

Still holding onto the rope, Alfie moved over to the block of ice. He picked it up and placed it carefully right behind Tony. Again, he applied more pressure on the rope. Tony's head craned to one side in obvious discomfort.

"Bleckmore, listen to me. Listen to me—okay? I can see you're very uncomfortable, and I think I can help you. Take a step backwards and up. Got a little platform here. Should ease the strain a little. Make you a bit more comfortable. Careful though. Might be a little slippery."

Again, Alfie pulled on the rope, and his smile reappeared as Tony placed first one foot and then the other on the block of ice.

"Nice play! Your best move yet!"

Alfie took almost all of the slack out of the rope and fastened the loose end securely to a nearby pillar supporting several overhead beams.

Tony's eyes were closed. His face was drenched in sweat. Never—never had he contemplated an end like this. Hogtied! Hogtied and completely outwitted by a turd who wouldn't have had a chance if only he hadn't been half asleep. What a shitty way to go.

Tony's bleary mind couldn't decide whether he was more upset about dying or not being able to talk. It wasn't a matter his mind dwelled on long, however, because absolute terror was rapidly obliterating his ability to reason.

Alfie moved to the door.

"I've taken the liberty of throwing another log on your fire. Should help compensate for the chill you're probably picking up from that block of ice you're standing on. I hesitate to add, though, that like most everything else in this world, there's a trade—off here. As you warm up, so probably will that good ol' block of ice."

Alfie picked up his suitcase, eased open the door and took a peek outside. Then he turned and gave Bleckmore one last glance.

"Goodnight, Bleckmore. Gotta go. My ten minutes are just about up. Enjoyed seeing your place. You should be very happy here. Take care."

The door closed, and Alfie was gone.

The only sounds left in the room were the ones emanating from the crackling fire in the hearth and from the stifled larynx in Tony's throat.

Tony was crying. It may well have been the first time in his life that Tony had ever cried. At least, this might have been the reaction of some if they could have witnessed his current plight.

Inadvertently, Tony moved his right foot a bit to the right. The slight shift in weight caused his other foot to slip. He tried to regain his balance, but he wasn't very experienced on ice, and suddenly, both feet went out from under him. Instantly, the slack left the rope. For a brief millisecond Tony felt the nauseating horror of a tightening noose. Then, almost before it came, the millisecond was gone and was replaced by a vast chunk of black nothing. The only sound now left in the room was the crackling fire.

CHAPTER THREE

Thursday, June 4th

Once a day, Sibyl lit up. Usually, it was in the late afternoon, at which time she ensconced herself in one of the soft chairs in her elegantly appointed office, pulled a pearl-handled cigarette holder out of a table drawer and let a match breathe life into a Virginia Slim. She never smoked at home—only at work—and then, as today, a late afternoon cigarette in her office was her single indulgence. She knew, deep down, that she didn't enjoy the actual cigarette half as much as she enjoyed the feel and the show of her glitzy holder. Somehow, this holder reminded her, as it did right now, that she was somebody— that she was a lady who was substantially beyond just the devoted wife of Kevin Tone and the mother of two grown children.

Sybil was proud of her past She was and had been a devoutly good wife to Kevin, and she had done a good job helping to raise their two children. But today, Sybil was even prouder of her present. It was relaxed moments like these which often prompted her to take stock of her recent accomplishments.

It hadn't been easy. Getting the money from Kevin three years ago to start up her gallery had been a bear. She had known from the beginning that the money, per se, wouldn't be Kevin's hang up. Kevin's lumber business had put more money in their bank than they would ever need. No, it was Kevin's old-fashioned ideas about women in the work place that Sybil knew would be the impeding mountain she'd have to somehow climb. Sybil also knew another thing—that when Kevin did finally capitulate to her wiles, he would come around full circle and become her biggest supporter. And, in fact, it turned out to be her ultimately well-disposed Kevin who helped her lure Marian away from a prominent East Coast gallery. Without Marian's twenty years of experience in managing art galleries, Sybil could never have mastered the innumerable complexities involved in running her own place.

Sybil smiled to herself. Today, after only three years in business, her establishment was generally regarded to be one of the most successful in the state.

Not bad. Not bad at all, she mused as she leaned her head back against the chair. She took a delicate drag on her cigarette and then stared abstractly at the holder between her fingers. Yes, and today was no exception. Another good day. She had sold two expressionistic Belvederes to a local collector, and this sale had assured her of a one year contract with the artist—a fantastic new proponent of blending triangles, circles and squares into subtle spellbinding chiaroscuro.

She smiled as she looked through the door of her office into the central part of her gallery. She could see Marian and a bearded customer standing in front of a Lattoeur landscape and could tell by the arch in Marian's back that the beard was tossing a low ball offer at her. Sybil glanced down at her watch. She suddenly remembered that she had an appointment with another low ball artist who was after an oil on hold for Tony Bleckmore, and who was also interested in a Seurrant still life. This eerily handsome, impish man with no last name and a Cheshire cat smile had said he'd be by at four PM to make her another offer. She knew what her answer would be, but at the same time, she was a little uncertain how imperturbable she could be while trying to stay firm. This man was certainly one of the most disconcerting gentlemen she had met in a very long time. Attractive. In his late thirties or early forties. But—enigmatic. Yes, definitely enigmatic—plus—yes, plus a capacity for intimidation. He was probably a man who would have instant appeal for younger women. Thank God she was in her sixties and happily married. Getting involved with a man like Mr. No-Name was, for sure, one good way to play the odds the wrong way.

Sybil put out her cigarette, rose and moved into her gallery. It was four o'clock exactly. She surveyed the rooms, and then her eye caught the front door swinging open. Her nameless man came loping into the gallery's foyer. Sybil moved to greet him.

"You are very punctual, sir," she observed good-naturedly. She proffered her hand.

He shook her hand enthusiastically.

"Long disciplined training, Mrs. Tone. Probably why I'm alive and enjoying your presence today."

Now Sybil knew what it was about this man that bothered her. That big pearly toothed smile It was difficult to fathom whether his smile was bubbling with amiability or was just a touch patronizing.

She quickly decided that the best approach at the moment was to be quite businesslike.

"I have the paintings you're interested in over here," she said crisply, pointing with her hand to a nearby niche. She led the way.

"Super!"

The man tossed his porky-pie hat on a passing chair and bounced along behind Sybil.

"You obviously can tell I come today bearing an offer of stupendous generosity. Guess I've always been an easy read."

Sybil stopped in an area where two chairs framed a small table. The table was placed in front of a V-shaped wall-screen on which were hanging two three foot square oil paintings. Each painting was lavishly framed in ebony with light overlays of gold and silver. She lowered herself into one of the chairs and studied the pictures as if she was seeing them for the first time.

"They are nice, aren't they," she observed earnestly.

The man bubbled as he eased himself into the other chair.

"Hey, you know, I like them both more every time I see them. Glad I decided to sweeten my offer. They kind of grow on you, don't you think?"

Sybil shifted her gaze to the man.

"Sir, these are registered paintings. It's customary, when dealing with works of art of this value, to have some idea of whom you are dealing with."

"You talking about me?" The man pointed delicately to the tip of his nose with his index finger.

Sybil laughed in spite of herself.

"I am, Sir. I have been referring to you as Mr. No-Name, since our three previous visits, because of your obvious reluctance to identify yourself."

"O-ma-gosh! Now, isn't that something? I have this fantastic memory, but I can't remember your asking me for my handle."

He stood up and gallantly took her hand.

"My apologies, Ma'am. Name's Alfie."

"Alfie?" She chuckled again.

"Alfie."

He returned to his seat.

"It's the only name I have. Most people, I find, kind of like it."

"Well now—" Sybil tried to recompose herself. "I don't believe I've ever met another Alfie."

She studied him for a moment. "I'm not exactly sure what Alfies are supposed to look like. But I never would have won a name-guessing contest over you."

"Alfie, Ma'am, stands for the sweetest, most lovable chap in the whole wide world. I fit these attributes to a T. I'm the most thorough-blooded Alfie you'll ever meet."

"You have a last name to go with Alfie?"

"Nope."

"Please—a last name would help. I always like to deal with customers on that basis."

"No last name," Alfie replied quizzically. "Sorry, don't even own part of one."

"You had no mother?' Sybil decided to tease back a bit.

"No mother. No father. I just happened. Been plain Alfie ever since I was a foot long."

Sybil shifted uncomfortably in her chair and tried to bring herself back to reality.

"All right, Sir. I yield for the moment. Let's see where we are with these paintings."

Alfie's smile broadened. "Love it. I'll take both."

"Sir—a—Alfie, I'm afraid we're still going to have to wait on the Simkins." She pointed to the angelically oiled face of a young girl studying a fish bowl

"Oh?"

"Yes. If you recall, I told you last week that Mr. Bleckmore still has a hold on that painting."

"Yeah, I remember you telling me that. But he's overdue in making up his mind. Right?"

"Yes, he is. But in spite of the man, I feel I must give him a little more time—as I would to any other valued customer."

"I'll betcha a quarter he won't take it."

"What makes you think that?"

"Instinct. Just instinct."

"Are you still interested in the Orange Madonna?"

"It's mine?"

"It's available, yes."

"I'll take it. Got my cash cow right on me."

"Cash? Sybil raised her eyebrows. "We're talking about quite a sum of money here, I hope."

"Fifty thou. That's a tremendous sum, I agree."

"Fifty-seven, Mr.—a—Alfie," Sybil countered softly. "The Orange Madonna is not on sale."

"Okay. We got a deal. I'll split the difference. Let's see—Fifty-seven less fifty divided by—"

"Fifty-seven less fifty is fifty-seven, Sir."

"It is?" Alfie appeared to be in shock.

"I am sure you'll love the Orange Madonna. I think it's one of the best things Boueluvex has done.

Alfie reached into his pocket and extracted a roll of bills.

"You're one tough hombre, Ma'am."

"Thank you. You certainly know how to compliment a lady, Sir."

Alfie nonchalantly laid a number of bills on the table.

"There you are. Fifty-seven bills. That's more than I'd pay for a good two-seater. And I love two-seaters."

"Thank you." Sybil picked up the money and carefully counted it.

"And hey—That was a compliment. You're an attractive dame, if you don't mind my saying so. To be a tough hombre and charming to boot— Well, you don't see that high-toned combination around so much."

Sybil stood up. This man was having an hypnotic affect on her, and she was uncomfortable with the feeling.

"I'll go and get the necessary papers ready for you."

Alfie leaped to his feet and faced the retreating figure of Sybil.

"A—Mrs. Tone—"

Sybil stopped and turned.

"Maybe I could pick up the painting and the papers tomorrow morning. Would that work?"

Sybil walked back to Alfie.

"Certainly, that would be fine."

"Super. I'll be here at ten." He stuck out his hand. "Privilege doing business with you."

Sybil shook his hand lightly. "Sir, may I ask you a question?"

"Question? Sure, fire away."

"Do you always pay for everything you buy in cash?"

He smiled expansively. "Is there another way, Ma'am?"

Sybil shook her head, paused a moment and then shifted her gaze away from Alfie.

"I'm surprised that you haven't mentioned Mr. Bleckmore."

"You're obviously not referring to that painting," Alfie replied, pointing to the Simkins' fish bowl.

Sybil's voice dropped to a whisper. "I believe your words were that you were going to try and jar a little sense into him."

Alfie's smile disappeared. "I never try."

"Oh?"

"I never fail either."

"Oh—"

"I didn't bring the matter up because there's nothing to talk about."

A long pause ensued while Alfie's smile gradually reappeared.

"What I'm saying is—mission accomplished—absolutely."

"Really?"

"Yes. I believe that I left Mr. Bleckmore deeply absorbed in thought."

"You didn't hurt him?" Sybil asked anxiously.

"Hardly touched him."

"I'm glad."

"When I left him he was as cool as a cucumber."

"He's such a very stubborn man," Sybil added pensively.

"My assessment, exactly."

"Well then—" Sybil's unsettled hands revealed her uneasiness. "We'll look for you tomorrow."

Alfie nodded and turned to go.

"I'll be here. Maybe we can talk about that fish bowl some more."

Sybil stood near the foyer, her eyes focused on the retreating figure of Alfie as he passed through the front doors. If all of her customers were like that man, she wouldn't want to be in this business. What a strange individual! Fascinating—but strange. And— gracious sakes alive—She stared at the money she was holding in one hand—can you believe it—he had just handed her fifty-seven one thousand dollar bills and hadn't even asked her for a receipt.

"Sybil, honey, this is an experience you've never had before. Really!" She was mumbling to herself as she headed for her office.

Marian turned her attention away from the bearded customer and glanced apprehensively at Sybil as she passed by. Marian couldn't recall ever having heard the boss talking to herself like that before.

Sybil walked into her office and was surprised to find her husband sitting in a chair by her desk.

"Darling, I didn't know you were here."

"Snuck in the back door."

Kevin Tone rose and greeted his wife by putting his arms around her and giving her a big hug. About the same height as his five-foot-ten wife, he somehow seemed taller. It probably had something to do with his dignified, I-know-who-the-hell-I-am carriage. Erect, square shouldered, head upright and crowned with neatly trimmed, thinning gray hair, a well-pressed three piece pin stripe suit—this all blended into a picture of the self-assured man.

Sybil moved over to her desk and unobtrusively stashed Alfie's money in a desk drawer.

"I'm glad you're here, Kevin. I'd like to leave early. Maybe we could get a bite on the way home."

"You look tired, Hon."

"I am—and I don't know why. Been an average day."

She retrieved her purse from the credenza behind her desk.

"Who was that man you were talking with just now when I came in?"

"A customer."

"I assumed that. I mean—his name."

"Oh—his name—Winchell. He didn't give me his first name."

"Nice looking guy—but you know what—I studied him a mite, and there's something about the man—I wouldn't trust that guy much further than I could throw my car."

"Really?"

"Did you sell him anything?"

"The Orange Madonna."

"Wow, that's a coup. Hope you got his money—all of it."

"He wrote me a check. He also wants to buy the fish bowl Tony's interested in."

"That son-of-a-bitch! I was kind of hoping you'd stopped doing business with Bleckmore."

Sybil smiled weakly at her husband.

Kevin came up to his wife with a broad grin and grabbed her by the arm.

"Come on. Let's go somewhere and get a drink and some hot food. One might think, looking at that glum puss of yours, that this Winchell fellow wrote you off instead of writing you a great big check."

Sybil glanced over at her husband as they walked together through the gallery.

He tossed a wide smile at her. It sent a warm glow charging through her. By the time they got outside, she could tell that she was already starting to feel better.

Yes—a drink and then some food. Maybe that would do the rest.

CHAPTER FOUR

Friday, June 5th

A beautiful, cloudless Friday in early June. Jeffrey Endecott was up early. The white-on-white turtle neck over a pair of black warm-ups felt good. Just right for the early morning nippy air. Jeff was about to leave the portico he was standing on and enter his study, when he had a change of mind. Early yet. Nice out here. Roam around a little more.

He turned and walked across the wide portico to a projected viewing area above his vast gardens and stopped. Every time he stood here and surveyed the imposing sight around him, it somehow seemed to sum up what he stood for—success and beauty all rolled up into one. *Magnificent.* This was the word most of the visitors to his estate applied to the view he was now looking at. Jeff agreed. Probably wasn't exactly modest to say so, but the extensive roses and peonies, scattered throughout a sea of conifers—all surrounding a posh cabana and swimming pool complex—were magnificent. *Magnificent!* That was the only way to describe it.

Jeff smiled as a blue jay landed nearby on the same railing he was leaning against. The bird was giving him the eye and saying, "What the hell are you doing here—this is my place—don't you know that?" Jeff smile broadened. Yeah, it's your place, little fellow—all yours. I'll try and not get in your way.

Jeff slowly swung himself around and let his eyes rest on the house he had been about to enter. Wow, when you looked at it from here, it sure seemed big. Yeah, well, that's because it *is* big—way bigger than he needed—except, that is, for his occasional bashes, like the one coming up tomorrow. Then, well, this spread almost's not big enough, Okay when the sun's out. The sprawling living room and expansive dining and kitchen complex on the first floor plus the spacious recreation area on the lower level soaked up plenty of people. But when rain knocked out his pool area, his bashes needed all of the dry space he owned.

Besides, Jeff mused, as he eased over towards the perched Blue Jay, he kind of liked the handle he'd acquired. *Country Squire*. Had a nice ring to it—brought to mind a certain amount of dignity, elegance, integrity, respect—the kind of things that really count in this world—two or three dozen acres of rolling farmland and something adequate in the middle to call home?

The Blue Jay flew away before Jeff could get close. He watched the bird until it flew out of sight, and then started back towards his house. Saturday's overnight soiree was only three days away. Time to sit down with Judson and go over the details one more time to make certain that all the bases were covered.

Good ol' Judson. How long had Judson been with him? Was it fifteen years? At least. Gosh, the guy was almost out of his sixties now, wasn't he Yeah, he was. Trouble was, he looked even older. Those twenty-five earlier years Judson had spent in the foundry hadn't been easy on him—obviously. Emphysema—and probably a bunch of other things Judson wasn't telling him about. Not the healthiest guy around—but well, the guy never missed a day—always Johnny-on-the-spot.

Another thing, Jeff reminded himself as he paused at his study door. Judson *liked* working for him—probably as much as he liked having Judson around. Jeff had to admit to himself that he was a pretty good boss—undoubtedly the biggest reason why Judson liked his job. Making Judson the head honcho, cook, valet and chauffeur—letting him superintend the maintenance requirements of the gardens and handle the hiring and bossing of extra servants when there was a need—this all worked. In spite of Judson's dour wooden face, Jeff knew he had a proud jack-of-all-trades working for him.

Jeff turned the door handle and entered his study.

"Howdy, Judson. You beat me."

Judson, in his customary black bow tie and short sleeve shirt, was seated somberly at the side of Jeff's large mahogany desk.

"Morning, Mr. Jeff."

"How you doing?" Jeff drawled as he moved to his desk. "Spry as a young colt this morning, I'll bet—eh Judson?"

Judson's somber expression didn't change as he slid a piece of paper containing a list of this weekend's guests across the desk to Jeff.

Judson looked away.

"We all set for tomorrow?"

"Yes Sir," Judson replied grimly.

Jeff eyed Judson closely. He then moved around the desk and put a hand on Judson's shoulder.

"Something wrong, ol' timer? You look a bit outta sorts."

"Nothing wrong, Mr. Jeff."

Jeff studied Judson for a few more moments and then returned to his desk and sat down.

"Yes, there is. You can't fool an old friend, Judson. Come on, what gives?"

Judson slowly looked up at his boss.

"Seems to me, Mr. Jeff, you got trouble coming here tomorrow."

"You talking about our friends, Judson?"

Judson lowered his eyes and looked away.

Jeff leaned back in his chair and smiled. "Hey, this bunch you're referring to are all close friends of ours. Why you saying that?"

Judson returned his gaze to the floor and said nothing.

"You know something about these folks I don't?" Jeff asked softly.

Judson shook his head.

"Jeff's face suddenly lightened. Yo—I'm with you now, Judson. It's Mr. Bleckmore. He's the turkey in your craw, now isn't he?"

Again, Judson was noncommittal.

"Should have known." Jeff paused and eased a smile of compassion on his trusted servant. "Well, Tony's my dear friend, Jud. I can't shun the guy simply because you don't like him—now can I? Besides, the rest of our guests are friends of ours who are right friendly people, don't you think?"

Judson looked up resolutely.

"Not when Mr. Bleckmore's around, Mr. Jeff. He never does me no harm. I jus' stay outta his way. He's a boot-shaker I'm real scared of. All the others—they nice folks. You got nice friends. But they ain't so nice when Mr. Bleckmore's around, and I don't think most of em like him much better'n I do."

Jeff threw his head back and let go with a loud guffaw.

"My friend, that's the longest speech I think I've ever heard you make."

Instantly, Jeff's guffaw dissolved into a gentle smile.

"And, I better quickly add—one of your best. I understand your feelings. Tony is a scrappy pit bull, I'll admit. But I think you're wrong about one thing. People like him more than you think. At any rate, please try and suffer him for my sake. He's a pretty good friend of mine, you know."

Judson nodded his head solemnly a couple of times as Jeff continued.

"As you are aware, I've decided to run for the Senate. This is a pretty select group we're having over this weekend. Sunday morning, over brunch, I'm going to ask them for their support. Not only are these people well-heeled, but just as important, they know tons of folks around the State whose support I need if I'm going to pull this thing off. You with me, pal?"

Judson straightened himself up a bit, stuck out his chin and again nodded.

"Thank you. Like always, eh."

Jeff switched to a crisper, more business-like tone of voice.

"We got plenty of booze?"

"Plenty."

"The usual line of hors d'oeuvres?"

Judson silently replied in the affirmative.

"And Judson—What you say we try that new punch I gave you the recipe for the other day. How about jazzing it up a little with that cherry filled block of ice we did once before. The ladies seem to like the looks of that—Okay? And I got one more idea. Let's not use that rolling bar table this time. Probably not big enough. Put the booze and set-ups on that long table with the ship's bell on it. That ought to be big enough. See how it works this time."

Judson started to speak, but frowned instead, as Jeff continued. "Let's see—what else is there?"

The front doorbell sounded.

Jeff glanced at his watch. "We expecting anyone?"

"No sir."

"Eight-thirty—must be United Parcel or someone."

Judson was already on his way out the study door. Jeff swiveled his chair slightly, placed his feet up on his desk and stared out the window at the various shades of green emanating from the pastoral enchantment of his back-forty. He was looking forward to this weekend. Yeah he was. Putting on the ritz with old cronies once in a while was what it was all about, wasn't it—especially in a place like this. A slight frown crossed his face. Not going to be easy to pull this thing off though. But if the old noggin keeps percolating and the timing's okay, things ought to work out just right. Yep, got to—

Suddenly, he became aware of the vibrating presence of someone else in the room. He turned his head and sucked in his breath. He knew what he was looking at. For sure. But never had his buddy looked like this before.

"Tony!"

Jeff's expression of shock turned into a big grin.

"Where'd you come from at this hour? A super surprise!" Jeff moved around his desk to greet his friend.

Tony Bleckmore dragged his bones into the room.

"Morning," Tony muttered hoarsely.

"Come on in and sit down. You look a little rocky. You okay?"

"No!"

"Gotta bug. eh?"

"No bug!"

"Well, you look a mite like you've got the horrible-horrible or something worse," Jeff observed lightly.

"Whatever the hell I got, I'm getting over," Tony spit out gruffly as he sank onto a hardback chair.

"Want a shot of something? Might help whatever it is."

Tony shook his head.

"Thanks. Tried the sauce in bed for two days. All it did was make me feel worse. I'm trying to dry out."

Jeff pulled out his pipe and pretended to direct his attention to the task of filling it with tobacco. Obviously, something was really bugging Tony. He'd never seen his friend so far removed from the swashbuckler he knew so well. And—well—Tony apparently had come over to unload something. Best thing to do was to wait him out and listen.

Several minutes passed in silence. Tony stared abstractly into space. Jeff played with his pipe. Finally, Tony broke the silence.

"Some sonofabitch tried to kill me."

Jeff's jaw dropped, but he said nothing.

"Some sonofabitch tried to kill me," Tony repeated, as if he hadn't heard himself the first time.

Tony glanced knowingly at Jeff as he continued.

"Funny, ya know—I always thought I was big enough and tough enough to handle anything or anybody if push really got down to shove. But this bastard somehow hoodwinks Oscar and then walks into my place two nights ago and wraps me up like I was a rag doll before I knew what happened. I mean—that mother had me hog-tied and gagged before I could flick a damn eyelid. And you know what? I still don't know how he did it.."

Jeff inched his chair up a little closer to Tony and leaned forward in rapt attention, his forearms resting on his knees.

"Oh, that ain't true, actually," Tony continued in a croaky, raspy voice. "I know how the prick did it. Jeff, baby, that SOB was a pro. I mean he was a top drawer pro and smooth as silk flowing through a hunk of honey. I mean—he was so damn smooth I could've probably enjoyed the hell out of watching this bird in action if the guy he was screwing around with hadn't been me."

"You know what the creep did? You wanta know? He put a half inch nylon noose around my neck, threw the other end over a beam, and then—" Tony's hoarse voice lapsed into a falsetto—"then—Sweet Jesus, you'll never guess what that bastard did then. He had me standing—I mean he had me standing on a crappy block of ice. There I was—can you believe it—strung up to one of my beams near the fireplace and standing on a goddamn freezing block of ice."

Tony rose slowly from his chair and began roaming listlessly around the room.

"You hear what I'm saying, chum? You hear me? There I am—a noose around my neck, my hands cuffed behind my back, and—oh, I didn't tell you what that insulting mother did that really blew my mind. He jammed a rubber ball, about the size of Aunt Tillie's tits, into my mouth so I could hardly breathe, let alone talk. Godamighty, I can't believe what I'm hearing myself say. There he was, the great Bleckmore, gradually hanging himself on a chunk of slowly melting ice."

Tony continued his aimless meandering in the room, obviously re-impressed with the enormity of the tale he was relating. Soon, he found himself standing in front of a stunned and quiescent Jeff.

"I know what you're wondering. I know what you're wondering. Why ain't I dead?"

Tony moved back a few steps and sat down.

"Well, shit—I don't know why for sure. All I remember is slipping on that lousy ice, feeling that rope tighten up awful bad and then, sometime later—I don't know how long—I wake up on the floor, and I'm lying in a pile of water. The rope's busted, and the other end's still dangling from that beam. Can you imagine that? Bleckmore split a half inch four ply line strong enough to hang a couple of bulls sky high on a meat hook."

Jeff stared, stunned by the bombshell Tony was laying on him. Suddenly, however, Jeff's eyes brightened, and his mouth widened into a quizzical grin.

"Hey, I gotta ask you something, pal. Was that critter hanging on the meathook full of bullshit?"

Tony's frown deepened.

"My God, you don't believe a damn word I'm saying, do ya?"

He stood up and walked over to Jeff.

"Look at this."

Tony pulled the neck cuff of his turtle-neck sweater down to reveal a reddish abrasive line circling his bulldog neck.

"I ain't bullshitting you."

Jeff stood up and moved in close to Tony and gasped at what he saw.

"Tony—Damn! That's god-awful! You aren't kidding. I'm sorry. My apologies, friend. But you understand—I've seen you play suckers with some pretty fantastic cock and bull—and when you got to the part just now about splitting a half inch line—well, man, it looks like you not only said it, you did it."

"I couldn't of. No way could two hundred and seventy pounds of Bleckmore bust that line. I lay in bed a whole damn day wondering about that. Finally, you know what I figured?"

"You didn't break it?"

"Yeah, you got it. I didn't break it. Couldn't of. When I looked closer, three of the four strands looked like they might have been split. Took me some time to come up with this, cause it was a hell of a while before I figured how to get that damn ball outta my mouth and the cuffs off. Hey, you wanta know how I finally managed that, for Christ sakes?"

A touch of the self-satisfied Bleckmore smile suddenly appeared.

"I had to stand backwards on a chair and push Oscar's buzzer a hundred times before he got curious enough to haul his ass upstairs to find out what 'n hell was the matter with me. Well, when I finally got my hands back, I took a good look at that rope to see if I could tell how it broke. Couldn't tell for sure, but I think three strands were cut—not split."

Tony paused to consider the significance of the verdict he had just rendered.

"Yeah—a cut rope. Had to be. But the big riddle's why. Why would some bastard try to hang me with a pre-cut rope?"

"I got one answer," Jeff said tentatively.

"Yeah, I know. The prick didn't want to hang me. But that don't make no sense—no sense at all."

"It might."

"Like—maybe he was trying to scare the be-Jesus outta me, you're thinking?"

"Maybe."

"Damn, he sure as hell succeeded if that was what was up his craw. But why? Naw, I—"

"Who was the guy? You know?"

"Haven't the damndest. Called himself Alfie. You know any Alfies?"

"What did he look like?" Jeff asked, shaking his head.

"A young punk with no curves. Thirty—maybe forty. Smiled like an idiot. Must have had a brain like Einstein. And oh, I forgot to tell you. He had a shooter with a silencer on me the whole time. Worse, the damn thing worked."

Tony pulled up his sleeve and showed Jeff the abrasive scar on his left arm.

Jeff blanched and turned away. Neither men spoke as Jeff slowly ambled over to a nearby bookshelf and pulled out a Waterford decanter. In his other hand, he picked up a goblet and turned back to Tony.

"Tony, I know it's still morning, but I need a thimble full of this stuff. Courvoisier. Sure you won't change your mind? Might make you feel better. Hope it does me."

"A thimble full—okay," Tony replied glumly.

"I know you pretty well, buddy. I can't believe anyone would want to kill you, scare you or even toy with a crazy idea like that."

"Yeah, sure—The whole world thinks I'm their pet canary."

"I don't know about canary, but I think people like and respect you. Deep down, you gotta know that."

Jeff handed Tony a shot of brandy.

"Hogwash, Endecott. You're dreaming."

Tony bottomed up his brandy.

"Okay, you tell me. Who would want to kill you?"

Tony moved over to a soft chair, sat down and swung one leg up over the arm of the chair.

"You won't like the answer."

"You're stalling, pal. Who?"

"Well, I got some names in mind, but I'll think on it a bit more before I sing em out to you. I doubt if you'll much like the sound of my music."

Jeff decided to back off.

"Hey, that cognac sent a little color upstairs. You're looking better already."

"You know, I think I'm beginning to get some of the picture. This bum Alfie's a hit man and a pro some of my business associates like to hire once in a while to handle their sticky problems. I'm thinking someone hired Alfie to send me a message. Only trouble is—I can't figure out why, and I damn well don't know who thinks I'm a problem—except I'm positive—yeah, I'm positive it wasn't the mob. Hell, I'm skin tight with those guys. Another thing, if my theory's right—what'n hell's the message?"

"Wish I could help. I'm more in the dark than you are."

"You're helping. Just talking to someone you trust helps."

"My suggestion is that we sit on this thing for a few days. I'll keep my antenna up and you just take it easy."

Jeff paused for a few moments, obviously out of ideas. Suddenly, his face brightened as another thought popped into his mind.

"I've got an idea. Why don't you try this out on Kevin over the weekend. That guy keeps his ear closer to the ground than a lousy snake."

Tony's scowl deepened.

"Glad you mentioned that bash of yours. I'm not coming."

"Come on, pal. Don't put me on. I'm counting on you."

"One reason I came over—to tell you I'm backing out."

"You're serious?" Jeff was aghast.

"Yeah, I'm serious."

"My God, why?"

"I know who's coming. That's why. It's a lousy list."

"I don't know what list you've been looking at—" Jeff shoved a piece of paper at Tony—"There's the official poop sheet on who's coming—a fantastic select few—and all our long time friends."

"Yeah—all my buddies. Great group," Tony said, glancing casually at the list.

"You're coming then."

"You asked me a bit ago who I thought would like to see me dead. Remember?

Well, here's a damn good start."

Tony handed the list back to Jeff.

"Wow, I can't believe this. My best friend vaporizing our bosom buddies right in front of my eyes."

"I told you, you might not like it."

Jeff appeared to be studying the guest list he was holding in his hands.

"To steal one of your favorite expressions, Bleckmore, I think you are full of pure unadulterated crap. Let's go through this list one at a time and you tell me why anyone of these fine people would want to touch a hair on your head—let alone blow you away. Let's start with your ex."

"Lena? She loves me so much, she can hardly look at me."

"Maybe—but she still loves your alimony. Right?"

"There ain't a helluva lot of love there, let me tell you."

"Okay—let's try another—*My* ex."

"Hell, I don't know this for sure, but I'll betcha a couple of quarters Ethel Endecott's kooky enough to think that with me out of the way, she could get you back. She's still got the red hots for you, Jeff baby. You oughta know that better'n me."

"I also know," Jeff argued quietly, "that Ethel's a tender little thing who has a hard time swatting flies."

"Come on, buddy. Ethel's not tender, and she damn well ain't little."

"Josephine! You're something else this morning. You'd think you'd been married to her instead of me."

"Who's next? We might as well do your whole damn list seeing's we got this far."

"All right. The Strabos. You got a problem with them?"

"Shit, man, I don't have a problem with nobody. It's everyone else who's got the problem. Okay. I agree. Marva Strabo wouldn't mind having a little of what I got. But that world famous shrink she's married to—Collin, he don't love me all that much cause he thinks he knows what I know about his wife."

"Tony, your imagination'll become a loose cannon if you don't grab onto it."

Jeff got up from his chair, walked over to Tony and ruffled his hair good naturedly. He then wandered aimlessly around the room while he tried to reason with his friend.

"Kevin and Sybil—You feel the same way about them?"

"No, by God, there's one gal that seems to like me for what I am. She's got a hell of an art gallery, you know, and she's one broad I enjoy doing business with. Bought my last six pictures from her. Her husband though—the bird you want me to talk to—how anyone would know what that mealy-mouthed four-flusher feels about anything is beyond me. He says what he wants you to hear and then— Well, I'll tell you one thing. I'd never want that self-righteous bastard behind my back any longer than it takes a fast owl to blink."

Jeff chuckled.

"Okay—I saved the best 'til last—A salt of the earth couple you've known as long as I have. They love everyone, by golly, including you."

Tony let out a raspy roar.

"You got to be talking about the Kennellys."

"Ah—you agree—finally."

"Hell no, I don't agree. They're the only ones left on that lousy list of yours."

"You're not going to tell me you don't like them either?"

Tony paused a moment and considered his reply.

"Well, let's see—I'll give 'em to you one at a time. First, that guy's wife. Anne Kennelly's a non-person. She's someone you'd have a hard time seeing if she was sitting nude on top of a flag pole. And when she talks, it's worse. You can't tell whether it's the wind or a croaking frog you're listening to."

"That's because you don't care which it is. Right?"

"All right—I don't care."

"Boy, you are in rare form this morning. I can't believe I'm hearing all this."

"You want me to finish?"

"I'm not sure."

"I will anyway. You got me started on this, remember. Sam's the number one hate-Tony on that list of yours. Personally, I like the guy. Liked him well enough, as you know, to cut him in for a piece of my cement action a couple of years ago. Made him a limited partner. The ol" geezer's been an absolute shit head ever since. Tells me he doesn't like some of the bums I associate with and wants out. I told Sam I'll damn well do business with any mick I wanta do business with and suggested he screw himself. I guess his anger really turned to steam when I told him I'd let him out, but not until I was damn good and ready. He thinks I'm ruining his lily-white reputation. If that isn't a crock."

Jeff gave Tony's arm a playful rap with his fist.

"I think that rope stretched your brains more than your neck ol' buddy. For my money, people like you a lot more than you think. Let's let it rest for a while. Tell you what—why don't you come back over here tonight, and we'll have some fun."

"Doing what?" Tony asked skeptically.

"I got the bobsy twins spending the night—just for you and me."

"Bobsy twins? We know a bunch of twins. Who you talking about?"

"Morra and Sorra."

Tony rose half way out of his chair with a raucous bellow.

"Morra and Sorra! Holy Shit! How'd you get them?"

"I got them."

"They take half the national debt to pry loose—and that's after you stand in line."

"I know. Trust me."

Tony turned away, gently rubbed the back of his neck with his left hand and grinned. "I'll take Morra," Tony finally muttered."

"You dog. Can't handle Sorra, eh?"

"Can't handle even thinking 'bout her."

"Okay—you get Morra. One condition."

Tony looked askance at Jeff.

"Yeah?"

"You spend the weekend here and let me change your mind about our friends."

"Aw, cut it out. You're bribing me."

"You got it."

"I'm incorruptible. You know that."

"Yeah, about as much as the devil himself."

"Come on , pal. You'll have more fun without me."

"I'll make you a wager. You'll have more fun this weekend than any of the rest of us."

"Morra, eh?"

Jeff nodded.

"What time?"

"Seven. We'll have a snack."

"Okay, you conniving mother, I'll be here."

Tony's moue reflected the ambivalence of his feelings at the moment. No one—no one but Jeff could have moved him off the hard rock stand he had taken with himself before he came into this joint, and no bribe but Morra could have gotten him to change his mind. Tony rose and lumbered towards the door.

"I gotta go. Thanks for hearing me out. I had to dump on someone."

"Call me if you need me. I'll be around. You know that."

Tony turned at the door.

"There won't be a next time. I got that figured."

"Great. I'm sure there won't."

"Gonna pick up a rod and hire me some muscle."

Jeff waved at his friend.

"Maybe you should."

Tony waved back and then turned to go.

"I wonder which one of those birds we been talking about was the turd that hired Alfie," Tony tossed back over his shoulder as he disappeared down the hallway.

Jeff watched his friend disappear with considerable poignancy. He knew that Tony's reference to *those birds* was a telltale sign that Tony was down on the whole human race. Well, after what Tony'd been through, who wouldn't be in the pits. Would have probably driven most men completely bananas. Tony, though—he's a pretty tough ox, isn't he. He'll bounce back. Tonight'll help. Yeah—a smile crossed Jeff's face—he deserves tonight after agreeing to tomorrow.

But just as quickly, the smile faded.

"I wonder who in hell Alfie is," Jeff muttered aloud to no one in particular as he sat back down at his desk.

CHAPTER FIVE

Saturday Morning June 6th

You know, honey, you've still got a knockout face.

These words were being muttered by a usually unassuming fifty year old lady who, at the moment, was smiling at herself in the mirror in silent self-assessment. She was standing in Jeff Endecott's spacious living room and enjoying a moment of private reflection.

Ethel Eendecott was not bragging. She was merely reacting realistically to what she was looking at. She did, indeed, have a very pretty face. Her clear, unblemished skin would add pride to any woman of her age. And her large blue eyes, full wholesome cheeks and short cropped curly blonde hair gave her an almost angelic appearance.

Ethel was unassuming about her appearance for a reason. She knew that she was prettiest and most attractive when sitting down. When she was standing, her awesome size made it difficult for bystanders to concentrate on her face. Below the neck, Ethel was nearly curveless. Broad square shoulders tapered down to robust arms and a waist which didn't exist. Even her ample bosom seemed to project more brawn than it did femininity. Ethel saw herself as others did, but she was helpless to do anything about it. She loved to eat.

She knew her distinctive feature was her smile. She relied on it. It was her confidence builder. It was a radiating, infectious smile and one that undoubtedly played a critical role in helping her hook the perennial bachelor, Jeff Endecott, nearly ten years ago. Even though this same smile was only paper thin today, it was, Ethel was certain, responsible for helping her maintain the cordial relationship she'd had with Jeff since their divorce two years ago. It was this smile and the pretty face she was looking at right now which filled her breast with eternal hope that one day she could win Jeff back.

As she turned away from the mirror, Ethel's smile was in high gear. She was swaying dreamily on the top of a gentle bubble. She had, per request, come in early on this beautiful Saturday morning and, in compliance with Judson's instructions, had dropped her overnight bag off in Jeff's bedroom.

How sweet! No, it was more than sweet. It was a heavenly thing for Jeff to do—turning over their old bedroom to her for the weekend. Yes, heavenly!

Ethel searched for an even more superlative adjective as she glanced in the mirror one more time to check her hair. She then floated over to a nearby chair which had a needlepoint picture on its seat depicting the front facade of Jeff's manor. Jeff had said over the phone that he wanted to chat with her about something before the party. But he hadn't said what. Ethel had been using all of her considerable self-control to avoid speculating too long about the dreamy alternatives.

She sat down and let her head rest on the back of the chair. She could feel a warmness welling up within her, and she knew what that feeling was all about. It was good to be home.

Precisely at nine a.m., she heard Jeff's familiar footsteps clicking authoritatively on the terrazzo floor of the long first floor hallway.

Jeff bounced into the room.

"Hi, Eth! Hey, you look smashing."

He moved quickly over to where she was sitting.

"Hi!" she purred, as her cheeks blushed from the compliment she knew deep down probably wasn't sincere.

Jeff leaned over and gave her a light buss.

"I didn't hear you come in. Just bumped into Judson. He said you were in here."

"You said nine. It's nine. I'm here."

"Yeah, you're always on the dot. I remember that," Jeff said affably. "Guess I learned that good habit from you."

"Thank you for giving up your bedroom. That was very nice of you—although it does bring back soulful memories."

Jeff settled into an adjacent chair—another needlepoint—this one of the swimming pool area as seen from an upper terrace.

"Hey, you brought some pretty good weather with you, Ma'am. Neat day, eh?"

"Yes, isn't it—but don't give me that credit. I'll bet you still don't allow it to rain when you're throwing a party."

Jeff laughed. "I pray a lot—and it seems to work, doesn't it. Every time I throw a bash like this one today, the sun seems to shine. You suppose it's a good omen working—I'm just lucky or what?"

"You decide."

"All right, if you say so, I will. I say, today it's a good omen, and I'm going to win."

"Have you ever lost?"

"Yeah, you know I have," Jeff added emphatically, "But I'll tell you, I don't want to lose this one. I don't want to make any mistakes—starting with this bash. S'why I asked you if you could come over early this morning. I'm hoping you'll help me out. What I'm saying is—sort of like the old days."

"Of course I will. What can I do?"

"Well, you remember how these overnighters go. There's a million details need taken care of to make things smooth—the kind of stuff I'm all thumbs with and requires an elegant hand like yours. You know what I mean?"

"Yes," Ethel whispered. "And thank you for asking me."

"How 'bout that! Neat! Tell you a secret. I already bet Judson you'd do it. Know my girl pretty well, don't I."

"Yes, better than I know you, I'm afraid."

Ethel's gentle smile was protecting the slight tremor creeping into her voice.

"I feel better, though, hearing you say yes. This is an influential bunch coming in here today. I want to wine and dine the heck out of them—show them how much I love 'em. And then tomorrow, I'm hoping we can get them all hopped up to help me get my campaign off on the right foot. Here—here's the list of who's coming."

"I know who's coming," she said, as she placed the list in her lap.

Jeff chuckled. "Huh, for a moment, I forgot who I was talking to. Course you'd know—just like you'd also know that—"

"Jeff, can I ask a favor of you?"

"You bet. You name it."

"Can we sit down somewhere quietly late tomorrow and talk?"

41

"Talk? Sure. My gosh, Eth, we can talk anytime, anywhere you want. Right now, if you want to."

"No, tomorrow—after everyone else leaves. I'd like that better."

"Tomorrow it'll be."

Jeff studied his ex-wife for a moment.

"Hey, nothing serious bothering you, I hope."

"Of course, there's something bothering me," she said sweetly.

"There is?"

"I always have something bothering me."

"Huh—you do?—I don't remember that. I'm sorry." Jeff was obviously puzzled.

"It's you," she said softly.

"Me?"

"I thought you knew that."

"Me, is it." Jeff shifted uncomfortably in his chair. "That's what you want to talk about tomorrow—something ol' Jeff's done. Whatever it is, Eth, I'll tell you right now, I'm real sorry for."

"I would just like to sit down with you tomorrow after all the hub-hub dies down and talk quietly for a few minutes about our future. Could we do that?"

Jeff's beaming countenance faded into a studious frown. He rose to his feet.

"Eth, I'll talk to you anytime you want. You know that. And about anything you want. But there's one thing we oughta stay away from. It won't do either one of us much good to try and resurrect the past. I got great respect for you, Eth, but my heart's beating to a different drum now. I wish it weren't—" Jeff moved over to Ethel, leaned over and took her two hands in his—"I wish it wasn't the way it is—but it is."

He leaned over and gave her a light kiss on the forehead.

As Jeff slowly straightened up, his ebullience returned. He smiled down kindly at the pretty lady with hope in her eyes.

"Well, I gotta get cracking. If I know these birds, some of them'll get here before twelve. Can't tell you how much I appreciate your coming in early and agreeing to help me out this weekend. Owe you one. Really do."

Jeff turned and made his way towards the hallway entrance.

"Feel free to make changes if you see something you don't like." He turned at the door. "And oh—holler and I'll come running if you need any help. Okay?"

Ethel raised one hand slightly from her lap to signal comprehension. Then, as Jeff disappeared down the hallway, she let her hand fall back onto her lap. She folded her hands and shifted her gaze from the doorway to an adjacent window. The soft glow radiating from her face had faded and was supplanted by a harsh look of grim determination.

"Damn!"

This was not a word Ethel used or even thought very often. It was, however, a word she was thinking and using now. It passed almost inaudibly by her tightly drawn lips.

If only that monstrous creature would drop dead somewhere—then— I'm sure my Jeff would come back to me. Damn! Damn! Damn!

Ethel shook her head sadly and struggled to her feet. She stood very still for a few moments. Then she angrily smoothed her skirt, lifted up her chin and assumed the mien of the temporary hostess of Endecott Manor.

———————

Jeff was right. A few of the weekend guests did come early.

At a quarter to the hour of noon, Collin Strabo swung his large yellow Lincoln Town Car under the impressive arched Endecott entrance. Seated beside him in a black satin pant suit, accented with red piping, was Collin's very pretty wife, Marva.

Marva was wearing the self-confident smile of someone who was looking forward with eager anticipation to the coming fray. She considered any gathering of more than a few people a fray wherein she could outwit her own gender in flirting with the opposite sex and thereby win for herself the most compliments and the most attention.

Marva reasoned instinctively. She usually got her own way the same way. Her greatest success in this regard was, paradoxically, her husband. She manipulated this erudite psychiatrist like a rag doll. To all of their friends, the wonder was how their marriage had managed to assume such durable proportions. Surely, no two more dissimilar organisms had ever shared the same pod quite so blissfully.

Marva's mind was ever subjugated to her constantly changing feminine instincts. She was the one thing in this world Collin was certain he didn't understand. He marveled that he derived so much enchantment from this feminine perplexity.

There had been very little conversation since they left home for Jeff's this morning. The half hour drive had been an unusually quiet one. Marva glanced over at her husband as they began the drive up Jeff's long serpentine drive. He seemed intense this morning. Not like Collin at all. His tiny, hairless head and long nose seemed more prominent than usual. Marva wondered for a moment why he looked so different and then quickly decided that it was a waste to be wondering about such silly things. She pulled out her compact for one last look.

"I'm glad we decided to come. Aren't you happy you changed your mind?"

"No," Collin replied apathetically, keeping his eyes firmly glued on the winding driveway.

"Yes, you are. I can tell," she said impishly.

Collin looked askance at his wife. "It won't work, hon."

"What won't work?"

"Your whitewashing our sharp differences of opinion here. I'm accommodating your wishes today—not the other way around."

"Well, you're so terribly sweet about it, I can't tell the difference."

"I told you before—I have a bad feeling about this weekend."

"Collin, this is a horrid thing to say about all of our dear, dear friends—and on such lovely, beautiful day too."

"The day's got absolutely nothing to do with what we've been talking about. You know that."

Jeff's home came into view as they rounded a bend in the driveway.

"Ah, I knew we wouldn't be the first ones here. Look at that."

Several cars were parked in front of the house. Kevin Tone was standing at the rear of one of them and was pulling some luggage out of the trunk.

"Oh what fun. There's Kevin," Marva squealed. I wasn't sure they were coming."

"Yes, thank God for Kevin and Sybil," Collin added solemnly.

He pulled the Lincoln up next to the Tone Cadillac.

Marva threw open the door and hopped out.

"Kevin, darling, I was so afraid you weren't coming, I think I would have gone home if I had found you weren't here."

Kevin dropped the bags he was holding on to and grabbed Marva as she flew up to him. He gave her a playful embrace.

"And if I hadn't known, for sure, that you were coming, sweet lady, I wouldn't have showed. But don't tell your ol' man. He's a very jealous guy. Okay?"

"Don't worry," she giggled.

Collin walked around the car and shook Kevin's hand.

"Hi Kev. Good to see you. You playing around with my wife already?"

"I am and thank you for approving."

Collin grinned. "Yes, you're right. I do approve. Otherwise, my wife would be irrepressible, wouldn't she?"

Marva looked up at Kevin. "You see what I have to put up with, Kevin dear? Being married to a distinguished psychiatrist has its price, let me tell you. He's so clever at taking the sting out of my fun."

Kevin chuckled. "Never tell him he's winning, Marva. Then he'll never find out."

"Well, you boys have fun with the luggage." Marva reached in the car for her purse and then started walking up the flagstone path towards the house. "I'm going on up and see who else is here."

Collin stood absorbing the retreating figure of his wife for a moment.

"I was rather cool to the idea of coming here today, Kev, but Marva talked me into it. You know why I think she insisted on coming? It gives her the opportunity to ply her coquettish trade. My, how she seems to enjoy that."

"About as much as you seem to enjoy watching her—perhaps."

"Most of the time—most of the time," Collin mumbled dispiritedly.

Kevin slammed down the trunk of his car. "You cool to Jeff's candidacy, Col?"

"No. Why do you ask?"

"Oh, you just mentioned not wanting to come here today, I believe."

Collin pulled the Strabo luggage out from the rear seat of his car before replying. Leaning against the side of his car, he turned to Kevin.

"Jeff will get an arm and a leg from me if he needs them. I love the guy. You know I do. And I have good feelings about his senatorial aspirations. I just wish he wasn't so mulish about one of his countless number of friends.

"My God, don't we all," Kevin growled. "You know, Sybil summed it up pretty well for me one day when we were talking about

Jeff. She said she's always been so proud to be a member of the entourage Jeff was so loyal to until suddenly, about a year ago, it occurred to her that this cohesive group included the only man in the world she was very ill-disposed towards."

"Have you heard the latest rumors?"

"No." Kevin edged a bit closer to Collin—all ears.

"Someone tried to kill Tony."

Stunned, Kevin was speechless for a moment.

"If anyone but you, Col, told me that I'd accuse them of pulling my leg. But not you. You don't kid about things like that. A—you said, *tried* to kill him?"

"He survived, as far as I know. I think he's here today."

"Damn, I don't believe it. Who in the world would have the bloody nerve?"

"Actually, it's far better than just an ordinary rumor. One of my nurses at the hospital is an acquaintance of an old timer by the name of Oscar who, apparently, is the head gatekeeper at Tony's condo complex. Seems like she ran into Oscar in a cardiac ward at the County General a couple of days ago. Oscar had been admitted with a heart condition. According to his chart, his condition was symptomatic of some kind of emotional disturbance. When she visited with Oscar briefly, he mentioned something vague about an assassination attempt and then clamed up."

"On Tony?"

"That's the rumor part. Pretty good guess, though, don't you think?"

"If you're right, what makes you think he'll be here today?"

Collin pointed to a low-slung Alfa Romeo Spider parked nearby. "Isn't that his two seater sitting over there?"

"I don't know what he drives. That his?"

"You know who's coming this weekend. Who else in our group would drive a contraption like that?"

Kevin picked up his two suitcases. "Well, you certainly are full of fascinating information this morning. We might as well go up and find out how true it is. Sib's been here a whole five minutes since I dropped her off at the door. That's usually more time than she needs to ferret out any juicy gossip."

Collin grabbed his two bags and joined Kevin. Together, they traversed the short distance to Jeff's front portico. At the door, Collin dropped one bag and reached for the door knob. Before opening the door, he paused and turned to Kevin.

"I agree with you. I *am* full of a fascinating story this morning" He stared hard at Kevin—then lowered the other bag to the floor before continuing. "The odd thing, though is that I feel more like a prophet than I do a messenger.'

"A prophet," Kevin mumbled quizzically, still holding onto one of the bags.

"You know as well as I do, Kev, there isn't a soul gonna be here today that doesn't hate Tony's guts."

"Except Jeff."

"Except Jeff," Collin echoed quickly. "And I'm thinking that whoever failed the other night might be tempted to try again this weekend."

Kevin chuckled and put a hand on Collin's shoulder. "Except the two of us, eh friend."

"I can't speak for you, but you're no dummy. You know how I feel every time that clod lays one of his paws on Marva. I'd like to wring the bastard's neck."

Kevin smiled ruefully. "I thought you professors knew better ways to deal with men like Tony"

"You're right. We do," Collin said as he turned, opened up the door, picked up his two bags and entered the Endecott foyer.

"Wonder what the hell he meant by that," Kevin mumbled to himself as he slowly followed Collin into Jeffery Endecott's sumptuous mansion.

At about the same time the Tones and the Strabos were congregating in the foyer, Judson was cornering his boss.

"Mr. Jeff, Mrs. Bleckmore just arrived. I've taken her things upstairs. She's waiting for you in the living room. I told her I'd find you right away."

"She didn't want to go up to her room first?"

"No sir. She said she'd like to see you."

"Thanks, Judson."

Jeff quickly moved down the hall and into the presence of Magdalena Bleckmore, who was seated in a small settee at one end of the ornately furnished living room.

"Hi, Lena Babe. How are you?"

"Fine, thank you." Lena replied coolly.

Jeff leaned over and gave her a cursory buss.

"Gosh, you look great. You're the last to arrive. The others are either upstairs or on their way to the pool. Hey, how about this for some weather?"

"The weather's lovely." Lena turned to the window. "No, I guess you'd say it's very lovely."

Jeff was by now observing Lena very closely.

"You mad at me about something, honey?"

Lena fixed Jeff with a pair of steely green eyes.

"I think you stink, that's all."

If Jeff was shocked or surprised, his expression didn't betray him. Rather, he seemed entranced by what he was absorbing. Len's sudden spate of anger obviously wasn't even remotely detracting from the magnetic affect the combination of a truly stunning face, set off by shoulder length raven hair, and a lithe, trim figure was having on Jeff.

He moved over to a nearby cellarette.

"Lena, babe, how about joining me in a little early afternoon snifter You've always been partial to a vintage brandy."

Lena nodded affirmatively.

Jeff poured brandy from a crystal Waterford decanter into the bottom quarter of two large oval glasses. He gave one to Lena, picked up the other and then seated himself on the matching settee directly across from her.

He raised his glass and smiled ingratiatingly at his disquieted guest. "To this weekend. I hope you enjoy yourself."

Lena sipped a little of her brandy. "I'm not drinking to your weekend. I'm drinking because I like your brandy. As I said, I think the whole thing stinks."

"Look, honey — " Jeff stood up. "I'll close the doors and you can say what you want. I don't like people mad at me, especially on a beautiful, summery day like this."

He shut the doors and returned to his seat. "Come on now, Magdalena, what have I done wrong?"

"If you weren't so damned distinguished, I don't think I'd tell you. I'd let you rot with curiosity."

"I'm not so distinguished," Jeff said with a broad grin. "Incidentally, you've never called me that before."

"I call all senators distinguished, in or out of office."

"Oh, that. You know already?"

"It's not a secret."

"Yeah, I guess not. As a matter of fact, that's one of the reasons for this get-together—some of my oldest friends to hear it from the horse's mouth."

"Then why me?" Lena's eyes were drilling into Jeff.

"Because—like I said, Lena Babe—my oldest friends."

"I'm not one of your oldest or even you newest friends, if that's what you're assuming."

"I think you are."

Lena rose, her agitation showing beyond her voice for the first time.

"Jeff, you broke up my marriage. You seduced Tony into thinking that wine, women and song with you was better than Tony with me. And you have the gall to think I'm your friend. You must be going loopy-loony upstairs."

Jeff walked over to Lena and put one arm around her shoulders.

"That was three years ago. If you've been my enemy for three years, you certainly haven't behaved like one. And incidentally, You did accept my invitation for this weekend. That seemed kind of friendly."

"You know perfectly well that the last time I saw that lousy, lecherous ex-husband of mine, I indicated that I hoped the next time, he would be dead. All around the State, people are talking about you and the Senate. They like the idea. But everyone doesn't know how much Tony influences your life. I do, and I resent your hypocrisy. I resent you bringing me out here to be a part of it."

Jeff remained unruffled as he backed away from Lena a couple of steps.

"I suppose you're right. Maybe sometime this weekend, we can talk about it. Maybe I'll have to learn to temper my extra-curricular activities. I am a bit of a bounder, I'll admit. But I've got a streak or two of good in me too. Must have, or I wouldn't be playing around with this Senate thing. Maybe, I'll surprise you, babe."

Jeff moved up to Lena and faced her eye to eye. "Maybe, I'll surprise you, eh?"

"Like the second coming of Christ, Mr. Endecott."

"You'll stay this weekend and have some fun with us?"

"I believe you've already impounded my things."

"Good ol' Judson. Well-trained isn't he. Confiscate your baggage, and then you can't leave."

Jeff walked over and opened the doors. Then he turned to her curiously.

"Hey, let me ask you again—how come you came?"

"Do I need a reason to stay?"

"No. Of course not. Just curious, that's all."

"Well, let's say that—that, I came in spite of you—to—a—study Tony one last time."

"Ma'am?"

Lena was now the one who was smiling.

"I said I came to study Tony."

"I thought that's what you said."

"You don't like my reason?"

"Yeah, Lena, I like it. Don't understand it, but I guess I like it."

Lena picked up her purse and moved to the hallway door. She turned to Jeff.

"Senator, you want me to elaborate. So I will. I intend to study an unmitigated bastard to see if I can find a way to prick his balloon forever. As you say, if I apply myself, I might succeed, and who knows, it might even be fun."

"How do you know you can find his balloon?"

"I was married to the son-of-a-bitch, remember."

Lena smiled demurely as, purse in hand, she gracefully glided up the hallway's circular staircase to her room.

"I'd almost forgotten," Jeff mumbled to himself.

He then moved a few steps over to the doorway and absorbed Lena until she could be seen no more.

CHAPTER SIX

Saturday Noon June 6th

As Lena's footsteps died away, Jeff jarred himself back to reality. He checked his watch. Twelve-fifteen. Time he moved his butt down to the pool with the rest of his guests. Yeah—things were under control. Maude and James, those super gourmet cooks Judson had picked up for the weekend, were percolating in the kitchen. Ethel undoubtedly had her finger on the pulse of things. Everything copacetic. Time he started having a little fun at his own bash.

Jeff could hear faint fragments of poolside chatter as he opened the door to the rear piazza and briskly stepped outside.

"Yo, Sybil!"

Jeff's eye had caught sight of the lady. She was wending her way along the path which dropped gradually downward to the pool area through a seemingly endless tunnel of Rhododendron shrubs.

Sybil stopped and turned.

"Jeffrey, dear. My, if you don't look delicious."

"Not as nobby as you, babe. Even in a cover-up you out-pizzazz the rest of the world."

He gave her a warm hug.

"I'm going to suggest to Kevin that we get you some glasses for your birthday, Sir. You obviously need a pair."

Jauntily, Jeff took Sybil by the arm and together they ambled down the path.

"What's up? I assumed you were down with the rest of the gang."

"I had to call Marian at the gallery. I never seem to get that crazy place out of my mind. Isn't that terrible? Kevin tells me that if I don't slow down, I might turn him into a dependent."

"I agree with him. You ought to retire."

"And become a country squire like you, I suppose?"

"No. I like to think of you more as a mistress."

"Oh my, Kevin would love to hear you say that."

"I've already told him I'll take you over when he's worn out. I'll croon you serenades all night long."

Sybil giggled. "I think you have naughty thoughts, Mr. Endecott. Reminds me of an insidious friend of yours who has told me, on occasion, that I make him want to warble. I suspect that you two are in cahoots."

"Who else besides Kevin you been seeing behind my back, babe?"

Jeff was obviously enjoying his banter with Sybil.

"You know who I'm talking about. Tony's been buying a few of my paintings lately. I'm sure you are aware of that." Sybil's voice dropped into a more serious tone. "Honestly, Jeffrey, I know how close you two are, but I'll say it anyway. He's changing. And it's not for the better."

"Can't sing as well as me, eh?"

Sybil stopped and turned to Jeff. "Let's just say, Jeffrey dear, that I've heard Tony's rich baritone, and I would rather listen to you gargle."

"That's pretty complicated blarney you're throwing at me, but I think I understand you."

They continued down the path in silence until Sybil slowed down and turned to Jeff.

"We're so delighted you've decided to run for the Senate, Jeffrey. We want to help you all we can."

"Hey—Sounds like I already got a couple of votes. Toney votes. That's nice."

"I imagine Kevin would stuff the ballot box for you if he thought he could get away with it."

They continued down the path. The poolside chatter got louder. Another turn—then a few steps down some winding flagstone steps—and suddenly, the path gave way to a pastoral, motley scene of soft pastels.

"Now there's a pretty picture postcard if I ever saw one," Sybil observed as the large oval swimming pool, surrounded by an imposing array of variegated white wrought iron furniture came into view.

Tony and Marva were sitting on the diving board with their backs to the rest of the group. Collin, Kevin and Sam were standing, with drinks in their hands, near a large circular table filled with hors d'oeuvres and a variety of canapés. Ethel and Anne were tete-a tete in the shallow end of the pool. Judson completed the picture. He was at the bell-table stirring the contents of a large punch bowl.

"Hi folks!" Jeff's ebullient, stentorian greeting was accompanied with a broad smile. "Judson taking care of all of you? We got anything you want right here. Just ask."

Jeff walked over to greet Sam and Collin whom he had missed when they had arrived.

Sybil waved at her husband's two companions and then sauntered over to the pool to greet Anne and Ethel.

"Hey, Jeff baby—" Tony gave Marva a playful push and sent her squealing into the pool. "We were wondering if you'd been invited to this blowout. Where'n hell you been?"

"Who you think's been doing all the work around here?" Jeff shouted back blithely.

"Damn you, Tony. You've ruined my hair," Marva cried in a lighthearted petulant voice.

Tony grinned. "I'll fix your hair later, honey. Sorry 'bout that."

He hopped off the diving board and strode over to the other end of the pool to greet Sybil.

"Well now, how's my favorite gallery owner?"

Sybil smiled affably and offered her hand. "Hello, Tony. Nice to see you."

"Hey, no handshaking at this brawl, Madam Proprietor."

Tony grabbed Sybil playfully and planted a firm kiss on her forehead. Then, he pulled back a step and looked down at her with an impish grin.

"I make a practice of kissing all good lookers right on the kisser. But with you and The First Lady I make an exception."

Collin, Sam and Kevin came leisurely strolling over to join the group of ladies surrounding Tony.

"You know what?" Sam said. "Every time I see Tony kissing a dame, I thank God I'm a man." Sam's squat stature and generous stomach hanging over a pair of faded swimming trunks, made him the odd man out with the rest of the group. When he laughed, his roly-poly stomach usually laughed the hardest. But at the moment, Sam's stomach was quiescent as he glared at Tony.

"That sounds like my chummy partner talking. Sometimes, folks, he can't quite figure out what he's missing."

"I think you boys ought to quit picking on Tony." Marva had climbed out of the pool and had joined the group. "He's a nice puppy—even if he does push little girls into water over their heads."

Ethel chuckled. "If you're a little girl, Marva, I'm Mother Theresa."

"At least you were half right, Marva," Collin said with a wry smile.

"I was? Which half, Collin dear?"

"The nice puppy—that's you, Tony—to a tee."

"Thanks, pal. Cleanest eyewash you've probably ever thrown at me."

"You need help, Tony? Looks like you're a bit out-numbered," Jeff quipped. He handed Sybil a glass of punch and took a sip of his own martini.

"Naw, buddy. I'm almost taking a nap here."

"Tony, can I ask you a question?" Collin was nursing a vodka tonic from a cushioned wrought iron chair he had dropped into.

"Never heard you ask permission before. Sure, shoot."

"That chafe around your neck—it looks a little tender. Have you done anything for it?"

"Surprised you noticed." Tony gently rubbed his neck under his chin with the finger of one hand. "Yeah, it is a bit touchy, I guess. You got anything in your bag of tricks'll help?"

"Depends on what it is. Looks like a flesh burn from here. How'd you get it?"

"Necking. Some of the chicks squeeze me too damn hard. Gotta figure a way to slow 'em down a little. Right, Jeff?"

Jeff smiled uncomfortably.

"Sorry I asked," Collin said derisively.

"Doctor, I'd say your professional curiosity was right on," Kevin said.

"No!" Collin shook his head. "It wasn't professional curiosity, really. I just happened to recall, a few minutes ago, a cadaver I worked on in medical school years ago. Called himself Orville, as I remember, and he had a neck that looked like Tony's. Orville was—"

"Collin, PLEASE! That's a horrid subject to bring up at such a lovely party," Marva said sharply.

"Orville was a convict," Collin murmured. "He died from a hanging."

Sybil gasped and stared nonplused at Tony. Suddenly, her face paled to a chalky white. Her eye lids fluttered and wilted. Sam, who was standing slightly behind her, caught her in his arms as she fainted.

Collin leaped to his feet and instantly took charge.

Sybil was carefully placed supine on a chaise lounge. Then, using a damp towel, Collin gently bathed her face. No voices, other than that of Collin issuing staccato instructions, were heard from the group.

"Thank God!" A relieved exclamation from Kevin broke the ominous silence, as Sybil's eyes popped open. "You all right, hon?"

"What happened?" Sybil asked in a tiny voice.

Kevin leaned down close to her. "You just fainted for a second or two."

"Oh my, I'm so embarrassed. My word, Kevin, I've never done this before, have I?"

Kevin smiled and gave her a tender kiss on her cheek.

Under Collin's watchful eye, Sybil was soon on her feet. She decided that she needed a walk to help clear her head. Kevin went with her. The steady firm steps she took as she departed on the arm of her husband mollified the group's concern for her.

Ethel's voice called out from the side of the pool where she was sitting with her legs dangling in the water. "Something wrong with Lena, Jeff?"

"She's up at the house changing her things. You know Lena. Likes to make her entrance just right."

"Saw her for a minute upstairs," Sam said. "She didn't seem her usual bouncy self."

"She's bouncy. Take it from me." Jeff chuckled ruefully. "Her tongue was bouncing me around pretty good."

Collin leaned forward. "She's inimical about the company you keep perhaps?"

"You rascal, you were listening."

"No—just guessing as usual. I imagine, however, that she's enthusiastic about your senatorial aspirations."

"You are amazing, Col," Jeff said. "You read minds like you're inside em. No wonder you're the wealthiest shrink in America."

"You're giving Collin too much credit," Sam said. "Everyone in this state's for you, Jeff. Doesn't take a clairvoyant to know that."

"I wouldn't say everyone, Sam." Marva was standing behind the group of men and was shaking out her long red hair from its recent confinement in a wet bathing cap.

"Tony was telling me a few minutes ago, Jeffrey dear, how he' going to talk you out of this silly idea."

"Yeah, I know. Jeff turned his infectious grin on Marva. "He worked a little on me last night."

"Well, I think anything negative here today starts and stops with Tony." Sam said as he glanced over at Tony who was swimming laps in the pool. "Speaking of our dear friend—the nicest thing I can ever think to say about him is that he's all wet.." He chuckled. "Can't argue 'bout that at the moment, can ya?"

All heads turned as the magnificent figure of Magdalena Bleckmore hove into sight. The prettiest face belonged to Marva. But below the face level, it was no contest. Lena's lean, sultry figure stood alone, and when added to her long, black shoulder length hair, lucid green eyes and just the barest hint of make-up, the total picture Lena presented was decidedly provocative. She was wearing a large straw beribboned sun hat and a loosely tied yellow terry cloth robe which barely concealed a tiny red bikini.

"Hi fellas."

She waved at Sam and Collin—then moved over to the pool to greet the ladies.

"You missed all of the excitement," Anne called out.

"So I just heard. I passed Kevin and Sybil a minute ago, and they told me what happened. A fainting spell—of all things! Imagine! I thought they went out with hoop skirts. I'll tell you what, though— Not a bad idea. If I thought it would help me look as queenly as Madam Sybil does, even after she's just zonked, I might try swooning a little."

Jeff burst out laughing. "Hey, toots, you're not supposed to look like a queen. You're a siren. You're supposed to walk around pale as chalk and let those green eyes work their wonders. Also, it would help if you had a drink in your hand. What can I get you?"

"What goes well with brandy? I've never started this way before."

"How about a Blue Dragon?" Sam suggested.

"No thank you. I never do blue. Pink sounds better." Lena pointed to the punch bowl.

Jeff obligingly started walking towards the far side of the pool to get Lena a glass of punch.

Lena was absorbing Jeff's backside all the way. "To think I could be angry with a man who walks like that."

Marva giggled. "Haven't you ever noticed a senator's rear end before. They all look like that."

Collin patted the back of his wife's head. "I think what Lena is subconsciously wondering, honey, is whether a successful playboy can manage to become a successful senator."

"Dr. Strabo." Lena was smiling tauntingly. "You're so uncomfortable sometimes to be around. One never knows for sure how close your cute little mind will come to the skeletons in our closets."

Lena turned to Marva. "If I meant anything as earthshaking as your husband suggests, darling, it's that that shoe-in senator could get me real horny except for one detestable reason."

"Well, speaking of your first love, I'd say he's got that old look in his eye." Collin was glancing over at Tony who was out of the pool and headed their way. "Come on, Sam. If we're ever going to get wet without dying, now's probably as good a time as ever. It's probably not going to get any warmer than this today."

Sam and Collin moved away towards the pool. Jeff returned with Lena' s drink, and a moment later, Tony joined the group.

"Lena love. Good to see you." Tony had draped a towel around his ample torso.

His pearly white teeth were flashing a gregarious smile. And his curly black hair, handle-bar mustache and piercing black eyes were radiating an exotic mystique.

"Hi Tony."

"My God, you're not good to see. You're absolutely devastating." Tony turned his big grin towards Anne and Marva. Gorgeous ladies, I hope you won't be offended if I seem a little partial to this little chick who used to think I was the beginning and the end."

"I think she still does in a way," Anne said with a smirk.

Tony ignored Anne's remark and turned back to Lena. "I'm sure glad Jeff asked you here this weekend. I was afraid he wouldn't."

"Oh really? Why?"

"Hell, you know why. Jeff likes peace and calm hilarity at these blowouts, and lately you haven't been exactly hilarious with me."

"Dear Tony. I'm on my best behavior—honor bound not to disturb the peace and pledged to be peaches and cream with you. You didn't know this?"

"No I didn't. But even if you just made up all that hogwash, I like the sound of it, and I'm for it. Hey, how about eating with me tonight?"

Tony was referring to Jeff's well-known tradition of pairing up couples at small tables for two around the pool at dinner time. It was a tradition which obviously was going to be perpetuated tonight, because five small tables, complete with candles and table settings, were already in position at the side of the pool.

"Oh, I'd love to, Tony but—" Lena glanced at a partially submerged Collin at the shallow end of the pool—"But I just accepted the same invitation from Collin a minute ago. I'm sorry."

Jeff quickly jumped into the conversation and reminded everyone to stop negotiating dinner partners, as place cards had already taken care of this matter.

"Well, Jeff, buddy, look the other way while Lena and I go over and do a little manipulating with those cards. A little manipulation once in a while's good for the soul. Come on, baby." Tony pulled gently on Lena's arm.

"No let's leave the cards alone. I'll tell you what. Instead, let's take a walk. How about the rose garden? You show me the rose garden. That's manipulation of the prettiest kind." Lena eased into a beautiful smile. "Only, I'll be doing the manipulating."

Anne smiled sadly and eased away from Marva. This was easy for Anne to do without calling attention to herself, because she was intrinsically the lady who always blended. The unremarkable face, plain figure and a mousy low-pitched voice—all added up to characterizing a transparent woman. Anne found a nearby cushioned wrought iron chair, sat down and contemplated Tony and Lena as, arm and arm, they moved away from the group. Quickly, she lapsed into the same brown study which had absorbed her in the living room of their home the previous night. Her thoughts went back to the sweater she had nearly ruined when she absent-mindedly dropped stitch after stitch while waiting for Sam to come home. She never dropped stitches. Never. Why? Well, it was obvious, wasn't it? All because of that insidious Tony Bleckmore. Or maybe—maybe it was because she just didn't know her husband anymore. Sam said the gun wasn't loaded. But, dear heart, it must be loaded. Why else would Sam have hidden that dreadful thing at the bottom of his overnight valise? And why else would he have kept his intentions such a secret from his wife? Why else? Only one possible reason. Sam must be intending to kill Tony. Good Lord, that must be what he's intending to do. Anne shuddered as these thoughts repossessed her. She took a sip of her wine. Tears came to her eyes. Oh if Sam just hadn't decided to go into business with that awful man. Sam had never told her much about his relationship with Tony except that it would save them a bundle of money over the long run. Tony's cement was apparently what Sam needed in his construction business., and that's all she knew about their relationship—except that things had changed after they had become partners. Her sweet, good natured husband had rapidly become a man-possessed. She didn't know what possessed him. He would never tell her. No—no— that wasn't true, was it. Anne shook her head. Maybe the problem was—Sometimes she didn't really listen to what her husband was saying. She smiled sadly as she recalled Sam's words last night while they were in the throes of one of their more bitter arguments.

I suppose you're right. I am itchy sometimes—like right now. What started out nice between Bleckmore and me has turned into bad blood between us. Probably should have filled you in sooner. That SOB's reneged over and over on cement discounts he promised me. Worse, I found out some time ago he's doing business with some very unsavory people— mafia types I can't afford to be connected with. When I told him I wanted him to buy me out, like he originally agreed, he reneged on that promise too. We've been having some pretty heated words about it ever since.

Anne rested her head on the back of her chair, downed the rest of her Zimfandel, and closed her eyes. She shivered as she recalled how last night had ended. Silence! Silence! They never went to bed angry and not speaking. Never! Never! But that's what they did last night. And it was all because Sam was so pig-headedly stubborn. Over and over, she'd asked Sam to phone Jeff and tell him that they weren't coming to his party. Tell Jeff that they were sick—tell him anything— but please, tell him we'are NOT coming. And Sam had only smiled and said nothing, hadn't he. Smiled and said nothing. And that's the way they had gone so quietly to bed.

Anne sighed—then opened her eyes at the sound of steps approaching her chair. She turned and looked up. And there was that smile again. Only this time it was the smile of the man she knew, loved and had been married to for thirty-one years.

"HI, Hon. You all right? Whatcha been doing? Dreaming a little after the swim, eh?"

Anne stood up, gave her husband a tender kiss and didn't answer his question.

———◆◆◆◆◆———

Arm in arm, Tony and Lena wound their way through the garden and down a landscaped embankment to the dirt road leading to the back portion of Jeff's property. Down the road about fifty yards, a small stream passed underneath a narrow wooden arched bridge. They stopped. Tony bottomed up the martini he'd been carrying and then tossed the glass over the bridge and onto the rocks in the rippling water below.

"Tony!"

It was the first word spoken since they had left the pool area.

"Jeff'll never miss it."

"It's his BEST crystal!"

Tony frowned. "It's a lousy group. You know that, don't you."

"What is?"

"This group. These people here today."

"My God, Tony, you've known them a long time. They're supposed to be your friends."

"Not my friends. Yours maybe. But not mine."

"Is what you're saying—you don't like any of us?"

"No! I'm crazy about you, Lena. Always have been. If you don't know that, you're blind. Jeff's next, and that's no secret either. Today, he's about the best friend I got. The rest—you can dump 'em all in a sinkhole. Sam—that weasel'd bury me tomorrow if he could—And that other sonovabitch—he'd just as soon see me dead too."

"What other sonovabitch? My goodness, I didn't think you owned so many."

"Kevin. He asked me out to lunch a few days ago. Told me he was supporting Jeff for the Senate and asked me to leave Jeff alone from now on. Said Jeff couldn't win unless I did. When I laughed in his face, he put his request in much stronger language. And that's when I told him that if he ever threatened me again, I'd kick his balls right up through his teeth."

Lena was leaning back with her elbows resting on the top railing of the bridge. She stared for a few moments at her ex-husband who was standing a few feet away. She opened her mouth to reply, but in place of words came only a soft chiding laughter.

"What n'hell you laughing at?"

"Poor Tony. You poor little boy. You think the whole world's afraid of either your foot or your mouth. I don't think, Tony dear, you could *actually* kick the balls up through the teeth of a mosquito."

Tony leaped at Lena.

"Damn you, woman! You know fucking well you're the only person in the world who could give that kind of shit to me."

He had his huge hands around Lena's slender throat. His hands didn't move, but as Lena's laughter increased, a paroxysm of anger caused his face to twitch uncontrollably.

"Go ahead. Squeeze, little man. You haven't the guts. We both know that, don't we." Lena's eyes were riveted on Tony's.

"Stop your laughing at me, Lena," Tony bellowed. His fingers trembled and his head shook as, in a taunt, subdued voice, he repeated himself again and again.

Finally, Lena raised her hands up and pulled Tony's hands down. Then, she dropped her own hands to her side and wandered desolately back down the narrow dirt road towards Jeff's home.

Tony Bleckmore sagged onto the railing of the bridge and let his head drop so that his eyes were resting on the flowing water below. He studied his rippling reflection for a moment—then abruptly turned his head aside in deference to a glower he found rather intimidating.

CHAPTER SEVEN

Saturday Evening—June 6th

The soft orange overhead lights bouncing off the swimming pool's bluish-green water was having a mesmerizing affect on her. Sybil shook her head, as if to clear it, and then glanced upwards at the black, starlit sky. Slowly, she allowed her eyes to drop down to the lovely dusky foliage enveloping them. As she did so, she silently concluded that truly, at this moment, she was a part of an exquisite, very peaceful scene.

At least—a relatively peaceful scene. The magnificent prime rib had done its work and neutralized the effects of a voluminous flow of alcohol during the late afternoon hours. Yes, now, all was quite sedate and, Sybil decided to herself, much more comfortable. Jeff's traditional way of serving poolside dinners, Sybil liked. The small tables for two were placed close enough together around one end of the pool to make group conversation convenient if desired. The relative intimacy of one's dinner partner made it also easy for a more low keyed tête-à-tête. Sybil's dinner partner was Collin. This delighted her no end, as she found his intelligent approach to the art of conversation utterly fascinating and quite singular from the witty, urbane approach most men seemed compelled to use with women. She and Collin had been sipping Irish Coffees when Collin was called to the phone. So—as the conversations seemed to be pretty much paired up at the moment, Sybil was enjoying herself by assimilating the tranquility around her.

Tranquil? But was it really tranquil?

Sybil wondered. She had long ago learned to trust those nebulous, mysterious waves of intuition which would occasionally engulf her.

Tonight, her senses were operating on a higher frequency than normal. Although the cause was as usual nebulous, she did make a mental note of a couple of specifics.

Ethel, bless her soul, was anything but herself. Obviously pleased that Jeffrey had placed her with him for dinner, Ethel was, nonetheless, a far different Ethel than the bubbly sophisticated hostess Sybil had greeted when they had met at noon. As she sat talking with her ex-husband, Ethel was smiling but seemingly only on the outside. Sybil glanced over at the object of her concern. Yes, inwardly, dear Ethel seemed decidedly tense.

Sybil's other specific was her husband. Kevin adored parties. Oh, he rarely looked forward to going to them. That's true. But once there, especially at a party where he was with well known friends, he always loosened up and enjoyed himself immensely. Characteristically, Kevin should be thoroughly immersed in these old friends he was with on this delightful summery weekend. Sybil knew, however, that he wasn't. He was guarding his drinks, and particularly, he was guarding his speech. Sybil also noted that Kevin was avoiding Tony.

Strange! Kevin was never this reclusive.

Oh yes—Heavens above—There was one other specific, wasn't there. Herself! This afternoon! Fainting! What an absolutely embarrassing thing to do! Had she ever fainted like this before? Goodness no! Why? Silly question. That scar on Tony's neck had reminded her of Alfie. That's why. Kevin had told her about the rumors regarding Tony's neck. Could there be a connection? Could there? Ridiculous! No point in dwelling on such a foolish idea a minute longer.

Sybil sat back in her chair and relaxed. In spite of everything, it had been a lovely day, a lovely evening, and she was looking forward to more of Jeff's after-dinner hospitality. In fact, if Collin didn't finish that phone call soon, she was going to excuse herself and head up to the house by herself. The early evening breezes were becoming uncomfortable on her bare shoulders.

Suddenly, Jeff's voice interrupted her thoughts.

"Folks, you all had enough to eat?"

The assent was unanimous.

"Good. How 'bout making your way up to the lower level. Judson's up there with a variety of liqueurs. Okay?"

Okay? My oh my, I think I'm being pickled for posterity—and what's worse, enjoying every minute of it.

As if by magic, Collin was her side and drawing back the chair for her. As she gained her feet, his elbow moved in front of her to encase her hand, and they headed for the house. Soon, they found themselves in an invitingly warm, cozily ornate recreation room. There, as advertised, was Judson behind an assortment of cordials which were pretentiously and elegantly displayed. At the other end of the room, Sam, Anne and Marva were seated on the floor. They were nursing cordials and luxuriating on an enormous snow-white Alaskan over-carpet in a large semi-circular bay window area. Their backs were supported by cushioned window seats, and they were gesturing for Sybil and Collin to join them. Lena was standing, with her back to them, sipping a cognac and absorbing a nearby collection of three Picassos. Sybil kicked off her shoes, eased down next to Marva and wondered where her husband was. She turned to Lena.

"Lena, dear, what did you do with that magnificent dinner partner of yours?"

"I tried to take Kevin upstairs, honey, but he wouldn't go So he brought me in here." She turned her saucy stare towards Sybil. "Sorry, that was a naughty answer. You know I'm lying as usual. Actually, I don't know where he is. Said he'd forgotten something back at the pool. So, he rushed out the door. That's all I know."

Jeff came puffing into the room and paused for breath.

"Howdy all. Looks like you all are way ahead of me.Excuse the panting, but I ran up here instead of walking—a dumb thing to do after all that food."

"Join the crowd. I can't even move," Collin mumbled lightly as he joined his wife on the Alaskan carpet. Jeff picked up a pousse-café of Danziger Goldwasser Judson had left for him at one end of the bar and then quickly moved to the other end of the room where he touched a small electric wall switch. A sizable movie screen slowly descended from the ceiling. He turned to the group with a broad grin. "Well, obviously, you now know what this evenings entertainment's going to be. Ya probably suspected a movie all along, didn't cha?"

"A movie?" Sam groaned. "Hey, you turn out the lights, and we'll all fall asleep, Jeff."

"NO, ya won't," Jeff bubbled. "Not when you find out how much this movie's going to cost you." Jeff's grin disappeared as he quickly surveyed the room. "Hey, looks like we're missing a few. Who's missing.?"

"Not me," Ethel said cheerily, as she entered the room through the hallway door.

"Just Tony and my husband," Sybil said.

"Yeah, you were eating with my ex, Anne? Drowned him in the pool, I hope." Lena deadpanned.

"It's Kevin I'm worried about. He's got the film I'm about to show you folks, and it's a dandy. Kevin put the whole thing together with a top drawer TV outfit out of New York that specializes in campaign propaganda. We've been wrapping this up for a couple of weeks now, and it's a beauty. Only one minor detail. It's not paid for. I'm hoping you people will like it well enough to bail me out. Gosh, I hope Kevin remembered to bring it with him.

"You want me to go out and see if I can find him, Jeffery?" Ethel asked.

"Naw. I'll go and take a look for him." Jeff put down his cordial and headed for the terrace exit. "Be right back." He pushed the door open and disappeared into the darkness.

Silence filled the room for several awkward moments.

Collin broke the silence with a harsh whisper. "Crazy evening."

Marva laughed. "I was just thinking the same thing, darling."

Ethel raised her eyebrows. "What's the matter, you two. Aren't you having a good time?"

"Ethel dear, we're being treated like kings and queens," Marva purred. "How could we be having anything but a delicious time?"

"I share Collin's feeling," Lena snapped. "I was telling Jeffrey the same thing when I got here this noon. This is a lousy, stinking group he's got here this week-end. I told him this, and I told him it's all because of one person."

"My God, Lena, I hope you're not talking about me," Kevin said quietly from the terrace door.

"Oh, there you are, darling," Sybil struggled to her feet and greeted her husband affectionately. "Where on earth have you been. We've all been wondering. In fact, Jeff just went down to the pool looking for you."

"He did" I'll be darned. Well, he'll never find me there for two reasons. One, I'm up here. The other—it's darker than night down there. The pool lights are off. Went back looking for my cigarette lighter and nearly fell into that damn pool. Jeff should have left a few lights on."

"Jeff wasn't looking for you, Kev," Sam said blithely. "He was looking for the movie you're going to show us tonight."

"It's set up in the projection room and ready to go. I told him that at dinner." Kevin glanced around the room. "Incidentally, I notice Tony's not here. I didn't run into him either."

Sybil grabbed Kevin's arm. "Probably a good thing. Come on, dear, let's sit down for a couple of minutes and rest your feet." As she was speaking, she noticed the glass terrace door slide silently open. Tony came through the door, chin down and slightly stooped. He walked deliberately to the hallway door. His back was to the group, but Sybil didn't have to see his face to know that he didn't feel at all well.

"Hey, Tony—you okay?" Sam called out, as Tony disappeared down the hall.

"Sam, you had better see if he's all right," Anne intoned softly.

"He'll be all right," Ethel said. "He's just had a dozen too many dry, dry martinis."

"I think your number's a little low," Collin offered dryly.

For a few minutes, the conversation waned. Several of the ladies took time out to freshen up in the nearby powder room. A couple of the men made similar trips. Jeff returned, spotted Kevin and asked him if he had the movie. Kevin reminded him that they were all ready when he was—except for one thing. Tony was still missing.

"Jeffrey, you had better send Judson upstairs and see if Tony's all right," Marva said. "He came in while you were out and didn't look like he was feeling very well."

Jeff glanced around. "Hey, Tony's not here is he. Good idea. He revives, you know, in a fraction of the time it takes him to get oiled, but it won't hurt to see how he's doing."

Quickly, Jeff dispatched Judson to find Tony and see if there was anything he needed. Then he turned to Kevin and asked him to brief the group on the campaign film they were about to see. Kevin complied and concisely filled in the group on the movie's content and how and when TV was going to be brought into the picture. He then paused for questions. Almost immediately, however, all conversation came to a halt when Judson re-entered the room with a look of conster-nation on his wrinkled face.

"Mr. Jeff, I don't think Mr. Bleckmore is in the house. I've looked all over, and I can't find him."

"Is his car still in the drive?"

"I looked there first, after I found his room empty."

"Then he must be out in the back somewhere."

"If he is, Mr. Jeff, then he's in some real dark. I turned off all the lights by the pool."

"Maybe he's wandering around in the gardens."

"I turned off those lights too."

"They were on when Tony came in a bit ago," Kevin said. "I could see the reflection of the lights on the door when Tony opened it."

Jeff started for the hallway door. "Judson, turn on all the back lights and take a look out there. I'll check again where you've already looked."

Ethel followed Jeff indicating that she would help him look. The rest of the group remained in the recreation room, except for Kevin who indicated he needed a walk.

"You know—this guy we're pretending we're worried about—" Sam was at the bar getting himself a glass of water—"Funny thing, ya know—if I was asked to write one nice thing about one Tony Bleckmore, I don't think I could do it. But you know, it's more than that. I've known Bleckmore for maybe fifteen years, and I don't think I could put together two revealing sentences about the guy. He's a mystery—a lousy mystery."

"You know he likes girls and booze," Collin said.

"In which order?" asked Marva.

"Ha, that's easy," ventured Lena.

"Yeah, but that's what I mean," Sam said. "Most guys like booze and women. But what else do you know about this guy. I mean he's kind of a mystery man, now isn't he. How about it, Collin? You're the expert. How do you figure him?"

"Well, I guess he's as much of a mystery as you'd like him to be."

"What do you mean by that?"

"I mean that's the product he's selling—mystery. If you buy into his product, he's a mystery. If you don't, he's really quite simple."

"REALLY, Collin," Marva chided her husband, "you talk in

riddles. Not even I understand what you're talking about, and I've been listening to you for a long time."

"I think Collin's right." Lena stood up and walked over and glanced out the terrace door. "Tony is simple. Tony's for Tony. And nobody gets mixed up in his web and survives without being for Tony too."

Sybil smiled knowingly. "Touché! You see, Sam, Tony's really no mystery after all. It's all in the eye of the beholder. Incidentally, where did my husband go?"

"I think Kevin's out in back with Judson," Anne said.

Jeff rejoined the group. "His car's locked. Doesn't look like he's been out in front. He must be somewhere inside and we've missed him."

"Ethel'll find him asleep in a chair in the living room, and we'll all feel pretty silly," Anne observed.

Sam moved to join Lena and Sybil by the door. "I feel pretty silly already. I wonder how many of you would look for me if I ducked out somewhere for five minutes."

"I would, dear," Anne said softly.

Ethel re-entered the room from the hallway.

"This is a mystery! Tony's not in this house!" Ethel, for the first time, was showing concern.

"You sure?" Jeff asked anxiously.

"Not unless he's found a hiding place I don't know about. I've looked everywhere."

Marva stamped her foot petulantly. "You people are making me nervous. I agree with Sam. This is rather silly. Tony's probably sobering up and enjoying himself immensely in the rose garden. If he knew we were carrying on like this, I imagine he'd be having hysterics."

Suddenly, there was a commotion at the terrace door. The door flew open and Judson pounded into the room. His eyes quickly found Jeff.

"Mr. Jeff, Mr. Tone's down by the pool. He wants you to come right away." Judson was speaking in a hoarse, barely audible whisper.

"What's the matter? What's wrong?" Jeff was already on his way, following Judson down the path towards the pool.

"Judson, for God's sake, speak up. What's happened?"

Judson mumbled a reply, but Jeff couldn't understand him and quickly gave up trying. Instead, he rushed on by Judson, leaping down the steps two and three at a time. He sped along the curved path through the gardens until the pool came into view. Then he slowed down. He spotted Kevin standing motionless at the far side of the pool, leaning against the long table where the ship's bell usually sat. Quietly, Jeff walked up to Kevin. Kevin was looking down. Jeff's eyes followed Kevin's. And there, at the bottom of six feet of water, was Tony Bleckmore, face down, legs slightly apart, the ship's bell lying beside his head, its chain tightly wrapped around his neck.

CHAPTER EIGHT

Midnight Sunday—June 7th

Sybil felt like she was about to faint for the second time in one day. Her usual sunny complexion had dulled to an ashen white and her eyes appeared to be on the verge of yielding to tears. She was being led to a quiet, seclusive nook in the corner of Jeff's spacious lower level recreation room. Her arm was in the firm grasp of her husband, whose somber expression was at odds with the disposition of this normally self-possessed, perceptive, somewhat up-beat man.

"Here, sit down. I'll get some of that coffee over there, and we'll try and collect ourselves a bit."

"Won't that keep us awake?"

"Probably can't sleep anyway. What's the difference?"

Kevin walked over through the semi-darkened room to a coffee urn. He filled two cups and started back to his wife, glancing out the back windows as he did so. The glow highlighting the tops of the conifers indicated that all of the backside lights had been re-lighted.

He handed a cup to Sybil and then lowered himself into a chair beside her.

"Damn, they got here fast, didn't they. I'll bet every cop in the county's crawling around that blasted pool."

"Who was that man who just talked to us? I didn't know policemen could be that polite."

"Can't tell you his name. He introduced himself, but I'm so discombobulated, I can hardly remember my own name. He's the guy in charge—s'all I know."

"He said we didn't have to stay here tonight."

"But that he'd appreciate it if we would. Remember?"

"Let's go home, Kevin. I can't stand this place. It's giving me the creeps."

"We can't do that. Someone here tonight killed Tony! If we go high-tailing it out of here, it will put us in a stronger spotlight than we're already in."

"What do you mean, 'than we're already in'?"

"I mean that we were here tonight when murder was committed, and no matter what we do, we're bound to be prime suspects. Let's not go out of our way to make matters worse than they already are."

Sybil's hands began to tremble, causing coffee to spill into her cup's saucer and onto her dress. Startled, Kevin quickly reached over and relieved her of the cup and placed it on an adjoining table. As he did so, Sybil's damn broke. She dropped her head onto her hands in her lap and convulsively burst into tears. Kevin stood looking down at her in complete bewilderment. This wasn't like Syb. She'd never sobbed like this before.

Not even when her mother died had she lost her composure. This can't possibly have anything to do with Tony's death. If anything, they should both be dancing a jig—not weeping, for God's sake.

He leaned over and took his wife's hands in his and gently pulled her to her feet. She let her head drop on his shoulder. Finally, her sobs subsided, and she looked up at the concerned face of her husband.

"Oh Kevin," she quavered in a tiny, unfamiliar, high-pitched voice, "I know who killed Tony. I know—I know—I know—"

Her head returned to Kevin's shoulder, as once again the tears began to flow.

Kevin's head jerked back. "Sybil, damn it. What in the devil are you saying—you know who killed Tony? Come on—what on earth's gotten into you?"

Sybil reached for her purse. First, she applied a handkerchief liberally to her eyes. Then, she methodically used a lipstick and dusted on some powder. Kevin stood by, transfixed. He knew his wife—a hell of a strong woman—no use rushing her. She'd talk when she was damn good and ready—and not before. Sybil carefully returned everything to her purse and then turned to her husband.

"Do I look all right?"

Kevin smiled. "You look a ton better'n that. Dumb question."

"Is there anyone around here listening?"

"We're alone. The police are all down at the pool, as far as I know. I have no idea where our friends are. Probably in bed." He glanced at his watch. "You know what time it is? Past midnight."

"Can we whisper?"

"My God, Sybil," Kevin barked, "Are you going to tell me what you—"

Sybil put her hand over his mouth.

"Please, whisper."

Kevin staggered to a chair and dropped down into it.

"Damn! If I don't sit down, I think I'll fall down," he stammered.

He looked up at his wife in frustration and tried to whisper.

"Are you about to tell me you had something to do with Tony's death?"

She nodded her head as she knelt by the side of Kevin's chair.

"Oh my God!"

"Please, darling, don't be angry with me. I did it for you."

"You did *what* for me?"

"Kevin—Oh, please understand, dearest—I wouldn't have done anything if it hadn't been for you. I just couldn't stand to see that man make you as miserable as he has for the past many weeks. You've always been the sweetest thing this side of heaven—and—and—Oh, I know—it has been Tony who has been so much on your mind lately, hasn't it?"

"Sybil, please," Kevin hissed. "You're usually the most articulate woman I've ever known, but right now, you're not making a damn bit of sense."

"Do you remember that strange man you saw me talking to a few days ago in my gallery? The one you asked me about?"

"Yes. What about him?"

"We killed Tony." Her whisper had become almost inaudible.

"Sybil, you're mumbling. Say that again."

"I said, we killed Tony."

Kevin relaxed and leaned back in his chair with a sad-eyed grin.

"Syb, this is NOT the right time to be funny. Those are frightening words to use under any circumstances."

"I'm not being funny," Sybil mouthed almost inaudibly. "I know who killed that hateful man."

Kevin straightened up and eyed his wife closely. "I think it's time you start talking a little more plainly."

"Alfie killed Tony," Sybil hissed, "and I put him up to it."

"Alfie? Who in hell's Alfie?"

"The man in the gallery I just mentioned. The one who bought *The Orange Madonna*."

"You told me his name was—was Winchell."

"Whatever I said, his name is Alfie."

"You're saying this—this Alfie killed Tony tonight," Kevin echoed skeptically. "How do you know that?"

"I don't know *how* I know. I just know."

"I think you got bewitched by the man's good looks."

"That's not fair."

"Ah, I'm right, aren't I?"

"You don't believe a word—" She interrupted herself sharply and paused. A sheepish smile slowly replaced her moue as she continued.

"All right, as usual, you're right. The man's both enchanting and extremely uncomfortable to be around. He's been in my gallery many times. Apparently, he's a genuine art aficionado—especially of expressionistic oils. He bought a few small things and then started looking at some of my registered paintings. That's when he and I started getting acquainted. He became interested in two oils, one of which I had on hold for Tony. This got us into a conversation about our—our dead friend."

Sybil paused and struggled for self-control. "I still can't believe I did this. The conversation he and I were having about Tony was very negative. You know I never carry on like this—not even with close friends—let alone with total strangers—but—"

Kevin put an admonishing finger to his lips.

"You want me to stop talking, Kevin?"

"It was your idea to whisper. You're almost shouting."

"Oh my goodness," she exclaimed, once more in a barely audible whisper. "That shows you the affect that man Alfie has on me."

"You're saying this guy Alfie, whoever he is, didn't like Tony? That doesn't make him very unique," Kevin observed cynically.

"That's what I told him. Everyone seems to complain about the man, but no one ever does anything about it. I added that I thought it was too bad someone couldn't take the time to jar some sense into Tony before Tony tried to jar the sense right out of most of us. That's when Alfie turned that beguiling smile on me and indicated that he had plenty of time. At first, I thought he was teasing me. But then—

when he asked me if I would like him to help me out, I lost my head—and, dear God in heaven, Kevin, I said yes."

"I can't believe I'm hearing this." Kevin was bending over, holding his head in his hands.

"Isn't that dreadful?" Sybil moaned, as she applied her handkerchief to her teary eyes again.

"Yes—yes, it's all of that!"

"It gets worse," Sybil whispered intently. "I should have forced our conversation back to the paintings, but I didn't. Like a complete idiot, I asked him what he meant by "helping me out." He laughed and mumbled something I couldn't understand—something like it might be fun trying."

Sybil leaned over and whispered in Kevin's ear. "The night you saw Alfie in my gallery, he told me that he had taken care of what I wanted."

Kevin rose from the chair, placed his hands on her arms and leaned near her ear.

"Are you saying you think this Alfie tried to kill Tony?"

"I didn't until I saw Tony at the pool this afternoon with that hideous scar on his neck, and Collin said something about hanging. I tried to forget about it afterward but—"

"Oh—*that's* why you fainted!"

Kevin peered deeply into his wife's eyes. "Have you told me all you know about this guy Alfie?"

"I don't even know his last name. He wouldn't tell me."

"I think your imagination's running away with you. Just because a man's got a killer smile with women doesn't mean he's a killer of men."

"I know that. But his eyes tell you something, don't they. I'm never wrong about a person's eyes. You know that. When I stop now and think about what I should have been thinking about then, I'm saying that this mesmerizing man has the capacity for murder. His eyes say so. I think there's a good possibility he tried to kill Tony the other night, and when he discovered he had failed, he stole in here tonight and finished the job."

Once more, Sybil's eyes began to water. She reached for her handkerchief and then continued in a loud whisper.

"If I'm right, then that makes me an accomplice. And—oh dear God, if I'm an accomplice, and if they catch Alfie, then that man will point his finger at me. You know he will—you know he will."

Kevin put his arms around his wife. "Honey, even if that Alfie character is somehow involved here, which I doubt, you're not an accomplice just because you sold him a few paintings. You ought to know that. You're usually much smarter than I am about what makes people tick."

"Oh my," Sybil sighed wistfully. "I did much more than just sell him a few paintings, I'm afraid. I told him where Tony lived. And I even told him about Oscar and Tony's back entrance. Oh, Kevin, that man could charm the devil himself. He asked me all of those questions and I—My mind—I just—I just lost my mind completely. I'm so ashamed."

Kevin held his wife tightly. They remained silently locked in each other's arms for some time.

Finally, Kevin drew his head back and smiled sadly at his wife. "I vote we spend the night here and talk to whoever wants to talk to us in the morning. Okay?"

Sybil nodded.

"And if that man's name comes up—which it won't—all you know is that you sold him some paintings. Right?"

"Kevin, I'm so nervous about this stupid thing I've done."

"Come on, let's go upstairs. Maybe at least one of us can get some sleep if we're lucky."

Kevin took his wife's hand and they walked towards the lower foyer.

"My, this has been a dreadful evening, hasn't it," Sybil murmured.

"Depends on how you look at it."

They climbed the circular stairway and then made their way down the wide hall to their room. They passed several bedrooms which were still emanating a dim yellow light through the cracks under their doors.

When they reached their room, Kevin turned the handle of their door and frowned.

"Locked. Did you lock our door?"

"No. I don't have a key. Do you?"

"No." He tried the handle again, this time putting his shoulder against the door. "It's not stuck. Must be locked. I'll be damned."

"What are you going to do?"

"Find Jeff, I guess."

Kevin took his wife's arm and together they started back down the hall. The sound of a latch turning in their door stopped them after only a few steps. They turned to watch their door open slowly and a familiar form appear.

"Judson, what on earth were you doing in our room?" Sybil glanced at her husband who was saying nothing.

"Excuse me, Mr. Tone—Mrs. Tone—I didn't know I locked the door. Was just turning back your bed. Yes, Ma'am—just fixing up your bed. Sorry. Very sorry."

Judson bowed his head slightly in their direction and then quickly shuffled down the hall.

Sybil and Kevin walked through the open door into their room and, as advertised, into the presence of two freshly turned down beds.

"Darling, don't look so mean. Nothing seems to be missing. He's the same sweet old man we've known for years."

"My eye, Syb. Never have trusted that guy."

"I like him."

"I don't. Guys that never smile bother me. Always have. Judson always looks like he knows something you don't—" Kevin sat down on the edge of his bed—"Especially tonight."

CHAPTER NINE

One AM Sunday—June 7th

At about the same time Kevin and Sybil were saying goodnight to each other, Jeff was sitting at his desk in his study wide awake. The door had been closed for nearly an hour while he brooded about the gruesome death of his friend. A lone desk lamp lighted the room. He was staring at a wall clock on the other side of the room and was well aware of the lateness of the hour. He knew he was mentally and physically exhausted and should be in bed. He also knew that he could not close his eyes until he had first resolved his quandary.

Jeff had his feet propped up on a leather ottoman which he had dragged across the room and placed beside his desk. He was holding in his hand his favorite pipe—*Watson's Special*—thus nicknamed by Jeff after he had watched Sherlock Homes a few times smoke a similar one on television. Somehow, the warm bowl of this curved-stemmed pipe in his hand always gave him a feeling of strength and confidence.

He needed strength tonight. Jeff knew this beyond doubt. To have a man murdered on your premises, especially when this man was your close friend—this was a shattering experience. Jeff realized too that his senatorial aspirations now hung on a delicately balanced scale—one which could be easily tipped either way by any rash of impulsive actions by himself or any of his house guests.

Dignity. Yes, dignity. This seemed to be the key to making the most of the days ahead. Whether they found the murderer or not (and surely, someone would be apprehended), dignity must be preserved. The sorrow, the loss which he and his friends felt as a result of this dastardly act—this would be expected and understood. But somehow, dignity would add a redeeming dimension to what had happened. Yes, surely—this is an element almost completely lacking in the well-publicized murders you keep hearing about.

Jeff had been arriving at these subtle conclusions on the fly. He had been god awful busy since that awful moment at the pool—busy doing a million things—including taking the time to think. After the initial shock of seeing Tony's lifeless body lying at the bottom of his pool had worn off, and after he had called the police, Jeff had started analyzing, as objectively as he could, everything that had happened, was happening and, conjecturally, would happen in the days ahead.

Seated in his study, Jeff had been ruminating long enough to require two refills of his pipe with Dunbar #3. The smoky atmosphere in the room was beginning to resemble his tired and hazy brain. The phone on his desk rang sharply and jarred him back to the here and now. He stared at the phone for a moment without answering it. Who the hell? Not another—Suddenly, he remembered. The call he had placed to California. He picked up the phone.

"Hello! Yes, speaking. Yes, operator, put her on—Hello! Mrs. Rossetti? I don't believe we've ever met. Jeff Endecott here. I'm a good friend of your brothers. Oh, really—thank you—Yes, there is something the matter. I have some very bad news, in fact—What?—I said I have some bad news. Your brother Tony died this evening, Mrs. Rossetti."

Jeff removed his feet from the ottoman and leaned forward on his desk, listening intently to the voice on the other end of the line.

"Yes, that's right. This evening—Well, Mrs. Rossetti, I'm afraid I can't tell you exactly what happened. It was quite sudden. Here at my home. He was spending the weekend. He was—well, what I'm trying to say is that we had the police out here as soon as Tony's body was discovered and—What?—I said the police have been here and well, Ma'am, they're telling us that it looks like Tony's death was not an accident—Yes, that's right. The police suspect he may have been murdered. I agree. It *is* unbelievable. Yes, inconceivable. I agree with that too—What?—Oh, yes, just a few people for the weekend. Very close friends. Seems impossible that anyone here disliked Tony enough to have wanted to kill him. We've all known each other for a long time."

Beads of perspiration were beginning to form on Jeff's forehead. He pulled out a handkerchief with his free hand and wiped his brow.

Explaining all this to Tony's sister was proving to be more difficult than he had imagined.

"Perhaps, if you could come out here tomorrow and assist in some of the technical arrangements, we'll have more details for you, Mrs. Rossetti. Yes—Yes, it certainly is a terrible thing. He was a very close friend of mine, and I can appreciate your feelings. It's been very difficult for all of us to comprehend what's happened—What's that?—Oh sure, you bet. I'll wait."

Jeff leaned back in his chair and dropped the speaking end of the phone from his mouth slightly in deference to a temporary recess at the other end of the line. His eyes caught the dim glow emanating from the decanter of brandy at the far end of his study. He needed that. Right now. He felt like a dog on a leash. Nothing he—The instrument in his hand came alive again. Instinctively, he re-positioned the phone.

"Yes, Mrs. Rosetti—You will?—Fine. That will be fine. If you'll let me know what time in the morning, I'll have someone meet you at the airport—Yes—yes, you're welcome. Goodnight."

The telephone receiver automatically found its way back into its cradle.

God, what an evening! Must be getting loco from the strain. Huh, that woman—Tony's sister. His only sister. She certainly didn't seem paralyzed with grief, did she. Strange. Tony always mentioned her as a woman he had rated right along with Lena. Lena. Wonder how she's taking this. Didn't see her much tonight. Didn't see her at all after they'd found Tony, come to think of it. Maybe she'd been around and he just couldn't remember seeing her. He'd been so damn busy. Those cops sure got here fast enough, didn't they. And those monkeys from the paper. My God, they're no different than a bunch of vultures. Good thing he knew the publisher, or those leeches would probably still be here. Box—that's a surprise. Not a bad cop, but he's kind of new. Decent enough chap, but—

Jeff leaned back and relaxed for a moment. Once again, he was ensnared by the provocative idea that had lured him into the study in the first place. A few minutes later, his decision was made. His mouth settled into an expression of firm resolve, and his eyes once again discovered the dimly radiating red hue of the brandy at the opposite end of the study. He got up, moved quickly to the brandy and then back to his desk with a glass in his hand. He sat down and lifted the brandy high enough to intercept the light shining from his desk lamp. Then, focusing through the glass and lamp to some nebulous point beyond, he whispered, "I'm sorry, Tony. You were a good friend. I'll miss you. Jeff remained motionless for several moments. Then he lowered his glass and checked a small brown leather address book lying open in front of him.

He picked up the phone and dialed the eleven digits necessary to connect him with a gentleman by the name of Cornelius Pire, a man who at the moment was sound asleep in his native state of Rhode Island. After three rings, a raspy high-pitched voice was on the other end of the line.

"Corny! Jeff Endecott! How are you?"

Jeff laughed heartily.

"No. No, I'm here at home—Yes, Corny, your clock is right. It's one in the morning here too. Hey, friend, how about splashing some water on your face and wake up. Got to chat with you. Kinda important or I wouldn't be calling you at this hellish hour—Yeah, I'll wait."

Jeff sipped his brandy.

My God, he was tired. Thank the Lord for this brandy. It was all at the moment that was keeping his failing batteries alive. Gosh, he hadn't seen this man he was now calling more than four or five times since the war, but even so, he could think of no other man he instinctively trusted more. At least twenty-five years older than he was too. Corny by now must be in his middle or late seventies because—

"Yeah, Corny, I'm here. Sorry about this. It's an awful hour to wake up anyone, especially a friend like you, but I'm in some trouble, and—What?—Oh yes, I remember. You told me a long time ago that if I ever got in a jam, I could count on you—Yes, well, that's why I'm calling. Didn't want to bother you, but after stewing over it for the past hour, I decided I need your help. Remember Tony Bleckmore?—No? Oh, I thought you met him last time you were here—Yes, a close friend of mine. One of my closest, I guess you'd say. Well, I guess you can guess what I'm leading up to. Corny, someone killed him here tonight—Yes, here at my place. I was having a small overnight party of ten, and a few hours ago—I guess it was around nine-thirty, we found poor Tony at the bottom of my swimming pool. I—What?—Oh, yes, sure, they came right away. Took lots of pictures. Asked a few questions and then said they be back tomorrow to question all of us. As far as I know, everyone's spending the night here. And that's what's got me really worried. It seems rather obvious that the police suspect that this was what they call an inside job—Why? I don't really know why. But I do know that I tend to agree with them. You remember my dogs?—Yep, still have the two of them. Well, they're cooped up in the back, and if there'd been any strangers around tonight, I'm sure I would have heard them barking up a storm—What?—Oh, I figured you ask me that. I don't know how. Suppose he drowned. He was lying at the— Oh, I almost forgot—You remember the ship's bell you gave us for a wedding present?—Yeah, well, whoever killed Tony wrapped that bell's chain around his neck. That's the way we found him."

Jeff downed the rest of his brandy with several intermittent sips. He had the telephone receiver clamped to his ear and was grunting affirmatives to what he was listening to.

"You got it right. You know about all I know. I suppose by now you've figured out why I'm calling—What?—Well, no, the police around here are pretty decent. They've got a fellow on this case that is new, I guess. Name's Box. He seemed all right to me, except that, when he left tonight, he looked a bit puzzled. This is why I decided to call you. My God, Corny, this thing's got to be solved in a hurry— for Tony's sake—for everyone's sake. If there's any chance you could come out here, I'd sure appreciate it. I think we're going to need your touch here bad—Yeah, I know that, but I'll tell you, friend, I'd rather have one retired Pire around than forty of this county's best—You will? Oh, that's great, Corny! That's great!—Yeah, tomorrow's perfect. That's almost right now, in case you haven't looked at your watch—Thanks. Really appreciate this. Give me a call before you leave, and I'll pick you up at the airport—Right! Goodnight."

Jeff wanted to lean back in his chair, kick off his shoes, put both feet up on his desk, close his eyes and not move for a hundred years. His bleary mind was still sufficiently focused, however, to realize that at the moment what he needed was a bed, not a chair.

He looked at the telephone receiver he was still holding in his hand. How strange life is. Weird! Who would have dreamed a few hours ago that a retired, world famous detective would be arriving her tomorrow to look into a murder involving an antique ship's bell this detective had given to Jeff and Ethel as a wedding present so long ago.

Crazy world!

Jeff replaced the receiver in its cradle and struggled painfully to his feet. He'd been sitting for a long time. Too long. It was an effort to even move. He dragged himself out of his study and shuffled down the long hallway towards the foyer stairway. He glanced out one of the back windows and noticed that the pool lights were still on. Don't those guys ever go to bed Apparently not. And Box had said he'd be here bright and early Sunday morning for one-on-ones with his guests. Well, if that Lieutenant can be up and at'em after five minutes of shut-eye, then by golly, so can he, Jeff resolved as he passed slowly by the entrance to the living room.

What was that? A whimper? Someone in the room? Jeff stopped, cocked his ear and peered into the semi-darkened room. His mental faculties suddenly went on red-alert. He walked into the room and snapped on a light.

His eyes immediately found Anne Kennelly. She was curled up in a chair in the corner of the room.

"Annie! You all right?"

He strode over to where she was sitting, leaned over and looked into two very moist and woebegone eyes.

"I'm all right." A delicate, indecisive whimper.

Jeff smiled down at her tenderly.

"Well now, you don't exactly sound like the Anne Kennelly I know. But then, I don't suppose any of us tonight sound much like ourselves. So you got company. Not much fun being some place where a good friend gets murdered. But don't worry, Annie.

This place is crawling with cops. Whoever murdered Tony isn't going to hurt anyone else. Come on, I'll walk you up to your room."

Jeff reached for her hand, but Anne didn't move.

"I want to stay here, Jeffrey. Thanks."

"You do? It's late—way after midnight."

"I know what time it is," Anne murmured bitterly. The trouble is Sam doesn't."

Anne pointed to the backside of a sofa in the center of the room. "He's over there."

Jeff walked over to the sofa and gazed down at the supine form of Sam Kennelly, mouth ajar, eyes closed—lifeless except for the barely perceptible rising and falling of his stomach.

"He can sleep here if he wants. Okay by me. Or would you rather we woke him up?"

"You can't wake him, Jeffrey. I've already tried."

"I can't eh." Jeff was shaking Sam vigorously. "Come on, Sam baby, time to go to bed. Wake up, pal."

Anne's eyes were once more welling up with tears. "He's dead to the world, because he's—because he's drunk."

Stunned, Jeff gawked at Anne. "Drunk?"

Anne nodded her head.

"You're joshing me. Sam's never been drunk a day in his life."

"I know! Never! Anne echoed vehemently.

"Your one-shot husband's about the most temperate guy I know. You sure he's snoozing off booze?"

Anne rose from her chair and padded over to Jeff. She took his hand and stared down at her sleeping husband.

"I never wanted to come here this weekend, but Sam insisted. We had an argument. When he softened a little, I finally agreed to come. Oh, it wasn't you we were arguing about, Jeffrey. You're one of the dearest men on earth. It was—I don't like to speak ill of the dead, but, well, it was Tony. I know how close you two were, but to some of us, he wasn't a very nice man. Maybe at one time Tony was different, but—well, I'll say it even if he *is* dead—He was a terrible man. Terrible! And he was doing terrible things to Sam. Yesterday, I had this feeling that if we came here today, something awful would happen, and I was right."

"Gosh, Sam seemed chipper enough to me this afternoon."

"No, Sam hasn't been himself for weeks—especially the last few days. After they found Tony's body, I couldn't locate Sam anywhere. I looked all over the place until, finally, I found him sitting on a settee in a corner of your side portico. He had a bottle of whiskey in his hand. Oh, Jeffrey, I've never seen him drink from a whiskey bottle before."

"No, neither have I."

"He just kept drinking from that bottle and mumbling to himself, 'I can't believe it. I can't believe it.' He said this over and over. I couldn't tell whether he was laughing or crying. It was just dreadful. I was numb. Finally, I got him to agree to go upstairs to bed. But when we got inside, he saw this sofa and made a bee-line for it."

Anne paused and looked up at Jeff with a pleading look in her eye.

"Help me get Sam in the car, so I can drive him home—Will you, please?"

"Has the Lieutenant talked to you recently?"

"Yes, he wanted to know where Sam was."

"Well, he must have stumbled into Sam too, because Box told me that he had talked to everyone and they had agreed to stick around tonight so he could talk to them in the morning. You don't have to stay, Annie, but like I say, everyone else apparently is. You'll stand out a bit if you run off."

"They want to talk to Sam and me? Gracious, I didn't know that. I don't think Sam does either."

"Everyone. Not just the two of you."

"Why? What on earth did we do?"

"Routine, I suppose. Someone killed Tony. All of us were here when it happened. So, I guess they want to know what we know."

"Are we—suspects do you suppose?"

"Suppose we are."

"Oh dear!"

"Don't stew about it, kiddo. We got some of the county's best prowling around here, and by tomorrow, we'll also have one of the country's best. They'll get whoever killed Tony real quick, I'll wager, and then we can all breathe easier. Come on, let's get this sack of potatoes in bed."

Ten minutes later, Jeff eased a comatose Sam onto his bed and received a grateful peck on the cheek from Anne for doing so. He let himself out of their room and trudged down the length of the hall to his room. Moments later, he was leaning against the wrought iron railing and was gazing abstractly out over the broad expanse of his gardens. The evening was enchantingly beautiful. But not to Jeff. It was ugly to him because all he could see as he stared at the moonlight trees was the image of his dear friend Tony lying grotesquely at the bottom of six feet of water. Suddenly, he felt very uncomfortable. Nauseous pangs had snuck into his belly. Instinctively, he shifted his eyes elsewhere in an effort to block out the oppressive image tormenting him.

He looked at the trees towering above him. He looked at the expanse of gardens spread out below. No matter where he rested his eyes, the churning inside his stomach increased. He let his eyes drop and studied for a moment the white knuckles of his hands which were grasping the balcony railing. And then it happened. His volcano erupted, and he leaned forward over the railing and let his anguish fall on the gentle bed of petunias some twenty feet below.

Jeff struggled back into one of the balcony's padded lounge chairs. He rested his head on the white brick wall of his home and stared at the black sky, his mind thoughtless, his stomach still heaving, still protesting. Several minutes later, he stood up, went inside and sat on the edge of his bed.

Funny, I thought tossing your cookies was supposed to make you feel better. I still feel like lousy hell.

His head fell back onto a pillow. His eyes closed. Soon, he was deep asleep.

CHAPTER TEN

Two AM Sunday—June 7th

"I used to sing in the boy's choir there an awful long time ago."

"Collin," Marva screamed, "you must be losing your mind!" She stared at her husband, almost unable to believe what she had just heard him mutter. Instantly, the whole nightmarish scene of their abrupt departure flashed through her mind.

They had left the Endecott home some twenty minutes earlier in a state of disarray. More importantly, they had left in violation of specific instructions from the police not to leave the premises. They had not packed. In fact, they hadn't even contemplated leaving. Collin had merely risen from his chair in the drawing room where the two of them had been sitting alone while the police were carrying on their investigation down at the pool. He had walked over to her, taken her hand and said, "Let's go."

And compliantly, she had followed her husband until they were halfway to their parked car. Suddenly—my goodness, it should have been a lot sooner—she became alarmed and pulled her hand away from Collin and questioned his intentions. And what had been his answer? Nothing. Weird. Not like Collin at all. Nothing but his uncharacteristically harsh demand. Demand? Yes, that's what he did—demand she get in the car. She had obeyed meekly and without thinking. Her servility, however, had lasted only as far as the front gate. First a few questions. Then objections. And finally, urgent pleas for her obviously obsessed husband to please exhibit a more rational behavior.

And what was Collin's reaction to her near hysterics? Again, nothing! He knew that they were running away. But he insisted they were not breaking the law. And, by

God, he knew what he was doing. The more he had repeated himself, the louder his voice had become. Soon, her voice had intermixed with his into one shrill crescendo. What a horrid sound that must have been.

And then, all of a sudden, they had passed the sign, "Lancaster— Village Limit," and all was quiet. As if by some spell of magic, Collin had abruptly stopped talking completely, carrying Marva into silence with him.

She had heard Collin talk about Lancaster. She had only been there a few times, but she liked the tiny village where her husband had spent a few years as a boy. It was quaint, pretty and charming. And certainly, one reason for its charm was its century and a half old Anglican Church, easily recognizable by its towering bell tower which formed a part of its western wall. As she recalled, visitors came from miles around to see this old historic site, but never, Marva was certain, had any visitors pulled up next to the Church at two in the morning and stopped to study its outline by moonlight.

Yes, weird! She could just imagine what the caretaker inside was doing at this hour—probably staring at the car lights reflecting off his bedroom window and wondering what in the world that large automobile, with a man sitting motionless behind the steering wheel, was doing parked by his church. And who was that at his side? Looked like a woman who was staring off into the nebulous darkness in an entirely different direction. Strange, that caretaker must be thinking. Of course, that poor man would have no way of knowing that what he was looking at was the lull before the storm involving two people who at the moment were completely out of sync with each other.

On the other hand, perhaps this church is finally driving some sense into Collin. Dear Lord, she hoped so. She had never, never seen Collin behave this way. Oh, sure, he had a temper—sometimes a nasty temper. But most of the time, he was kind of cute when he was mad. Tonight—tonight he wasn't mad, and he certainly wasn't cute. He was just plain stupid. Leaving Jeff's the way they had—their clothes still in their room. Honestly, what would the police, what would their friends think?

Well, there was one good thing. Sitting here was better than getting all the way home and then being arrested by the police. If Collin would just turn back.

She glanced over at her husband. He appeared relaxed. His hands were off the wheel, folded in his lap. He was just staring at the church. Perhaps he was trying to rationalize his behavior. Marva smiled to herself and looked away again. Yes, her husband was an expert at helping others. No doubt about it. But when it came to understanding himself, he could act a teeny bit like his patients once in a while.

Like right now! Oh especially like right now! If Collin had suddenly announced himself as the next Messiah, Marva would have been no less surprised than she was to hear him refer to his choir boy days. This was a subject he rarely alluded to. Indeed, she wondered if Collin was in control of himself. She decided to probe further.

"Collin, are you sure you are all right? Would you like me to drive?"

"I am not losing my mind, dear." Collin's voice was soft and firm. "One does not judge another person to be insane just because this person enjoys reminiscing about a sentimental moment in his past, especially if this person is your husband."

"Really, Collin! This is no time to be sarcastic. Every minute we sit here, we're getting deeper and deeper in trouble."

"We're not bothering a soul that I can see."

"You know perfectly well what I mean." Her voice was rapidly regaining its high pitch and intensity. "You had better start this car and drive us back to Endecott's. Just being there when a man was murdered is trouble enough. What you've done by running away — well, I just don't know what you've done. Everybody, including the police, probably thinks we're implicated in some way. It's hideous! Oh, please, please, Collin — " Her voice cracked. "Please let's not sit here any longer. Let's turn around right now and go back."

Marva broke into uncontrollable sobs.

"Yes, yes, I think that's a good idea." Collin looked at his wife and took a hold of one of her hands. "Get this out of your system. Crying will certainly make you feel better."

He gazed tenderly at her for several minutes while her tears slowly ebbed and finally ceased. She was left with a pair of watery, vapid blue eyes.

"You know we're not implicated. I know we're not implicated., Collin intoned listlessly. So, in spite of what others may think, I can't see why we shouldn't relax and enjoy this peaceful scene here and then continue on home."

"You—you haven't really heard a word I've said, have you?"

"It would have been a little difficult for anyone not to have heard either one of us, I'm afraid."

"You have no intention of returning to Jeff's, do you?" In spite of everything I've said—my pleading with you—you're not going to take us back to Endecott's tonight,"

Collin started the car.

"Let's go home and have a drink. What do you say. Let's have a drink and then we'll get a good night's sleep. I'll send someone after our clothes in the morning and—"

Marva looked sharply at her husband. His mouth was open, but he had left his last sentence hanging in midair.

"Collin—Col—what's the matter?"

"My God!" He was staring straight ahead.

Marva put her hand on her husband's arm. "Are you all right?"

"Damnation, we've *got* to go back!" He glanced, alarmed, at his wife. "I've left a vial of methylbenzethonium chloride in my valise in our room."

Marva slowly turned away from Collin. She leaned back against the seat, clutching her purse in her lap in a viselike grip. As she stared straight ahead, she felt the car move forward. She was only vaguely aware that the car was turning around, and that they were headed back from whence they had come, seemingly hours before. She saw the blur of shadows slowly passing by their car. She sensed the tense form of her husband next to her. She knew that in a few minutes they would be back at the Endecott home. But as a tear formed and then steadily made its way down her cheek, she began to wonder. And as she continued to wonder, words began to form—words which she found very difficult to say.

"Collin—Collin, did you kill Tony?"

His face impassive, his eyes unwaveringly straight ahead, Collin paused before replying.

"What I'm trying to figure out, Marva dear, is whether you're asking me this foolish, rather unusual question out of anger or out of joy."

CHAPTER ELEVEN

Sun-up Sunday—June 7th

Sunday mornings were the best. Whether or not Mr. Jeff had house guests or not, Sunday morning was always Judson's favorite part of the week. He could stay in his room dozing until the Sunday paper came. Then, attired in his bathrobe and slippers, he could sit down by himself in the breakfast nook with a freshly made pot of coffee and be the first to digest the Sunday paper. He guessed that he was the only human in the whole world who could read through the multi-sectioned paper, reassemble it into its original form and then later lay it, seemingly *untouched*, on the table for Mr. Jeff.

Yes, Sunday mornings were worth all the rest of the days of the week—especially when they were beautiful cloudless mornings like today. But not *this* Sunday morning. There was nothing beautiful about what he was looking at today. He had been up for nearly two hours now, and already, he longed to crawl back into his brass-poled bed. He felt sick—sick in his belly and sick upstairs. He had never seen a dead man before—well, er, leastwise not a dead man who had been murdered—and especially not a dead man he'd been too close to so often.

Mr. Bleckmore spread-eagled in our pool—Lord above!

Judson, a devout Catholic, inadvertently crossed himself each time that dreadful sight crossed his mind—which was about every three or four minutes as he went about his duties on this early Sunday morning. The two policemen, who had arrived at the crack of dawn, hadn't helped ease his mind either. Judson couldn't see the police from the kitchen, but he knew they were somewhere down by the swimming pool. They had been down there for nearly an hour and a half now.

90

More out of curiosity than anything else, Judson decided to take them a pot of coffee. He threw in a couple of cinnamon rolls for good measure and then shuffled his way down the stone steps and through the rose garden. He paused cautiously when the pool came into his view.

There they were. Just like he figured. Talking together. Friendly-like. They probably wouldn't mind if he brought them some coffee.

He proceeded over to the pool where his coffee and buns were received with considerable appreciation.

As Judson disappeared back up the path towards the house, one of the men said to the other, "That's about the most religious man I've ever seen. I'll bet he's crossed himself a hundred times since we've been here. Did ya see him just now when he brought us this pot of coffee."

"Probably from some convent, Jake," the other man replied. "They get jobs at places like this when they fly the coop, poor devils. Nice enough chap, though. And not bad coffee. Come on over and sit down for a minute and let's see where in hell we are. Want a cup?"

"Yeah, thanks. Leave a little room for cream."

Jake Reston walked over to the glass table, behind which Lieutenant Bill Box was sitting with a pad full of notes.

Jake was a slender, wiry, competent young man whose twenty-six year old head didn't have a hair on it. Some kiddingly asked him once in a while if he'd been bald when he was born—to which his standard snort was, "Yeah, even before that." He'd been with the County Sheriff's force for the three years and had enjoyed working with Box, an ex-linebacker out of Notre Dame, for about nine months now. Most of their work had been routine. Three cases had been sticky. They had solved two of those—which, according to the old-timers, wasn't too shabby a record these days. It was probably too early to tell, but this one they were on right now looked like it might make a dent in their average. A thorny one. Make no mistake about that. Something might break, but Jake's instincts at the moment were betting against it.

Jake poured a touch of cream into his coffee, picked up his cup and carefully sampled the steaming brew. Not bad. He glanced at his boss, who was studiously absorbing the notes he had in his hands, and then walked over and sat down beside him.

Bill Box had two characteristics which required understanding, Jake figured. Well, actually, it was probably more accurate to say that his boss was loco on two things, and you'd better get hep to them damn fast. Box didn't like to be interrupted when he was thinking, and Box wanted to be the boss. A large, brawny man with deep-set brown eyes set underneath a small forehead and sandy short cropped hair, he looked like a boss. He was friendly enough, but his decisive step and his firm, authoritative voice left no doubt as to who was in charge of a case. Box's strongest attribute seemed to be that he knew the limits of his own capabilities. He knew that the unknown adversaries he was up against might well be smarter or cleverer than he was. It was to his credit, therefore, that he was not afraid, when stumped, to ask for help.

At the moment, Box wasn't stumped—just a mite puzzled—a familiar feeling. He was seated at the same oblong glass table which Tony had used as a prop just before somehow making his one way trip to the bottom of the pool.

Box glanced at Reston and repeated himself. "Let's see where we are here."

"Looks like a sticky wicket so far, don't it?"

"Yeah, maybe. But we got a few things, at least. Listen—one, we've got a lady's heel print where it doesn't fit. Don't know whose yet, but we'll know before long. Two—we've got a couple of burnt paper matches, and if they end up not belonging to Endecott, this might mean something."

Jake nodded in reply.

"Three—we got a vial of stuff that our lab people say is a poison for which antidotes are real hard to come by. And we know damn well who that belongs to."

"Yeah, but we still don't know whether any of that junk got into Bleckmore. Right?"

Box nodded his head and continued.

"Four—we know the owner of that vial left the premises late last night for about ninety minutes. Right?"

"Right."

"Five—we've got a six once drinking glass with unknown prints which was pitched to a spot not far from where Bleckmore dove into the pool."

"Those prints won't be unknown for long. We got enough last night to cross-reference to someone."

"And we know that glass was thrown into those ferns over there, but we don't know exactly where the person was standing when he or she threw it, do we?"

"Negative, boss. We know the direction of flight of the glass by the way it landed in the dirt. Whoever threw it had to be standing somewhere near where we are right now. Any further away would have put him on the other side of the pool. The dent in the dirt isn't that deep. Besides, from way over there,"—Jake was pointing to the other side of the pool—"If it had been thrown from over there, the glass would have busted when it hit."

"Okay—so we've got a live glass, but so far no owner."

"Check."

"And six—we've got a lady's hair brush with a nice clear dent in it. What is it? Looks like silver to me."

Jake nodded his head. "Probably silver plate. I'll have it checked out."

"Any blood on it?"

"Negative."

"Well, Jake, that's my list. Now tell me, my friend, who's our murderer? Let's see how smart you are."

Jake laughed. "Easy. I'd say we're dealing with a man or a woman somewhere between five and seven feet tall who may or may not have been a guest at this house last night. What else you want to know?"

"Hey—you know, I think you're right. It could have been a man or a woman."

"I'd say so."

Jake got up and walked to the other end of the table and sat where Tony had been sitting the night before.

"Look here. Only a foot or two from the water. The guy was stewed. Wouldn't have taken much of a shove. Just a solid rap on the head with something and then, plop."

"Like with this brush, maybe."

Jake returned to his cup of coffee. "Maybe."

"Yeah, I guess it could have been a woman. He was a big sonuvabitch, but—could be."

"And it could have been a man," Jake said with a dry smile.

93

Box chuckled. "We're moving like a snail, aren't we—but I guess it's better than standing dead still. What'd they come up with last night? Any tracks out back?"

Jake consulted his notes.

"I didn't check that out with the fellas this morning, but I don't think so. Oh yeah, you know the dirt road which crosses the creek about fifty yards back?"

Box nodded.

"Well, there's two sets of footprints running to the creek on that road. The victim's shoe matches one set of prints. The other belongs to a lady."

"Who?"

"Dunno. But it'll be easy to check. There were only five broads here last night s'far as I know."

Box poured himself another cup of coffee. "My hunch is that it's an inside job."

"You going to play it that way?"

"With one ear. The other one I'll keep married up with my wandering eye. Which reminds me—Guess we'd better start talking to some of these people that were here last night and see if we can't get our feet on a little cement. They're all here, aren't they?"

"Yep—far as I know."

Box checked his watch. "Wonder what time these yokels rise and shine?"

"If they ain't up yet, why don't we start pounding on a few doors?"

"Good idea. Let's go."

Bill Box got off his chair, picked up his notes and headed for the house. Reston followed behind. They reached the outdoor terrace and then started up the outside stairway to the kitchen. Box was met at the door by Jeff Endecott, who was holding a glass of tomato juice in one hand.

"Ah, Lieutenant, good morning. I was just heading out to find you. Judson said you fellows have been here for a couple of hours. Don't you ever sleep?"

Box grinned. "Anything over two hours dulls my senses—especially when I'm working."

"Wish I could do that. I've had four hours, and I'm still sleeping." Jeff nodded at Jake as he came through the door. "You fellows making any progress?"

"A little." Box looked around to see who else was up.

"Good to hear. Anything I can do for you?"

"Yes, there is. As soon as possible we'd like to chat with you and your guests."

"Sure thing. In a group?"

"One at a time."

"Fine. Wanta start with me?"

"I am wondering if there's a little nook where we can talk—a little privacy somewhere?"

"You bet. I'll tell you what. Why don't we go down and sit by the pool. That's about as private a spot as any at this hour."

Box turned to Jake. "Why don't you start with the help. I'll catch up with you later."

Jake nodded to the backs of the two men who were already headed out the door. The Lieutenant and Jeff proceeded in silence down the winding path. As they neared the swimming pool area, Box turned his head and eyed his companion.

"You've got quite a layout here."

"Too big. Way too big. I'd get rid of it if I didn't enjoy entertaining so much. This pool here is tailor-made for—"

Jeff grimaced. "No—no, not anymore—not anymore. I don't think I'll ever be able to use that damned pool again. Nope—nope, I'm not sure—"

Jeff put his head in his hands as he sank into one of the poolside chairs.

"Mr. Bleckmore was a good friend of yours?" Box sat down next to Jeff, pencil and pad in hand.

"Yes—yes, he was. A hell of a good friend."

"Mr. Endecott, you know I'm compelled by law to advise you that you aren't required to answer any of my questions without your—"

"Fire away! I'm as anxious as you are to get to the bottom of this stinking mess. Oh say, there is something I don't want to forget to mention to you. An old friend of mine is flying in here this noon from Boston. I called him last night. You may have heard of him. You're working cousins. His name is Cornelius Pire. Before he retired, he was a pretty well-known private investigator working out of Boston"

"I've heard of the gentleman. I'd say he's a little better than well-known. He's been text book material for us for some time."

"No kidding. I didn't know you boys had such a close fraternity. Your boss had heard of him too. I took the liberty of checking this out with Wilcox when I got up this morning. Asked his okay to have Corny do a little prying around with your boys. Gave me the green light and said he'd get in touch with you this morning."

"Already has."

"Hope you don't mind."

"Not a bit. I'm not married to this case. The sooner we can wrap it up, the better I'll like it. Besides, who knows, I might even learn something from Pire."

"Good. You two ought to work well together."

"Sir." Box's voice had modulated into the dead serious frequency of the prying cop. "Can you tell me why you threw this party?"

"Sure. I invited these people for the weekend to celebrate my decision to run for the Senate. No secret, actually, but these people are some of my oldest friends, and I thought before any real news publicity or anything, it would be fun to have a gathering of the clan, so to speak."

"How'd you celebrate?"

Jeff chuckled. "Oh, a very conservative party. Just a little booze, dinner and swimming—not necessarily in that order. Actually, we didn't really celebrate. Just enjoyed ourselves until—"

"You didn't celebrate?"

"No. Found out everyone wasn't too gung-ho for this senate thing. So I hardly brought the matter up yesterday."

"Some of your guests were against your running?"

"Yes. Yes, they were. Well, it was only one, actually. Tony. He was here Friday evening. We discussed the matter briefly, and to my surprise, he didn't like the idea. So, yesterday, as I said, I left the matter alone."

"Did Mr. Bleckmore say why he was cool on your running?"

"No. No, I'm sure he would have. But as I said, we only had time to discuss it briefly."

"Did all of your guests arrive here on Friday?"

"No, just Tony. The rest got here yesterday noon."

"What was Mr. Bleckmore doing here Friday evening, Sir?"

Jeff shifted uncomfortably in his chair.

"Tony and I had a mutual love for booze, Chinese food and women, Lieutenant. I imported all three Friday night.

"The ladies' names?"

"Will this get them in any trouble?"

"Academic question. It will save me a little digging if you tell me."

"Morra and Sorra. I expect you know their real names. I don't."

"I know 'em. Were they here all night?"

"Took them home before breakfast."

"You were on what kind of terms with Mr. Bleckmore?"

"Tony? He was a very dear friend. Our relationship was warm. He was an expert at enjoying life, a hobby in which I also have an avid interest."

"Do you know anyone here last night who didn't like Mr. Bleckmore?"

"No. Near as I know, everyone likes—liked Tony."

Jeff thought for a moment. "No—no, I guess that's not quite true. Lena—his ex wife—I guess you'd say she didn't like him much."

"Do you know why?"

"I don't *know* why. I imagine it's because she didn't approve of his life style."

"He ran around a lot when they were married?"

"Yes."

"Anyone else who didn't like Mr. Bleckmore?"

"Not as far as I know. Thought we had a real friendly group, or I wouldn't have asked them out here. Probably made a mistake with Lena, though."

"Why?"

"Oh, don't get me wrong, Lieutenant. Lena's a real sweet gal—sharp sometimes, sure, but she wouldn't hurt a fly. I just don't think she was happy yesterday, and Tony's got to be the reason."

"Mr. Kennelly—He part of your friendly group?"

"Sam? He's a long time buddy. Why you asking?'

"He was the only one of your guests I couldn't communicate with last night. I assume you know why."

"I know, Lieutenant. Blato! Zonked! Surprised the hell out of me. I've never seen him that way before."

"You're saying he usually holds his liquor?"

"Yeah, he does. One drink a night, and he always holds that one real well. One's his limit. Never've been able to talk him into another. Tony's death must have gotten to him."

"Mr. Kennelly a good friend of Mr. Bleckmore?"

"They were partners, Lieutenant. As far as I know, they both benefited from that relationship."

"Let's see—" Box studied the notes he'd been making. "One other couple I'd like your opinion about Mr. Endecott—The Strabos."

"Just like the rest. Old, old friends."

"Of whom?"

"Of whom?" Jeff seemed surprised by the question. "Of everyone here last night.

As I've said, we've all known each other for some time."

"Dr. Strabo's a psychiatrist."

"A Who's-Who shrink—Yep."

"An expert in parapsychology."

"Hey, you guys move fast on your homework, don't you?"

"As you say, he is pretty well known."

Box paused and considered his next question."

"Are you aware, Sir, that the Strabos disappeared for a couple of hours late last night?"

"You mean they left this place?" Jeff asked, obviously surprised. Box nodded.

"No, I didn't. I thought the whole gang had tucked themselves in for the night."

"They all did, eventually. The Strabos returned about three in the morning. They'd have been a little smarter, however, if they had never left—or at least had let us know they were leaving."

The Lieutenant reached into his briefcase and pulled out a small plastic vial neatly encased in a plastic wrapper.

"Otherwise we wouldn't have been inclined to search their room and find this."

"What is it?"

"Methylbenzethonium Chloride. It has several commercial uses. It's also a very lethal poison."

"My God! That's Collin's?"

"I assume so. It was stashed away in his room."

Jeff smiled ruefully. "I sometimes wonder if shrinks aren't often loonier than their patients."

"I'll leave that one alone."

Box suppressed the faint trace of a smile. He replaced the vial in his briefcase and then shifted in his chair and faced Jeff.

"Mr. Endecott, have a go at outlining your day yesterday for me."

Jeff eyed Box curiously. "How close do you want it?"

"As close as you can recall it."

Jeff leaned back, put one leg over the arm of his chair and for a few moments let his eyes rest on the tops of some of his towering oaks.

"Well—they all started arriving here around noon—"

Methodically, he recounted his perspectives on the group's afternoon and early evening activities up to and including Bleckmore's disappearance and the eventual discovery of his body at the bottom of the pool. Jeff emphasized repeatedly that, until they found Tony, the day had been pretty uneventful.

"That's about it. You now know about what I know, which isn't much."

"You mentioned that Mrs. Tone fainted. She do that often?"

"Don't think so. She sure doesn't seem like the fainting type to me."

"Nor to me," Box bit off tersely. "So why'd she faint? You any idea?"

"I'll give you a good guess. Tony had a flesh burn running most of the way around his neck. I'm sure you saw it."

"Yeah, we saw it. I was wondering when you were going to mention this."

"I think Sybil fainted when she heard Collin indicate that he'd seen burns like that on a corpse fresh off a hangman's noose."

"She told you this?"

"No. Like I said, I'm guessing."

"Well, our coroner isn't guessing about Mr. Bleckmore's neck. He reached the same conclusion as Dr. Strabo."

Box's eyes were riveted on Jeff.

"So where do *you* figure this leaves us? Mr. Bleckmore died of drowning, not strangulation."

Jeff took his time replying. He was leaning forward in his chair and staring dully at his feet.

"Yeah, well—I was going to get to this. It's not an easy thing, you know, when the guy we're talking about's a close friend. Tony showed up over here Wednesday morning all shaken up. Not the Tony I'd ever seen before—not by any stretch of the imagination. He claimed that someone busted into his condo earlier in the week and tried to hang him. He said that whoever this was hog-tied him and strung him up to an overhead beam in his family room. That's about all he could remember when he came to. He told me that the way he figured it, he busted the rope when he fell, and that was what saved his life."

"Sweet Jesus!" Box was regarding Jeff with rapt attention. "Take me through this hanging bit one more time—and slower."

Laboriously, Jeff repeated his story.

"You say, Mr. Bleckmore thought his assailant was a pro. He have a reason?"

"I don't know for sure. The man's gun had a silencer on it. Knowing Tony, that probably meant a pro."

"This hangman have a name?" Box asked cynically.

"Yes, as a matter of fact. Alfie."

"Alfie?"

"Alfie. That's all. Just Alfie."

"Shit!"

"Mean something, Lieutenant?"

"Yeah. Probably means his name's not Alfie—especially if the guy's a pro. Only—it couldn't have been a pro."

"Why not?"

"The rope wouldn't have snapped."

"Oh, I forgot to tell you, Lieutenant. Tony said he thought it had been cut."

"Cut?"

"That's what he said. He thought, I guess, that whoever this guy was, he was trying to scare the crap out of him."

Box rose from his chair, strolled to a spot several yards away, where he stopped. He leaned his back against a low-slung rosewood and became preoccupied in thought. A couple of minutes later he swung around and walked back to Jeff.

"Well, it looks like at least temporarily you've shoved me off in another direction,

If some stranger got in here last night, professional or otherwise, he probably left some kind of a calling card. So, we'll start looking a little closer."

"Even a pro leaves a trail, eh?"

"Somebody, somewhere, usually leaves a trail. Usually. Not always. Which leads me to my last question. I still don't follow you on Mr. Bleckmore's trail last night. See if you can help me here. Let's start with that game you said you were playing after dinner. Did everyone arrive at approximately the same time?"

"Can't remember. Far as I know, they did—except, I guess, Tony. Someone told me later that Tony was one of the last to show up and passed through the recreation room without stopping. Apparently, he was going up to his room. Nobody thought much about it at the time as we all knew Tony had had a snoot full."

"You didn't see him?"

"No, I didn't. Like about everyone else in the room, I had to go to the can. He came up when I was taking my turn, I guess."

"And no one, as far as you know, saw Mr. Bleckmore after that?"

"Nope. There's a million ways Tony could have made his way back to the pool. The question is—why in God's name did he go back, unless someone forced him to?"

Bill Box placed his notes in his briefcase and stuck out his hand.

"Thanks. I'll be back at you again before the day's over. You've been a help."

"I've got one for you, Lieutenant. This restriction thing you set up—How long?"

"I told you last night, anyone can leave any time they want—But Id rather talk to them here first. Ought to be able to do that by the middle of this afternoon."

Jeff acknowledged Box's reply by raising his hand, waving and turning to leave.

"I'll be around here all day if you need me."

Box picked up his briefcase, and then, head down and prepossessed, he ambled up the path behind Jeff.

Cornelius Pire. Huh, now it's coming back. The Belladonna murders. That's when he had first heard about this guy Pire—He'd read about how this pip-squeak of a private dick had wrapped up a case in a few weeks that had hamstrung East Coast authorities for more than three years. Something about a Mother Theresa type who turned out to be a rancorous old lady. Yeah, that was it—This old biddy got her kicks out of sprinkling various kinds of blackberries around the neighborhood with deadly results. How had Pire gotten to the nub of that one? Can't remember. Have to ask him. Yep, probably a good thing the ol' codger's coming. If there was any kind of Mother Theresa hanging around this place last night, it wouldn't hurt to have Pire around.

CHAPTER TWELVE

Late Morning Sunday—June 7th

Damn!

Lieutenant Box's head snapped up and out of its reverie as he lumbered up toward the Endecott home after his interview with Jeff.

Why in bloody hell are you crawling along this path like a wooden Indian and daydreaming about the imminent arrival of one Cornelius Pire? Get your butt in gear, man. You're never gonna catch a killer when your head's up and locked.

Box immediately picked up his gait and was at Jeff's kitchen door almost before he had completed chastising himself. He walked inside and spotted Reston talking with Judson in an alcove off the kitchen. Box motioned Jake to follow him. Moments later, the two men were standing together on the outer terrace.

"I gotta leave for an hour or two. Something's come up."

Jake nodded.

"Fill you in later. Save me some time."

Again, Jake nodded.

"While I'm gone, talk to as many of these birds as you can. Loosen up their tongues. Soft soap em a little if you have to. Tell the Strabos to stick around. If they insist on leaving, let 'em know they better not be hard to find. Okay?"

Box didn't bother to look or listen for a reply. He was gone. A couple of minutes later, he had his patrol car speeding down a narrow two lane road toward the big city.

Several miles down the road, he screeched to a halt near a major intersection and pulled out his phone.

Box dialed a number automatically. He told the controller who answered to patch him through to his boss and NOW. Moments later, the voice of Sheriff Randy Wilcox was on the other end of the line.

"Randy—Sorry to interrupt you, but I may have a hot one—and then again, this may be just pissing in the wind. Don't know. But you remember that NCIC bulletin we got nearly a year ago referencing to an NCB Advisory about some hit man on Interpol's files? He was moving into our area somewhere."

Yes, Wilcox remembered. He put Box on hold. A minute later, he was back on the line with a piece of paper in front of him.

"I got it in my hand."

"What's the guy's name?"

"Romanareo."

"A.k.a. The Roman?"

"The Roman," Wilcox echoed. "What's this guy got to do with Bleckmore?"

"Don't know, for sure. I'm operating on hearsay, so far. Gonna chat with this guy if I can find him. Then I'll try and answer your question."

"Remember, Box, legally, the Roman's a saint in heaven. No one's ever caught the guy even jaywalking."

"I know what a sweetheart he is. That's how he got on Interpol's master assassin list, ain't it. What's his first name, boss?"

"Doesn't say."

"An address?"

"Where are you?"

"On 19 at the corner of Roosevelt."

"Well, he's holed up in a house he owns about five miles down the road from where you are now—just west of Cederville."

Wilcox gave Box the address and indicated that there'd been some casual surveillance on Romanareo since he moved in a little over a year ago.

"Thanks."

"Hey, Box," Wilcox snapped, "you got someone with you?"

"Negative. But I'm all right. I'll be by and let you know how I make out."

Box slammed his phone back in its cradle before the sheriff had time to argue. He pulled back on to Highway 19 and roared towards Cederville.

Easy to find. The house was set back about two hundred feet from the road. A freshly painted white picket fence extended around a spacious, neatly manicured lawn. A small sign was attached to the front gate indicating that, "The dogs are friendly if you are."

Box glanced around for the dogs but couldn't see any. So he proceeded up the walk to the front door.

No door bell. He knocked. Before his knuckles hit the door a second time, the door swung open. A tiny Japanese girl, hands clasped demurely in front of her, stood in the doorway looking at him.

Ma'am? Miss? What the hell. How old was this kimono standing in front of him? She wasn't much bigger than one of his daughter's dolls.

"Miss—" That's usually safe, he decided. "Romanareo live here?"

Slowly, the little slip of a miss floated backwards and to one side and beckoned him into the house.

Box took three steps into the house and stopped. He didn't have to ask *where* Romanareo was. A man was standing five feet away. It was obvious this guy wasn't the cook. A leather vest over a tan turtleneck. Jeans, boots and absolutely no fat. No fat anywhere. Box knew he was looking at the Roman, even though he had never seen even a picture of the guy.

"Lieutenant Box, I believe. Welcome to my parlor."

"You Romanareo?"

Box eased his partially extracted badge back into his pocket and critically scrutinized the man standing across from him.

"I knew Romanareo. He's dead, friend."

That damn smile! Box hated men who smiled a lot. Could never read their bloody minds. Always made him feel uncomfortable.

"When'd he die?" Box threw back a forced smile."

"About a year ago. You're looking at Alfie, Lieutenant." He moved up and shook the officer's hand. "Let me introduce you to my family."

Alfie motioned to the lady who was still standing by the door.

"Sing Sang, my wife."

Alfie then pivoted slightly and pointed to two other kimono clad dolls who had magically appeared at the far end of the large sitting room.

"And those are Sing Sang's two sisters, Sang Sung and Sung Sing."

Box nodded impassively. "Nice looking family. How do you tell them apart?" Box glanced around the expensively furnished room. "And incidentally, where are the dogs?"

"In the next room, Lieutenant—a pair of the prettiest Dobermans you'll ever see. Would you like to meet them?"

Box shook his head.

"I'd like to talk. Where can we go?"

"Ah yes, you came for a reason, didn't you. I almost forgot. How's right here?" Alfie pointed to a couple of soft chairs with oriental slipcovers.

Box nodded, moved to one of the chairs and sat down.

Alfie followed and sat across from him.

"Actually, the dogs are superfluous, Lieutenant. Don't really need them. Sing Sang has a black belt in Kung Fu. Sang Sung is a master in Tae-Know-Do. And Sung Sing has perfected both Jijitsee and Aikido. One of them's always awake. So you can see, I'm pretty comfortable here."

Box cracked a smile in spite of himself. He noticed suddenly that the three aforementioned ladies had somehow disappeared.

"You snap your fingers or something and things happen. That it?"

"What's that?" Alfie looked puzzled.

"Your singing Kimonos. You just give them the high sign and they disappear. Good trick."

"No high sign, Lieutenant. We talk with the mind." Alfie pointed to his head in emphasis. "It's easier that way. Also a lot more fun—especially when you get involved in other activities and you have the right partner—and especially when this right partner is an expert at indulging in a smorgasbord of mental intercourse, climax hovering and—"

Box coughed to suppress a laugh. "Alfie," he snorted, "you know Tony Bleckmore.?"

Alfie's smile broadened.

"Know of him. Never met him."

"You haven't? You sure?"

"Sure enough. Should I?"

"He's dead. You know that?"

"Great!"

"Great? Is that a yes or no?"

"That's a no, Lieutenant. When did he die?"

"Last night—which brings me to my next armchair question. Where were you last night?"

"I don't remember."

"You better try. Your name's come up in connection with Bleckmore."

"All right. You motivated me. I was right here with my three cherubs."

"All night?"

"All night."

"Next question. How'd you know Bleckmore?"

"I collect paintings." Alfie pivoted and pointed to a couple of dozen impressionistic and abstract paintings interspersed throughout the room.

"Bleckmore's got a hold on a fish bowl oil I want. Mrs. Tone won't sell it to me until the big man's made up his mind. From what you're telling me, sounds like Bleckmore's decided to let me have it."

"So you know Mrs. Tone," Box muttered suspiciously.

"Super dame. Four of these paintings in here come from her gallery. Got lots of moxie—Knows her business."

"You said, 'great, Bleckmore's dead'. What the hell's that mean?"

"It means—now I can have the fish bowl."

"He was murdered."

"Oh." Alfie frowned. "Another shocker, Lieutenant, but I can handle it."

"I won't ask you if you already knew this. I think I know your answer."

"You're reading my mind. Good play!"

"Endecott. You know him?"

"Our next senator. I've heard of him."

"What else you know about him?"

"Nothing. Why you asking me about that loaded gent?"

"Because he was a good friend of Bleckmore's."

"Not a way to win an election. That what you're saying?"

"I'd suggest that you tell the Roman to listen carefully. What I'm saying is that Endecott's claiming that Bleckmore told him that a man who called himself Alfie tried to kill Bleckmore."

"Snakes alive! Must be another Alfie somewhere."

"By hanging him."

"An execution. How 'bout that!"

"Only this Alfie we're talking about didn't succeed."

"I thought you said Bleckmore was dead."

"He is. Murdered last night at Endecott's. The attempted hang was several days ago at Bleckmore's pad."

Alfie leaned back in his chair and beamed.

"Sounds to me like you don't know who done it and you want my help."

"Like starting right now, Alfie, by telling me how many times the Roman's been to Bleckmore's."

"I told you—The Roman's dead. But I'll try and answer your question this way. However I choose to deny knowledge about anything you ask me, it's all pretty theoretical, wouldn't you say, unless, that is, you've got testimony from a witness that'll challenge my memory?"

"We'll have Endecott's statement from Bleckmore."

"Who's dead. I'll tell ya what—why don't I save us both a lot of time. I don't know how Bleckmore got his last night, and more importantly, I didn't give it to him. Honest! Scout's honor."

Alfie flashed Box the three finger salute.

"What do you do for a living?"

"I'm retired."

"From what?"

"I was a horticulturist, Lieutenant. Now, I'm in the process of seeking new cultures to conquer. And hey, I'll answer your next question before you ask it. I inherited my modest means from an Asian woman who took a shine to me and whose name I've managed to forget. That's my whole autobiography, Sir. Now you know all about me without having to open a book."

Box jumped to his feet.

"I know about the Roman, Alfie. He was good. Very good. He made a ton of money knocking off a variety of odd types around the world, and so far, he's never had to account for his actions."

Box glared at the unblinking eyes of Alfie, who had also risen from his chair.

"I say—so far, Alfie. But you never know when the Roman might make his first mistake, do you. I'm telling you right now, I'm going to have my people comb Endecott's joint, inside and out, like it's never been combed before. And if we find even one minuscule pinhead that's got your name on it, I'll be back."

Alfie bowed low.

"So don't go anywhere. Okay?"

"If I leave the country, I'll drop you my address."

Box moved to the door and swung around.

"Don't even leave the county until I get back to you."

Alfie stuck out his hand which Box shook mechanically.

"Glad to meet you, Lieutenant. You're the first live police officer I've had the pleasure to meet and visit with in a long time. Enjoyed it."

Alfie continued as Box let himself out the door.

"Tell you what. When this Bleckmore thing blows over, why don't you come back for a longer visit. I'll show you my flowers and give you a glass of the best Pomerol out of St. Emilion you ever wet your tongue on. How's that?"

"When you hit me with your real autobiography someday, I'll consider it," Box tossed back over his shoulder as he headed for his car.

A minute later, he was speeding towards town to see his boss.

CHAPTER THIRTEEN

Forenoon Sunday—June 7th

Sam checked his watch.

Eleven-thirty—exactly. Too darn late to go to church. But, well—at least he and Anne were getting out of this place. Anything was better than staying here one minute longer.

Where the devil was Anne? She'd said she'd be right along.

Sam glanced out the side window of his car at Endecott's front door. The door was still partially ajar just like he'd left it a few minutes ago.

Damn! He was always waiting like this for her to show up. Wonder if she knew how frustrating it was to wait like this for someone who was always an inch behind you when you walked out the door. For forty years, he'd been doing this. Must be over a million hours of waiting. Probably more.

Sam turned on the radio and picked up a voice telling the world what a beautiful day it was.

Yes, beautiful to some—but around here it sure was crummy. *And*—the day wasn't even half over yet. That cop—what was his name? Heston—Reston—something like that. A damn unpleasant cuss. Asked questions like he was interviewing a condemned man. What were you doing here when? How well did you know the dead man? Do you have a drinking problem? Drinking problem—God, that one was the limit. Wanted to tell that fuzz that whatever problems old Sam's got are none of his business. Probably would have too, if Anne hadn't chimed in and—What was it she said? Oh yeah—*My husband's a very modest drinker, Officer, and last night , he ate something that disagreed with him.* Ha, good ol' Anne. Good thing she hadn't said something about the fact that her husband had *seen* something that didn't agree with him.; Lord knows, she probably would have spilled the beans if she'd known what was really bothering him. That would have popped Heston's eyeballs for sure. No wonder people didn't like cops. Impertinent, nosy bums—even when you try to be nice to them. Like this morning—Even took the time to write down a chronology of just what happened around here last night and exactly when it happened. Thought it might help those birds get to the bottom of things. But—Was there any kind of thank you-very-much? No, there was not! Just a suspicious look or two and some more insolence. Like—*How'd you figure all this by the minute stuff out, Mr. Kennelly, if you spent the whole evening swacked?*

Someone ought to invent a charm school for cops, Sam decided, as he caught sight of his wife coming down the front steps.

She opened the car door.

"Did you tell anyone we're leaving?"

"No, let's go! Get in!"

"Don't you think we ought to?"

"Why?"

Anne snuggled up next to her husband.

"Oh Sam, I'm so worried. I'm glad we're leaving, but I keep thinking we should be staying. It seems like everyone else is and they're all so suspicious. I—Oh my goodness, did you hear—did you know Collin is in terrible trouble?"

"Collin? You serious?" Sam pointed the car down the driveway.

"Yes. Kevin just told me. I ran into him in the hall. That's why I'm late. He told me that the police found a bottle of arsenic in his room and they're going to ask him all kinds of questions."

"Arsenic? Collin? You sure?"

"Yes. It was either in his room or they found it on him. I'm not sure what Kevin said. Oh Sam, maybe it's a good idea we're leaving before they find your gun. I wish you had listened to me. I pleaded with you. I—"

"Anne! Damn it! I didn't bring that gun here. I told you that."

Anne gasped in surprise.

"I didn't. Honest."

"You didn't," Anne breathed softly. "Oh my, that's nice. I don't remember your telling me that."

"You asked me not to bring it, didn't you?"

"Yes."

"When you told me Friday that you hadn't called Jeff, I figured the least I could do was to leave the gun home."

"Thank you."

"No big deal. Even if I had brought it, it wouldn't have meant anything."

"How can you say that?"

"They haven't found any bullet holes in Bleckmore, have they?"

"Was he strangled, you think?"

"Sure—probably by the same guy who tried to get him earlier in the week."

"Sam, stop the car!"

Sam glanced over at his wife, not sure he had heard correctly this rare *command* from his wife.

"Please, pull over. I want you to look at me."

"You all right?" Sam was wearing a frown as he pulled the car over to the side of the drive. He turned and faced his wife.

Anne was staring sternly straight ahead.

"We've been married nearly forty years, haven't we, Sam?"

"Now, what in the world's this all about?"

"You're not answering my question."

"All right—all right. So we've been married a long time. I agree. So what?"

"And you've never ever had too much to drink before, have you?"

Sam's frown deepened.

"In fact, I can hardly recall a time when you've had more than one drink—not even when we're at one of Jeffrey's parties. Am I right?"

"I suppose so, but—"

"Then tell me what happened last night. I'm your wife. I deserve to know why you behaved so strangely. Something bad was bothering you. Whatever it was, I want to share it with you."

"Give me a few minutes to collect my thoughts, Anne, and I'll tell you. You're right, as usual."

He eased their car back onto the driveway. When he reached the highway, he turned right and headed for home.

"Anne, you remember that game we played last night?"

Anne nodded her head.

"You remember anyone missing while we were playing it?"

"Yes."

"You do? Who?"

"Tony."

"I mean—besides Tony."

Anne thought for a moment. "I'm not sure. Why?"

"Probably the same kind of an answer I'd have given normally. But after we found Tony, I started thinking. I remembered going to the bathroom after we had gotten started on that stupid game and noticing that somehow my pocket watch was missing. I knew I had it down by the pool, so I figured I must have dropped it somewhere coming up to the house. I slipped out one of the back doors and headed back down to the pool to see if I could find it. That's when I ran into Kevin. He had my watch in his hand and said he'd found it just off the path where, apparently, I had dropped it. I thanked him and wouldn't have thought anymore about it, except for Tony. Afterwards, bumping into Kevin popped back into my mind, and that's when it hit me like a ton of bricks. I mean—"

Sam paused and took a deep breath.

"What hit you, Sam?"

"Kevin was carrying his suit jacket in his hand. His tie was loosened and askew. And one sleeve of his shirt was soaking wet."

"Oh dear. Oh, my goodness." Anne was whispering. "Do you suppose—do you suppose—"

"I didn't suppose last night, Anne. I knew. That's why I went berserk with that bottle. So far, I haven't seen anything or heard anything that makes me think I was wrong."

"Kevin couldn't have. He's too nice a person."

"You're wrong. He could have. He was mad enough at Tony. I know that for sure. But—Oh, how I sure hope he didn't. I can hardly stand the thoughts I'm thinking. He's one of the most honorable guys I know. But—well,. no matter how you slice it, it looks to me like he's been involved in something screwy."

Anne turned her head away from Sam and stared aimlessly out her side window.

"No. No, I don't believe it. Kevin's Kevin. A dear man. I saw him in the recreation room, and he looked like his normal well-groomed self to me."

"You did? Was he there for long?"

"I don't know. I wasn't keeping track of who was where any more than you were."

Anne touched her husband's arm lightly.

"When I stop to think about it, Sam, I don't even remember seeing you in the room all the time. Everyone, including you, was moving about quite a bit."

Sam remained quietly morose for several miles. Then he glanced over at Anne and sputtered gruffly, "If anyone asks you where I was last night, you tell them I was in that game room every minute. Never left it. Didn't even go to the can. You tell them that. Okay?"

"Yes dear. I will say that—even if you whisper to me that you know who *really* murdered Tony."

Sam slowed the car down and eyeballed his wife.

"Say that again."

Anne folded her hands in her lap, let her head fall back onto the seat's headrest and ignored Sam's request. She closed her eyes and her mind at the same time. It was the only way to block out the quivers which had been running crazy inside her ever since last night. She had to block them out. She didn't want to cry again.

CHAPTER FOURTEEN

Noon Sunday—June 7th

By the time the Kennellys reached their home, Box was back at Endecott's. He had not lingered long at the main office—just long enough to fill in Wilcox on his Alfie visit and secure a promise from his boss to break loose a half a dozen men. For as long as it took, Box intended to comb Endecott's estate for evidence of any outside intrusion—especially by one Alfie, a.k.a. the Roman.

In response to Wilcox's "What'd you find out?" Box had hedged.

"Well, I'll tell ya. Not a hell of a lot. All I know for sure is I wouldn't want to go one-on-one with the guy. He looks lethal enough to be our man, but beyond that, I couldn't read him. One thing, though. I want to look at the Endecott spread real hard—real damn hard."

With that summation, Box had excused himself and hurried back to Endecott's. He located Reston quickly, filled him in, and then informed his assistant about the extra men who were arriving at noon.

"You're in charge of that detail, Reston. If you find anything even faintly resembling outside intrusion of this property, I want you to shoot off a large cannon. I want to know sooner than now. Got it?"

Box then headed for Endecott's study where, according to Reston, the Strabos had been waiting for him for nearly an hour.

The interview with Collin and Marva started out poorly, then steadily regressed to lousy. Collin was obviously used to doing the interviewing and didn't like being on the receiving end of questions. That he had been made to wait an eternity for this snooping police officer had added insult to injury. Box was able to get in only a few routine questions before Collin's fuse ignited.

"Lieutenant, let me make this very clear. I am not going to reply to any more of you idiotic imputations."

Bill Box was seated behind Jeffrey's desk. The study door was closed. His eyes were glued on Collin Strabo who was standing in front of a chair on the other side of the desk and who, at the moment, was on the verge of losing his cool. Box had always pictured shrinks as being possessed with more self-control. Strabo on the edge might mean something. Worth pushing the guy a little more. He glanced at Strabo's wife, who was sitting in a chair at one side of the desk. How 'bout that now! Looked like she was as angry as her husband. Her eyes were straight down on the floor. Angry eyes. Sure looked like it. And her ears seemed to be intently following Strabo as he paced back and forth in front of the desk.

"I repeat, Sir, I am through cooperating."

Collin stopped pacing and faced Box.

"You have broken into our room, confiscated our possessions, put us under house arrest without provocation, and now are subjecting my wife and me to interrogation like—like common criminals. Your manner is impudent, and I resent the association you are obviously attempting to make between Mr Bleckmore's untimely death and our presence on these premises."

Collin paused for breath.

Quickly, Box jumped in.

"That association you're referring to is not mine. It is, I'm afraid, a fact that Mr. Bleckmore was murdered here last evening and you, among others, Sir, were on the premises at the time."

"Lieutenant, that doesn't make me or my wife a murderer. I—"

"Dr. Strabo!" Box's voice had suddenly become hard. "This interview is terminated. You're free to leave. I have no further questions. For your information, before you go—if I thought you were the murderer, you would have been behind bars long ago."

Box reached into his pocket and produced a small plastic vial. "Here, this belongs to you, I believe."

Collin, startled and somewhat subdued, reached for the vial. "You're returning this to me?"

"It's yours, isn't it?"

"Certainly. It 's registered in my name."

"Yes, so we noticed."

"Then why did you enter our room and take it?"

"As long as you're asking, I'll tell you why."

Box rose from the desk, walked around the desk to where Collin was standing and looked sharply down at the surprised psychiatrist.

"In the first place, we were under the impression, when we entered your room, that you had voluntarily vacated the premises. We assumed this after listening to the report of our man on duty late last night who described your rapid departure to us. In the second place, we don't often find an exotic poison in a home where a man has been murdered—especially when the owner of that poison has suspiciously fled the scene."

Collin backed up a couple of steps for air.

"I was not aware that Mr. Bleckmore was poisoned."

"He wasn't."

"Then, I still don't understand."

"Neither to I, Doctor. I was hoping originally that you'd have an inclination to explain why you brought poison to an overnight party."

"Do I need to explain?"

"Not to me. Maybe to a court. But not to me."

"Well, I'll wait for the court then."

"Officer!" Marva was on her feet facing Box and standing near to Collin. "I don't understand my husband at all—"

"Marva, for God's sake, will you—" Collin had his wife by the arm.

"Collin, stop!" She pulled herself free. "Please, be quiet for a minute!"

Collin complied, obviously surprised by her uncharacteristically brusque manner. Marva turned to Box.

"I don't understand my husband at the moment. I love him dearly, but I don't understand him. I guess you are giving us permission to leave. Well, when we leave, we're going home. You have our address and if you have any further questions you'd like to ask, I'll be glad to answer them. Lately, I haven't been too fond of Mr. Bleckmore, but I never wished him dead. If there's any way I can be of help to you in discovering how he died, please call on me."

Marva turned to Collin and took his arm.

"Thank you, dear, for letting me make my little speech without interrupting me."

Collin, with Marva beside him, turned his back on Box and walked slowly toward the study's closed door. When they reached the door, Collin turned back to Box. He had reacquired the impassive expression of a doctor who is about to articulate an opinion.

"I still say that a man is innocent until proven guilty—at least that's the way I understand things still work in this country. I am not sure you look at it this way."

Box walked over and opened the door for them.

"You are absolutely right, Dr. Strabo. If I assumed every man was innocent of the crimes we investigate, I'm not sure I could ever prove that anyone was guilty."

Collin walked out of the room without pausing for a reply. Neither did his wife pause, as Collin had a firm grip on her arm. But Box saw Marva's eyes linger long enough to catch his.

Now what the hell did she mean by that look? It was a look which was neither friendly or hostile—but it was a look. No question about that. A man likes to understand what the hell he's doing—especially in this lousy cops and robbers business. So far, this morning, it seems like he understood very little of what he had been doing, except that just about everyone he'd talked to so far wasn't leveling with him—which, come to think of it, is probably the way the ball bounces more times than not.

Box glanced at his watch. Time for an early lunch. Good. He was hungry. Perhaps a ham sandwich and some pretzels would improve his disposition as well as his stomach—temporarily. Yeah, only temporarily, if that long. His next interview was with that ex wife of Endecott's—which means that things could go from the way they are right now to considerably worse.

———◆◆◆◆◆———

"Mrs. Endecott!"

Bill Box was choosing his words with the same care he had used to choose the screened in verandah as a place to meet. He didn't want Endecott's ex to feel oppressed. The information he was relating to her was, in itself, oppressive enough. The open aired, tree-shaded comfort of this verandah—well, this might be enough to keep this volatile woman's emotions intact. Box sure hoped so.

"Mrs. Endecott, there's no need to get alarmed about what I've been telling you. It may mean absolutely nothing."

"Then why did you tell me?" Ethel was grim. Her eyes were boring into Box who was averting her gaze."

"No reason except I thought you were entitled to know."

"My fingerprints on a glass found near where Tony had been sitting. I still don't understand why this makes me guilty of murder."

"Obviously, it doesn't."

"Well?"

"We merely think it strange that yours are the only prints on a glass thrown into the foliage from a spot very near to where Mr. Bleckmore was murdered."

"I admit the glass is like one I was drinking from. But I did not throw that glass or any other glass into the garden."

"'What did you do with the glass? Can you recall?"

"No I can't! And I'll bet you can't find anyone else who can remember a silly detail like that."

"It may be a detail, Ma'am, but it's not silly."

Box reached into his briefcase, propped up against his chair, and quickly produced a silver-plated hairbrush, which was wrapped in a transparent plastic cover.

"This your brush?"

"No, it's Mr. Endecott's."

Ethel's response failed to conceal her apprehension.

"It's part of a bedroom set in my room. I used it yesterday down at the pool."

"Thank you. It has your fingerprints on it."

"Yes—So?"

"It also has a sizable dent in the heavy end of the brush."

Box held the brush up in front of Ethel.

"Do you recall seeing this dent before, Ma'am?"

"No, I don't. I don't know—I may have dropped it or something. I can't remember."

"It doesn't appear to be that kind of a dent. You sure it wasn't already in the brush when you were using it?"

"I'm sure."

Ethel's voice was beginning to quiver. Box knew he had gone far enough. Time to retreat. He decided, for the moment, not to mention the heel print which Reston had told him had been matched to a shoe belonging to Mrs. Endecott and which was found in her bedroom this morning.

"You've been very helpful. I have only one more question, if you don't mind."

Box wasn't looking at Ethel for affirmation. His eyes were on his notes.

"Did you see anything, or do you know anything which would help us locate the person who murdered Mr. Bleckmore?"

Ethel was on her feet. She had her handkerchief gripped tightly in one hand. Her purse was in the other. Her lips trembled.

"Mr. Box, you call me out onto this porch, accuse me of murdering Tony Bleckmore, and then ask me if I have any idea who his murderer was. I find your approach appalling—very appalling. But I'll answer your question. No, no, no, I have no idea who killed Mr. Bleckmore. Whoever did, didn't consult with me. Now, am I free to go?"

"Yes, you are." Box stood up as Ethel moved towards the verandah door.

"You may be interested to know that I've just come to the conclusion that I don't like policemen. Does this surprise you?"

"Yes, Ma'am. Actually, it seemed to me you were quite fond of them."

The door slammed, and Ethel disappeared.

Box pulled out a cigarette and smiled sadly.

What a fun job you've got, pal.

He lit his cigarette, and then, after taking a long drag, he watched the smoke curl aimlessly above him and gradually fade into nothing.

CHAPTER FIFTEEN

Late Noon Sunday—June 7th

A lavish Sunday late noon lunch originally had been planned for ten people. The sudden demise of one of the house guests, however, had reduced this number to four. Maude and James had been instructed by Jeff to serve the original menu to anyone who stayed for lunch. And so, a five-course meal was served to four who barely had one-course appetites. The mood amongst the four guests was somber. The conversation was sporadic and, even after a light Sancerre wine began to take its bite, quite guarded.

Ethel was sitting at one end of the long dining room table. On either side of her were Sybil, Kevin and Lena. All four had decided to spend another evening at Endecott's in order to be of some assistance wherever they might be needed. At least, this was the Tones and Ethel's avowed desire. Lena seemed to be staying simply because she didn't want to return home.

Over after-lunch coffee, Lena asked Ethel why she was so flustered and angry after her brief conversation with Lt. Box. Ethel replied that the Lieutenant had pointed a finger at one of their party on such flimsy evidence that she could not control her shocked reaction. When pushed to elucidate, Ethel deftly shifted the conversation to Kevin, accusing him of being unusually quiet for a man with such an affable reputation.

"Ethel, I'm afraid we've all been behaving unlike ourselves since we've been here—not just me," Kevin countered.

"For one thing," Sybil added, "none of us have had much sleep."

"And another thing," Lena added, "these cops crawling around here are enough to give a hot toddy the shivers."

"How did you make out with the Lieutenant," Ethel inquired sweetly, looking at Kevin? "Are you free and clear?"

"As far as I'm concerned I am. And that's what I told him."

"You ought to have been able to tell him something more than that, Kevin dear." Lena was smiling, but her voice wasn't. "It seems to me you were afoot a great deal last night."

"Yes, that's what Box said." Kevin turned his head angrily and looked directly at Lena. "I wonder who told him that?"

"Darling, don't look at me. I haven't had the pleasure of the Lieutenant's company yet. But I am interested to observe your unusual lack of composure. It's surprising you don't care to reveal yourself more to your dear, dear friends."

Kevin paused to sip some coffee before replying.

"If I decide to reveal anything to anyone, it will be to tell our fine-feathered police officers that I think they're barking up the wrong tree. There's an obvious approach to slicing through the mystery of last night, and they're not taking it."

Sybil looked sharply at Lena.

"I think you are being a little harsh with Kevin, my dear. I'm on edge. I'll admit it. And I'm sure Kevin will admit he's on edge too. It seems to me that it's perfectly natural for all of us to be a bit jumpy under the circumstances."

Sybil threw a tender look at her husband.

"What is *your* approach, dear?"

"Simple. You remember last night—Tony came dragging into the room. He didn't stay—didn't say anything—just went right out through the hallway door. Not much later—fifteen, twenty minutes—Tony was found at the bottom of the pool. Well, now I'd say that we should establish who was in the game room during that short period of time and then absolve them of any complicity in Tony's death. Those few that are left, I say, are the ones the police should be looking at."

Sybil glanced around at the rest of the group. "My goodness, I can't recall *anyone* leaving the room. We were *all* there as far as I can remember. This theory of yours won't lead us very far, Kevin."

Ethel touched her spoon to her water glass to get attention.

"I don't remember seeing anyone who was in the room for the entire time we were there All I recall is a zoo full of people milling about the place. And incidentally, Kevin sweet, I can't picture you in the room *at all* last night."

"Probably," Lena added caustically, "because he wasn't there—at all."

"Yes he was," Sybil snapped. "I'll testify to that. It was quite dark. Jeff had the room rather subdued—maybe too subdued for any of us to be speculating about who was doing what last night."

"Yes, your theory's quite impossible, Kevin," Lena said. "Obviously, you'd starve as a cop."

There was a pause in the conversation. All stared into their coffee. Finally, Sybil broke the silence.

"Scary to think of last night, isn't it. Poor Tony, he should have gone to bed before the party started."

"Crap!" Lena pushed back her chair. "Tony's better off dead and your pretending otherwise is pure crap. Excuse me, boys and girls. Enjoyed the lunch, but I've got a date in less than an hour with a dandy. Lieutenant Box no less. Ta-ta."

Lena waved her fingers and left the room.

Kevin chuckled and glanced at the two remaining women who were eyeing each other knowingly. "Part of Lena's charm we've learned to love, isn't it. So beautifully direct."

He rose to his feet. "Where's Jeff? Either of you know?"

"Down at the airport picking up Corny as far as I know," Ethel replied. "Is there any more coffee in that pot?"

"Hand me your cup."

He filled Ethel's cup and offered some to Sybil. She refused, excused herself and left the room. Kevin filled his own cup and then gave his attention to Ethel.

"You know Pire well? Never's been here before, has he?"

"Yes I know Cornelius. He's the kind of gentleman whom you meet just once and feel you've known for ages. He was here three years ago. We had a party for him. You and Sybil were in Europe, I believe."

"Oh? Well, what kind of a chap is he? Never heard Jeff talk about him much."

"Corny is a very, very dear seventy-seven year old man. That's my simple description. Jeff will tell you he's a retired, very famous detective who he cherishes as a friend even though they don't seem to see each other very often. Jeff worked for Cornelius during the war in the Intelligence Department. They became quite close, and after the war, they stayed in touch. When we were married, Jeff asked Cornelius to stand up with him. But Corny was on a case and couldn't get away."

Ethel dropped her voice. "That beautiful ship's bell—you know, the one that's been on the table by the pool for so many years and the one that—"

Kevin was nodding his head.

"You knew that was Corny's wedding present to us."

"Yes, I knew but guess I'd forgotten."

Ethel smiled sadly. Ironic, isn't it—Corny coming here—what with that lovely bell of his being at the center of this lurid weekend."

"Why'd Jeff ask him to come?"

"I don't know. Jeff doesn't consult me anymore period. My guess is that it's probably typical Jeffrey. Nothing but the best wherever or whenever. I imagine he wants to leave no stone unturned, and Corny is about the best there is—or was."

"Whatever—it won't hurt. I still think these local country cops don't know what they're doing."

"Yes, I heard you."

"This guy Box—judging from the questions he's been asking, I don't think he's found out a thing about what went on last night— except that someone did a rather clever job of taking care of Tony."

"I think I disagree," Ethel replied very softly.

"You do?"

"Yes, I think he thinks he's learned quite a bit"

"What makes you think that?

"Intuition, darling."

Ethel pushed back her chair, picked up her purse and started to leave the room.

"Ethel, hold up a minute. You can't leave me hanging like that."

Ethel stopped and turned back towards Kevin.

"I believe that curiosity I hear coming out of you, darling, is sitting on pins and needles. My—oh my.!"

"If you think I'm the culprit, Ethel, your intuition's seriously on the blink.'"

"What *I* think obviously isn't half as important as what that nasty police officer thinks.

"True."

"If you must know, I think he believes that I'm the one who killed Tony." Ethel's face was grim. "I certainly hope he's wrong, don't you, Kevin dear?"

She pivoted, left the room and crossed the foyer to the large full length mirror Carefully, she checked her reflection. She needed to take a walk, but first, everything must be precisely where it belonged. She found a few stray hairs, which she carefully tucked back into place. Then she smiled joylessly at herself in the mirror as she thought of Kevin standing there back in the dining room with his mouth wide open.

Poor Kevin—Rock of Gibraltar Kevin—Rain, hail, tornadoes—no force on earth ever seemed to affect the imperturbability of the man—except, that is—

Ethel exchanged an understanding glance with herself in the mirror and smiled.

She could picture him still pacing back and forth in the dining room—alone—agitated—wondering why she had put the finger on herself—and was she telling him all she knew. Perhaps he was staring out one of the front windows and searching helplessly for a place to anchor his nervous hands. Yes, surely—if she knew Kevin, this must be where he was right now—gazing blankly out of some window and wondering intently about what he did not know.

Satisfied with the mirror's appearance, Ethel crossed the foyer to the front door. She walked outside and the moved briskly down the drive.

Tony's car. Yes, that silly looking little red toy car. Still parked where he had left it. Strange. You could do away with a man, but sometimes what he owned lived on forever. Sad. Very sad. Whenever she would see a little red car like this one, she'd probably think of Tony Bleckmore.

Ethel increased her pace and tried to put this terribly depressing thought out of her mind.

CHAPTER SIXTEEN

Early Afternoon Sunday—June 7th

"Looks the same as I remember it, Jeffrey. Very beautiful. Very beautiful."

"Thanks, Corny."

"Only this time, something is missing. Your lovely wife at the front door, maybe."

"She's inside, Corny, and just as lovely."

"Only not your wife, eh?"

"Not my wife. You're right. Sometimes, I wish she was again."

Mr. Cornelius Pire was standing by the open door of Jeffrey's car, which was parked on the circular drive in front of his home. The two had just arrived from the airport, and Cornelius was once again looking at the home he had seen only once before, some three years ago. The two men, standing side by side, presented quite a contrast in appearance—Jeff, a large robust, still youthful looking man in blue slacks and white turtleneck—and Cornelius, a cherubic, pleasingly stout short man with a rosy complexion and close cropped curly white hair. Corny's public attire seldom varied. A small bow tie and a seersucker (usually pale blue) suit in the summer. A small bow tie and wool slacks (usually light gray) with a contrasting blue sport coat in the winter.

To label Cornelius neat would be proper. But to refer to him as dapper would be even more precise. His jaunty air, on top of a bland disposition, infectious smile, soft high-pitched voice and tiny, deep set gray twinkling eyes—this was the essence of Pire.

Plus—self assurance! Absolutely! Self-assurance radiated from every fibre of his being. Long years of subjecting himself to unknown and dangerous adversity had left its mark. The preeminence which accompanies survival and success in this kind of environment had endowed Cornelius with self-confidence and a peace of mind to an uncommon degree.

To a casual nearby observer, this little old man, shuffling up the front steps to Jeffrey's home, surely must be a retired school teacher or, say, a nondescript relative who Jeffrey had temporarily plucked out of a convalescent home somewhere. It took a sharper, far more penetrating examination to discover the charismatic reservoir of enthusiasm which bubbled underneath that ruddy weathered skin.

Jeffrey opened the front door for Cornelius and stood aside as his guest paused a moment and then entered into the main foyer. Cornelius glanced around at the ornate surroundings—the overhead crystal chandelier; the black and white checkered marble floor; the Cezanne oils on either side of the front door; and the long winding carpeted staircase.

"Ah yes, it all comes back. With too much time you forget the majesty of an earlier visit. I shall try not to forget again."

Jeffrey closed the door and joined his friend.

"Majesty? Never heard this place referred to like that before. Suppose it might have a little of that—or did. But today, it's more like a sad pad, Corny—a sad pad. I was wondering last night if this place will ever seem the same again."

Cornelius put a compassionate hand on Jeffrey's arm.

"Time is a superb healer, Jeffrey. Be patient. Let time pass along and allow us to find the killer of your friend. I'll venture that you will start feeling better sooner than you think."

Jeffrey poured a sad smile down on his friend.

"Again—thanks for coming, Corny. Sure good to have you here."

He took Cornelius gently by the arm and began steering him towards the staircase.

"Let me show you upstairs to your room. Then, if you like, I'll introduce you to the cops who are roaming around here somewhere. What's your pleasure?"

"I have a small favor, Jeffrey, if you don't mind?"

"Name it. It's yours."

"If, after you take me to my quarters, I could have a few minutes to wander around your home and your grounds by myself, I would be very grateful. It is my way to get wet—to pick up a feel for what I will be looking at, maybe. Then—" Cornelius checked his watch— "Shall we say in an hour? I'll meet you right where we are now, and you can introduce me to this Lieutenant you've been telling me about. Would this be possible do you think?"

Ten minutes later, Cornelius padded quietly back down the circular staircase and slipped out the same door he had just entered. He swung to his left and plodded along a white stone path which wound its way around the side of the house and into a large flower garden defined on all four sides by some carefully pruned Japanese hemlocks.

Cornelius found a slatted wooden bench near the center of the garden, sat down and took a deep breath. A gentle breeze helped waft the fragrances from a sea of flowers by his sensitive nose. Slowly, he turned his head and absorbed the enchanting sight around him.

Lovely! Azaleas. Bleeding Hearts. Bluebells. Back in that corner, some honeysuckle. Oh my, look at that Chinese wisteria reaching up almost to the top of those tall pines. And—over there, roses, roses and more roses—including, would you believe, a bed of Variegata di Bologna, showing the same subtle shade of pink as his di Bolognas back home.

Cornelius rose to his feet and walked over to closer inspect the roses. He pulled out his pocketknife, cut the stem of one small bud and raised it to his nose.

Yes, his favorite flower. Incomparable! But—but even the hypnotic scent of this tiny wonder wasn't overcoming the sense of foreboding he was feeling right now, was it? It was a sensation he was very familiar with. Ah yes. Even though it had been four years, he could still remember that ominous feeling in the pit of his stomach. Off-beat homocides usually had this affect on him. They were challenges which always breathed excitement into his bones. But, alas, they were also challenges which often lead to an ugly murder being further darkened by the ultimate exposure of a virtuous killer. Cornelius smiled ruefully as he recalled one of the first truths he had learned about homicides—that most people who commit murder aren't any where near as concerned about the evil they have wrought as they are about being found out. Probably true here. He could smell it in the air. It was pervasive in spite of the flowers. And the aroma will probably be even more so when he catches the murder scene.

The swimming pool, Jeffrey had said. The deep end. Back below the rocky embankment. Well, better go find it and see what it has to say.

He returned to the white stone path and walked towards the large block of rhotodendrons at the rear of the house. He wound his way down some wooden steps through these arched shrubs.

No signs indicating the way. But this was the right direction, maybe.

Through the leaves, a glimmer of sunlight bouncing off some water caught his eye, and he knew he was getting close. Soon, he was standing at the pool's edge and staring attentively through the bluish-green water at the pool's bottom. The random thoughts running through his mind were being overwhelmed by the annoying rumbles coursing through his belly and the familiar and prophetic twitch of his pinkie. He decided he'd seen enough. Almost time to meet Jeffrey. But first, back to his room and some of those pills. His belly needed some help, maybe.

Jeffrey and Cornelius discovered Box standing on the small bridge at the back of Endecott's property. He was leaning against the rail, head down, watching the water go by.

"Lieutenant!" Jeff called out from a distance.

Bill Box turned to the pair approaching him. He smiled slightly.

"I was just wondering what the victim said to his ex-wife when they were out here last night."

"Lieutenant Box, meet Cornelius Pire."

"Hi ya, Lieutenant."

"Mr. Pire? Oh yes. Mr. Endecott mentioned you were coming. Nice to meet you. Told him your name wasn't exactly a stranger to me."

"Please, Lieutenant, try Corny. It will save us both time, maybe."

"Check—Corny," Box assented with a trace of a smile. "If you don't mind my saying, you don't look quite like your reputation."

"An opinion shared by others, Lieutenant, and one I always accept as a compliment. Jeffrey's been telling me all about the broken branches you're running into. Says you've been Johnny-on-the-job."

The three men made their way back to the pool, where Jeff excused himself and left Cornelius and Box together.

"Now Lieutenant—" The two men were sitting at the side of the long glass table—"I want you to know I got no business muzzling in on your ball game or taking any of your time. Just that Jeffrey's pretty worried about this whole thing and asked me if I'd take a look in and all—and well, when an old friend calls, I usually come and—"

Box interrupted. "I understand, Corny. The boss called me, and you're cleared to meddle all you want."

"Meddle. Ha, you used the right word, my friend. Meddling's about all this ol' man's good for now. But well," Cornelius winked, "to earn my bread and keep, I'll try and help a little too."

Cornelius glanced up towards the house. "Let's see, Jeffrey said he'd send me down a gin sour. Don't suppose you can join me?"

Box shook his head.

"No. Well, that's too bad. One of the advantages I have over you young fellas. When I'm on half duty like this, I can have a drink or two. Just think, Lieutenant, in thirty or forty years, you can booze it up a little on the job too."

"How you know I don't now?"

Cornelius grinned mischievously. "I'm reading your tea leaves, maybe."

"Ancient instincts, eh?"

"Don't sell 'em short. They're one of the best things you own. Your instincts told you anything yet?"

"Yeah, a smidge. Evidence so far hasn't told me diddle, but my insides *are* vibrating a little."

"That's important."

"Not in a court room."

"Oh my, but I don't agree, Lieutenant. Ah, here comes a fine gentleman, nearly as old as me, with a marvelous looking drink. Dear Jeffrey never forgets a promise."

Cornelius got up and hurried towards the rose garden to meet Judson. He returned a few moments later with a gin sour in each hand.

"I have taken the liberty of confiscating your drink, Lieutenant. You don't mind?"

Box shook his head good-naturedly.

"No, I don't agree. A few hours in the field by a sharp investigator who's got a sensitive nose and's not afraid to use it is worth dozens of hours of haggling in a court room."

"You know—a—Corny—I—a—what I'm trying to get at is I'd like to discuss this case with you, but I guess you'd better let me see some identification."

Cornelius handed his wallet to Box. "Look it over, Lieutenant. I'm who I say I am, but you've sure got a right to ask. Good for you."

Box returned the wallet to Pire.

"Okay, Cornelius Pire, I'll buy you. Last night we went over this place with everything but a high powered telescope. We found a cocktail glass with Mrs. Endecott's prints on it in the foliage over there, with enough of an impression in the dirt to indicate that it came on the fly from about here. Where you're sitting is the point from which the body entered the pool. We've got a high-heeled impression of Mrs. Endecott's shoe from the sand between those slabs just to the left of your foot. Mrs. Endecott was barefooted up until the time she changed for dinner, at which time she put on the shoes I'm referring to. We've got a heavy silver-plated hair brush with Mrs. Endecott's prints on it, which she admits to having used when she was swimming down here yesterday. The brush has a sizable dent in the end of it, which could have come from Mr. Bleckmore's head. I've talked to Mrs. Endecott. She's belligerent and won't cooperate."

"She won't admit to the crime?" Pire's eyes were twinkling.

"She wanted my head."

"As I recall, Mrs. Endecott—a very lovely, gracious lady."

"Maybe—but she definitely doesn't like me or Bleckmore."

"You know her better than I. Ah, a superb gin sour. You've talked to our guests, I take it?"

"All but one. I can't seem to hook up with the victim's ex-wife."

Box checked his watch. "But I've got a date with her in a few minutes. That'll make all of them."

Cornelius started to rise. "I shan't detain you."

"Please, Corny, don't leave. She'll wait. I'm enjoying the conversation. Probably won't hurt either."

"Thank you." Cornelius relaxed. "Did you learn anything from talking to any of these people?"

"Yes. They're all suspects in my book. Any one of them could have pulled this thing off. Mrs. Endecott—very antagonistic. Another couple, the Strabos—he's a world famous shrink who's got to be wound up tighter than any of his patients—very unfriendly. The

Kennellys—he's a walking chronometer. Don't know yet how accurate he is, but he can tell you what time someone coughed last week. Also, from what I hear, he's almost a teetotaler who got bombed last night for the first time in his life. Fishy, I'd say. The Tones—very cooperative to a fault. He wants you to think he can see through walls. He's already fingered Mrs. Endecott pretty hard and figures Mrs. Bleckmore's involved too."

"Why?" Cornelius was squinting softly at Box.

"Why? Why what?"

"This Mr. Tone—he accuses both Mrs. Endecott and Mrs. Bleckmore. I wondered why."

"Motive mainly. Said they both hated Mr. Bleckmore's guts. And doesn't remember seeing either one of them at the time of the murder."

"Do you have any pictures I might look at, Lieutenant?"

"Yeah, but they won't help you any. Pretty routine."

Box reached into his briefcase and extracted a dozen enlarged pictures taken of the body both in and out of the pool. He handed them to Cornelius who laid them all out on the glass table and studied them for several minutes without comment. Finally, he looked up dolefully at Box.

"First murder I've been personally involved in."

"Beg pardon."

"That bell—I—"

"Oh, yes, Mr. Endecott told me. A wedding present. Must chill your spine a bit, eh?"

"Sad, Lieutenant. Very sad for me to see a lovely bell used for such a criminal purpose. The only consolation, I imagine is that my poor bell tells us a little something about the murderer."

"It does?"

"Yes, it does. I would think we're dealing with an amateur here— perhaps, a clever amateur—but an amateur nonetheless. The bell wasn't really necessary, would you say?"

Box chuckled. "Never thought about that, but guess you're right. Someone was gilding the lily a bit."

"This is Mr. Bleckmore, I take it?" Cornelius was staring at a small snapshot of Tony which he was holding in his hand."

"Yes, that *was* him."

"A recent picture, maybe?"

"I guess so. Why do you ask?"

"He looks familiar. Maybe not, but somewhere I feel like I've met this man. Do you have an extra copy?"

"Keep that one. It's yours."

"Ah, thank you. If you can discover its vintage, would you let me know?"

"Will do. Here's what I thought you'd ask me for—my wild-ass approximation of what happened and when last night."

Box handed Cornelius a piece of paper with the following notes in Box's handwriting:

> Sunday noon—All guests arrive. People on premises the rest of the night include Mr. Endecott, Mrs. Endecott, Mrs. Bleckmore, Mr. Bleckmore, Mr. and Mrs. Tone, Dr. and Mrs. Strabo, Mr. and Mrs. Kennelly, and the servants Maude, James and Judson.
>
> 1:00 to 5:00 PM—All guests at pool.
>
> 5:00 to 6:00 PM—Guests changing clothes in their rooms at staggered times.
>
> 6:00 to 7:00 PM—Cocktails at pool.
>
> 7:00 to 8:30 PM—Dinner around pool.
>
> 8:30 to 8:45 PM—Guests move to house (recreation room).
>
> 8:45 to 9:20 PM—Guest chatting, waiting to see a campaign movie Mr. Endicott had made and wanted them to see. Mr. Bleckmore missing until approximately 9:10 PM, at which time he entered room from terrace and quickly exited through the hallway door.
>
> 9:15 to 9:30 PM—Random search for Mr. Bleckmore.
>
> 9:30 to 9:35 PM—(somewhere between these two times) Judson announced the discovery of Mr. Bleckmore's body which was lying at the bottom of the deep end of the swimming pool.
>
> 9:39 PM—Body observed by all guests.
>
> 9:46 PM—Sheriff's office notified by telephone.
>
> 9:55 PM—Police arrive.
>
> 8:55 to 9:10 PM—(some where in between) Coroner's official estimate of time of death. Cause: drowning.

Pire studied the chronology for a moment and then made a few notes of his own in a small black leather notebook he had pulled from his pocket.

"Interesting, Lieutenant. As you say, a little loose, but interesting. Your sources of information were the guests?"

"Only one—Mr. Kennelly."

"An objective observer, you think?"

"Not necessarily. He's a watch-watcher who apparently enjoys letting everyone know it."

Pire's eyes were again focused on the small snapshot Box had given him. "What kind of man was this Mr. Bleckmore?"

"A loaded playboy who worked his connections into his business. He ran a construction business. Cement. Had contacts all over the place."

"He has a connection with Mr. Endecott, maybe?"

"Purely social, as far as I know."

"Lieutenant, I've bothered you enough, but one last question. Do you know who was the last person last night to see or talk to Mr. Bleckmore?"

"Mr. Endecott figures he was. Says he left the man alive and soused at the pool. He said that Bleckmore told him he was going to mosey on up to the house a short time later. Apparently, he had indicated to Endecott that his head was bothering him. Mr. Tone had a significant variation to this story. He told me that he was one of the last to leave this area and when he glanced back, Bleckmore was still sitting by the pool."

"Hey, we got company."

Bill Box had swung his attention up towards the house, where a pair of figures were slowly making their way towards them down the winding garden path. Jake Reston had Lena Bleckmore's left arm lightly in his grasp and was gently guiding her towards the pool.

"I thought you were putting me on trial before lunch, Lieutenant."

"Sorry, Ma'am." Box was on his feet. "Was just on my way up."

"Well, I wouldn't have minded being detained if I'd known you were talking to this dear little man."

Lena smiled sweetly at Cornelius, who was standing next to Box.

"This must be your father."

She held out her hand to Cornelius.

Box revealed an embarrassed grin.

"This is Mr. Pire, Ma'am. I wish he was my father, but I'm afraid he's just another lousy cop."

"Mr. Pire?—Oh my—Jeffrey's friend. Lena, you big mouth! I'm sorry. I'm—"

"Delighted, Mrs. Bleckmore." Corny was holding Lena's proffered hand in both of his. "Your quaint manner of categorizing all of my attributes into three little words I find quite satisfying. Some prying policemen are referred to in a much different manner, you know. Won't you sit down? I was just leaving."

Lena lowered herself into a chair next to Box.

"Don't leave on my account, Mr. Pire. I'm not going to reveal any secrets, am I, Lieutenant?"

Box insisted on Pire staying. Reston excused himself and returned to the house. Lena indicated, in reply to several questions from Box, that she knew very little about what had happened last night. She'd had Kevin for a dinner partner and had paid very little attention to Tony. Mr. Tone had been a most engaging conversationalist. After dinner, she had gone directly to the recreation room and from there to the powder room. Had Mr. Tone escorted her up to the house? No, he hadn't, she said, because, as she recalled, she had preferred to walk up alone. Yes, she had seen Mr. Bleckmore enter the recreation room. It was dim, and she couldn't see too well, but she gathered that he was not well. He had hurried out of the room in the direction of the little boys' room as soon as he had entered. Was that the last time she had seen Mr. Bleckmore? Yes, it was, she said, and added an appreciation to the Almighty. She wasn't very fond of Mr. Bleckmore? Hell no, she wasn't, and without being asked, went on to explain to Cornelius and the Lieutenant that her ex-husband's obsession with his own self-interests was the reason why she had divorced. him.

Cornelius jumped into the conversation for the first time. "Mrs. Bleckmore, I'm glad I was able to listen in on this, because in the brief time I've been here, I was gathering the mistaken impression that Mr. Bleckmore was, generally speaking quite a beloved gentleman."

The barely perceptible twinkle in Cornelius's eye had slipped by Lena and her jaw dropped.

"Mr. Pire, is it? You *are* a funny little man. My ex was a first class prick, if you know what that is."

"Ah yes, the ultimate compliment for some gentlemen, maybe."

Lena cocked one eye as she studied the curious little Methuselah in front of her.

"Let me put it another way, Mr. Pire, if I may. My mistake was that it took me far too long to realize that Tony's schlong is where his brain was."

Box asked her if anyone at the party shared her strong viewpoints regarding Mr. Bleckmore.

"Sure, Lieutenant. Everyone knew Tony but you cops, it seems. You want me to go down the list?"

Box nodded his head.

"Well, you can start with Ethel. Tony took Jeff away from her. 'Nough said. Collin Strabo? You figure it out. Tony's wandering eye trouble has always included Collin's wife—even after he broke his engagement with Marva to marry me. Sam Kennelly? Listen to Anne. She'll tell anyone who'll listen what a screwing Sam's gotten from Tony's cement. Kevin Tone? He'd like the world to think he's above disliking anybody. But he's just like the rest of us. Yesterday, Tony unloaded on me the interesting tidbit that Kevin loved Tony so much that recently Kevin asked Tony to blow himself away somewhere until Jeff got elected."

"Elected?" Cornelius's eyebrows raised slightly.

Lena was likewise surprised that Jeff hadn't told Cornelius anything about his consuming passion to become a United States Senator. And what were Jeffrey's feelings for his murdered friend, Cornelius asked Lena lightly? Lena melted a little and replied that as far as she knew, Jeff had never really disliked anyone. The great puzzle to her, she said, was why he enjoyed Tony's company so much—this in spite of their obvious mutual interest in whoring around together.

Finally, Box asked Lena if she had any idea who might have wanted Tony dead. Lena smiled sweetly and replied that she certainly did.

"Take a look at everyone on the guest list, Lieutenant—except me, of course. Every sainted one of these people had Tony's eulogy written months ago."

"Except you," Box echoed cynically.

"Naturally, Lieutenant," Lena purred. "You can tell by just looking at me, I'm sure, that I am far too honest a person to have composed a eulogy full of the sweet kind of things you hear about a thug only at his funeral"

Box opened his mouth to pop another question but quickly closed it in deference to a wave of frustration which was smothering him. Instead, he perfunctorily thanked Lena for her cooperation—then turned to Cornelius and asked him if he had any questions for Mrs. Bleckmore."

Cornelius shook his head and smiled.

"Mrs. Bleckmore is far too beautiful a woman to interrogate. She should, I'm afraid, just be absorbed and appreciated, maybe."

"Now, Lieutenant, if you could dish out crap like that, you'd get promoted yesterday. Am I free to go?"

With a nod of Box's head, Lena was on her feet and sashaying her way back up to the house. Both men stood gaping at the sight of her retreating figure.

Box glanced at his companion and observed wryly, "You give a young guy heart, Corny."

"That so? What have I done?"

"Getting a bit older apparently hasn't diminished the ability of at least one of your eyes to roam a little, eh?"

"Ah yes, the sublime Mrs. Bleckmore. I suspect that she could easily wiggle the eye of a man even more feeble than I. It's my other eye you didn't notice, Lieutenant. It's the one more easily distracted by such mundane matters as the number of operatives you have prowling these premises. You are looking for something specific, maybe?"

"Yes and no, I guess. I'm prowling against my instincts a bit, Corny. You ever heard of a guy called Romanareo, a.k.a. The Roman, a.k.a. Alfie?"

"Yes," Pire replied quietly.

"You have?" Box was startled.

"Jeffrey mentioned a Mr. Alfie to me on the way in from the airport."

"Oh! For a second, I thought you meant you knew the guy."

"I do, maybe." Pire's countenance glowed with the pleased look of one who enjoys dabbling in a touch of one-upmanship.

Box looked puzzled but said nothing.

"Actually, Lieutenant, I know only one man who has ever claimed to know the man you ask about. The Roman and I have a mutual Hong Kong acquaintance by the improbable name of I.M. Tolerable. It was through this gentleman that I received a vicarious Romanareo introduction. It wet my appetite, but alas, in vain, because one of the Roman's hallmarks was his total inaccessibility."

"Well, he's not exactly inaccessible around here, Corny. I talked with him this morning. Are you aware of the Roman's possible involvement in this case?"

"Jeffrey indicated that he'd been told by the deceased that a gentleman by the name of Alfie had tried to kill Mr. Bleckmore."

"Yeah, that's what Endecott told me. Maybe that's Bleckmore's story—maybe not. We'll never know for sure, will we? However, at the moment, I gotta believe Endecott's on the level. That's why I got a microscope out around here looking for anything that'll show Alfie was afoot around here last night finishing a job he'd bungled earlier."

But your instincts are whispering to you that you are looking for something which does not exist, maybe?"

Box barely nodded his head in agreement.

"Is Alfie the Roman, Lieutenant?" Pire asked casually.

Box grinned. "You meet this bird and he tells you he's the nephew of the Pope. But at the same time, his eyes are telling you loud and clear that he's the Roman."

"Ah yes, the eyes—they always talk louder than the mouth, don't they."

"Yeah, they do. I was looking at an All American Boy, if you know what I mean. At the same time, though, I was reading a guy who could have iced Bleckmore just by snapping his fingers. Deep down, I don't think he did. I'd love to be wrong here and nail that bastard real good—but," Box added with a scowl, "the vibes are wrong."

Pire's pudgy hands slowly twirled the half empty glass of his gin sour, as his twinkling eyes studied Box intently.

Box stared abstractly at the ground in front of him for several moments and then looked up once more at Pire.

"What I'm trying to say, I guess, is that this guy Alfie's got a damn strong motive *not* to screw around where we can all see him. Now you tell me, Corny, why in hell would a man you'd think would be craving anonymity start fucking around with a small potato like Bleckmore?"

"Yes—as puzzling as the crime itself, maybe."

"And Bleckmore had a damn scar around his neck that's got to tell you he wasn't dishing out a bunch of cock-and-bull to Endecott. Right?"

"So we have a lovely bundle of conundrums, Lieutenant. This is the kind of case that stirs the cockles, maybe."

Cornelius savored the remainder of his gin sour and then carefully placed his glass on the table next to his chair. Assuming a more somber mien, he then turned his attention back to Box.

"I am wondering, Lieutenant, if you would have any objections if I paid a call on your devoted friend, Mr. Alfie?"

Box chuckled. "Hell no. Be my guest. Why don't you take him a box of candy from me. Might help you wring a confession out of him"

"A box of chocolates. Splendid idea. I'll follow your advice."

"Just on the odd chance you fail, though, I think I'm gonna keep the bird dogs prowling around here a little longer."

"Now and then, when someone fails, he succeeds, maybe," Pire observed lightly.

"Somehow," a preoccupied Box muttered to himself, "I think, if anyone of these guests would tell me what they know, I could break this damn case wide open today. I think they're all piss-ass lying."

Cornelius rose to his feet and stuck out his hand.

"Thank you, Lieutenant, for letting me bother you like this. I'll just mosey around and leave you alone."

They shook hands, and then Cornelius picked up the Bleckmore snapshot Box had given him and carefully placed it in his wallet. As he turned to leave, he lightly slipped his hands into the side pockets of his jacket and dropped his chin as though deep in thought.

Box watched him amble up the path until he disappeared behind some ferns. He then sat down in a comfortably padded chaise lounge. He glanced at his watch.

Miller time—but not on his watch—only in his mouth. Sometimes that damn minute hand crawled slower than his wife got ready to go out. Especially—yeah, especially when he seemed to be going nowhere—standing absolutely still like right now. God, what fun to be on a case sometime where the murderer would come up to him, stick out his hand, introduce himself and say, "Howdy, Lieutenant, I'm the guy that done did it. Lock me up and put me away, will you please." Just once. Wouldn't that be a ball? Then he could move on to the next case and—Box turned his head and gazed up towards the house.

Shit! That guy Pire. Wonder if he ever had time stop dead still on him? Probably not. He looked like he thought this baby we've got's duck soup. Well, I suppose that's just it. You can't solve these lousy murders unless you're damn sure—absolutely damn sure—that the answer's only five minutes away. Probably one big reason Pire made such a name for himself.

Box picked up his notebook from the table next to him, frowned and slowly started reading what he had written.

CHAPTER SEVENTEEN

Mid-afternoon Sunday—June 7th

"Good afternoon! I believe it's Mr. Judson?"

"Just Judson, sir."

"Ah yes—Judson. And I am Cornelius Pire, a dear friend of Mr. Endecott's. I am wondering if we, you and I, could have a few words together?"

"Yes sir."

The scene was the annex to the kitchen, more frequently referred to as the breakfast nook. It was Jason's favorite spot in the house—a cozy place where he could relax when his services weren't required by Mr. Jeff.

Judson had been eyeing the distinguished visitor from afar ever since Cornelius's recent arrival. At the moment, he was still recovering from the suprise of hearing his name called out and then finding the object of his curiosity standing only a few feet away.

He dropped the silverware he had been cleaning and rose from his chair.

Those eyes—Gosh, it was hard to look at this gentleman who was addressing him so kindly. Those eyes—they were little beads looking right inside you. Jason felt very uncomfortable.

"May we sit down here?" Cornelius gestured towards the table they were both standing next to.

Jason nodded and warily moved up to the table.

"Ah, fine." Cornelius sat down.

Judson, joined him, sitting in an adjacent chair.

"Jeffrey tells me you're a fine cook, Judson."

Judson's cheeks reddened, and he indicated that Mr. Endecott was very easy to please. Cornelius asked Judson what some of his favorite dishes were, and Judson, in replying, happily discovered that his interrogator was a lover of good food. What was it he called himself? A gourmet? All of a sudden, he found himself listening with rapt attention to Cornelius's description of how to prepare a roast crown of pork, with sausage and raisin stuffing, surrounded by glazed apple halves soaked in cranberry sauce. Judson was overawed. He sat and listened with a rare grin. When Cornelius asked him if he'd like a copy of the recipe, all Judson could manage was to nod his head.

"Good. I'll pass it along to you before I leave."

"Thank you. You want something from me?"

"Well, yes, actually, Judson, I do, maybe. I was wondering if you could tell me anything—let's say, anything unusual about the party here yesterday."

Judson shook his head.

"I believe you were helping Mr. Endecott with the party?"

"Yes, sir."

"Maybe you could describe your duties yesterday."

"You want *everything*?"

"Whatever seems important to you."

"Well, I helped the guests into their rooms with their luggage. Then I served drinks in the afternoon at the swimming pool, and—"

"Can you recall, Judson, what the guests were drinking?"

"Yes, I guess so. A—Mr. Endecott and Mr. Bleckmore," Judson crossed himself, "they drank martinis. They always do that. Mr. Strabo stayed with Scotch. Mr. Kennelly, he likes one Budweisier like always but—" Judson's face reddened. "What I mean is he had one beer in the afternoon—but later last night, he asked me for a bottle of bourbon. That's the first time I seen him ever do that."

Judson paused to collect himself.

"A—I left out Mr. Tone—he drank gin and tonics. And the ladies—I gave them some punch—all of them."

"I see. Do you remember anyone, other than Mr. Kennelly, drinking—a, how shall we say it—a heap?"

"Mr. Bleckmore, he drank more than a heap—like always. Yes sir, he did." Judson frowned as he crossed himself again.

"Anyone else drink a heap?"

"The women—seems like to me."

"Oh?" Cornelius raised his eyebrows. "What about the women?"

"They drained the punch bowl dry, sir."

"Dry, you say?"

"Yes—ice and all."

"Was it a strong punch, Judson?"

"Rum, Sherry, and some fruit juices. Made it myself. Mr. Jeff's own recipe."

"How big a bowl, maybe?" Cornelius was leaning towards Judson listening intently to every word.

"About like this, sir." Judson spread his hands about a foot apart.

"And you say they drank the bowl dry?"

"Yes sir."

"This seems a bit unusual to you, maybe, Judson?"

Judson nodded his head. "They even ate the cherries in the ice."

"Cherries?" Cornelius frowned.

"You know—a block of ice with cherries molded in it. Mr. Jeff always liked to serve a pretty punch for the ladies."

Cornelius leaned back in his chair and stared blankly at the chandelier hanging over their heads.

"Where was the liquor served from?"

"The large glass table by the pool"

"And the punch too?"

Judson nodded. He was staring nervously at the floor in front of him.

"Judson—" Cornelius leaned forward again, folded his hands, leaned his elbows on the table and fixed his eyes directly on the man sitting next to him. "Judson, your memory is most remarkable and very helpful. Do you recall any incoming telephone calls yesterday, maybe?

Judson thought for a moment.

"I answered the phone twice. It might have rung more, but I remember two times I answered it."

"Yes?"

"One call was for Dr. Strabo—dinner time. He took it at the pool."

"There is a phone at the pool?"

"Yes sir."

"You don't know who it was that called, maybe, Judson?"

"No sir—'cept Dr. Strabo said he'd been expecting the call."

"And the other call?"

"That phone rang jus' 'fore noon. It was for Mr. Bleckmore. He was still in his room. I wrote the number and name down on a piece of paper and gave it to Mr. Jeff in his study."

"I see. Judson, you've been too nice to me. I've bothered you long enough."

Cornelius rose to his feet and put his arm on Judson's shoulder. "Unless, maybe, you can recall anything else unusual that occurred yesterday."

"Can't remember nothing else, except—except—"

"Yes?"

"Except Mr. Bleckmore's dying."

"I agree. That *was* terrible."

Cornelius shook Judson's hand and turned to go.

"If you do think of anything else, I'd consider it very kind of you if you'd look me up."

"Yes sir."

Judson stood up. "A—Mr. Pire?"

Cornelius swung around towards Judson. "Yes, Judson."

"You say you are good friend of Mr. Jeff's?"

"A very good friend, yes indeed."

"I can tell. You're a nice gentleman. Mr. Jeff—he usually likes nice people."

"Thank you. He also hires nice people, I would say."

Judson walked over to Cornelius.

"You said *unusual* thing?"

Cornelius nodded his head.

"I'll show you something—probably nothing—but I thought it was kind of funny—if you want to see it."

"Certainly, Judson. I'd like to look at anything you'd like to show me. Where do we go?"

"To the laundry room."

"Where's that?"

"Downstairs near the recreation room."

"You lead the way. I'll follow."

Judson walked out into the first floor foyer, Cornelius right behind him. As they reached the circular stairway leading downstairs, Jake Reston entered the foyer from the front door.

Cornelius smiled affably. "Good afternoon, Sergeant"

"Thanks for the promotion, but it's just Reston, Mr. Pire."

"Sorry. You look like a sergeant, so I'm only half wrong, maybe."

"Thanks."

"I wonder if you'd be so kind as to do me a favor?"

"I'll try. What can I do for you?"

"Ask someone to check the filtration system of Mr. Endecott's swimming pool and see if by chance they run into any loose maraschino cherries. Would you please?"

"Cherries?" Reston's right hand was cupping his right ear.

"Little red cherries."

"Cherries, oh, sure—" Reston repeated mechanically.

"Thanks so much."

Cornelius turned and hurried down the stairs to catch up with Judson.

Jake Reston stood watching Pire disappear down the stairway. He shook his head. *Man, I hope to hell I'm in a box 'fore I become a flaky white haired old man like that.*

Judson was standing in the open doorway to the laundry room when Pire arrived. He walked over to a clothes washer-dryer appliance; Pire right behind him.

"I'm sorry. This is dumb, but you said anything."

"Yes—yes, of course, Judson. What have you got?"

Judson picked up an obviously used and faded article lying casually on top of the appliance and handed it to Cornelius.

"It's a life preserver. I've never seen it around here before this morning."

Pire looked it over and then returned it to Judson.

"You're suggesting, Judson, that Mr. Endecott does not own a boat?"

Judson shook his head.

"Any of the guests here last night own boats maybe?"

"I don't know. Don't think so."

"Yes—well, at least we can assume that they didn't bring their boats with them, can't we." Cornelius was smiling kindly at Judson. "Mr. Endecott's pool is large—but not that large."

Cornelius stuck out his hand and shook Judson's.

"Thank you again, Judson. Very interesting. Keep me in touch if anything else occurs to you, will you please."

Judson indicated that he would and excused himself.

Cornelius reached over and picked up the life preserver. He examined it cursorily and then put it on. After he had closed the zipper and fastened the four front clasps, he glanced down at himself. *Zounds! If I were ever to be caught in deep water with this thing on, I'd have to hang on to something for dear life. This contraption's almost big enough to hold another Pire.*

It wasn't until several hours later that a curious thought crossed Pire's mind.

That life preserver Judson had shown him was very old fashioned. They didn't make those vest type zipper models anymore, maybe. Have to check that out.

He sighed and then filed another loose end into the memory bank of his human computer.

CHAPTER EIGHTEEN

Late Afternoon Sunday—June 7th

Late the same afternoon, two men were standing by the Endecott pool, not far from where Bleckmore had met his demise. One of the men had his back to the pool and was standing not more than a couple of feet from it. This was a particularly hazardous position, because this man had crammed on his right foot a lady's high-heeled shoe. It would have been a bizarre sight, to say the least, had any casual observer been nearby. However, the two men were alone and,. therefore, their movements required no explanations.

The shorter of the two men lifted one leg and, with the assistance of his companion's arm, put all of his weight on his high-heeled shoed encased foot.

Jake Reston laughed. "My God, if the boss sees the two of us screwing around like this, I'll get canned, and you'll get thrown in the jug."

But the white-haired man whom Reston was supporting appeared unconcerned. He chuckled lightly as he shifted his weight, removed the shoe from his foot and returned it to Reston's satchel. Both men then knelt down and carefully examined the ground on which Cornelius Pire had been standing.

"You're right, Mr. Pire. A hell of a difference. I'll make a cast of the impression for the record."

"And note my weight at one hundred and fifty two pounds, Reston. I'll wager I'm within five pounds of Mrs. Endecott. Would you say that my impression in that sand is at least a half inch deeper?"

"Give me a minute, and I'll tell ya."

While Reston made a cast of the impression of the heel print manufactured by Cornelius, Cornelius was busying himself in the

146

foliage a few feet away. On hands and knees, he was running his hands through the loose dirt around an assortment of flowers.

Reston watched Cornelius out of the corner of one eye.

"With due respect, sir, I hope you don't maintain that position too long. What's sticking out of the garden makes a very inviting target."

Cornelius rose slowly to his feet and faced Reston with a grin.

"I'm indebted to you, maybe, for resisting temptation"

"Would you like to see this?" Reston was holding the cast he had made of the heel print.

"How does it measure?"

"Three-eighths of an inch deeper."

Cornelius sat down on the edge of a chaise lounge.

"A question for you, sir. If you were a lady, how would you throw your empty cocktail glass at that garden patch over there?"

"How?"

"Yes. How would you throw it?"

Reston chuckled. "I'd just throw it. I don't know how."

Cornelius rose to his feet. He picked up a glass he had borrowed from Judson's kitchen and held it in his right hand.

"I'll show you what I mean. Tell me if this looks nice and ladylike."

With a smooth underhand motion, Cornelius tossed the glass towards the garden and watched it land with a light thump in the soft dirt. He turned to Reston.

"Look okay?"

"You were darling, sir."

Cornelius picked up the glass. "Now examine the depth of the impression this glass made when it hit and see if you agree that, just before impact, our glass had to be going straight down."

Cornelius didn't wait for Reston's reaction.

"Now, let's try a slightly more masculine approach."

Pire moved to the pool's edge and with a quick overhand motion, he flipped the glass into the garden near to where the glass had landed the first time he threw it.

Reston walked over, knelt and studied the new impression the glass had made in the dirt.

"Which impression looks like the one the Lieutenant was telling me about? Can you recall, maybe?"

"The last one."

"Not the ladylike one, eh?

"Nope."

Reston stood up. "Well, it certainly fits. I'll admit that. I forgot to tell you. Box checked out that duplicate hairbrush from Mrs. Endecott's bedroom, and the handle bent about ten degrees when it was impacted on a slab of soft pine. Says he used enough force to produce a dent similar to the one in the original brush. He added, by the way, that when he straightened out the handle, it left a pronounced crease."

"Excellent."

"So we've proved Mrs. Endecott innocent, it looks like," Reston said skeptically.

"I don't know about that. But I'd say that we can reasonably conclude, at least, that a woman did *not* throw an empty cocktail glass, used by Mrs. Endecott, into the garden, either before or after *not* hitting Mr. Bleckmore over the head with a hairbrush."

"Makes you wonder, doesn't it—what in hell someone did hit him with. Coroner claims it was something with a good edge on it."

"Have you had a chance to have someone check the pool's filtration system?"

Reston looked up sharply, then smiled sheepishly.

"Damn! Forgot to show you. These what you're looking for?"

Reston produced a small plastic bag containing a couple of dozen or more small red cherries.

"These came from the pool?"

"Yep."

"Maybe you're holding the murder weapon, my friend—or at least what's left of it."

"Ice?" Jake Reston broke into a broad smile.

"Could be. Judson told me, as I recall, that the punch bowl was nearly empty when he took it back to the house. What better way than to pick up a sizeable piece of ice, use it, and then throw it into the pool, knowing that the evidence will soon melt away."

The two men started gathering up the paraphernalia they had been working with. Suddenly, Cornelius felt very tired. It had already been a very long day for him. The lack of a full night's sleep, the air flight, the trying experience of reintroducing himself to the kind of investigatory practice he had been out of touch with for several years now—all this was taking its toll

"If you'll excuse me, Reston, I think I'll head for my room. I'm a little weary, maybe. But we do make some progress, eh?"

Reston smiled on the outside and nodded his head. Inside, however, he was frowning. As he trudged slowly up towards the house behind Pire he was beginning to wonder just what kind of progress they *were* making.

Man, they had zonked a big hunk of their evidence, starting with their strongest suspect, Mrs. Endecott and had proven nothing else, except by the iffy guesswork. Yet, this old timer was calling this progress. Well fine. If Pire's encouraged, then that's the ticket. Might just as well feel the same damn way. Suppose it won't do any more harm than good.

When Reston reached the upper level of the gardens and pulled his head up from his thoughts to see where he was, he noted that Pire had disappeared. He paused, looked around, shrugged and then continued on. By the time he reached the house, Reston had again become preoccupied—so much so he forgot to look up in time to notice that he was rapidly approaching the kitchen door. A moment later and the collision between his head and that door sounded like a rifle-shot as it echoed through the conifers.

Damn!

Reston wasn't sure whether to laugh or cry as he rubbed his head. He also wasn't sure which hurt the most—his head or just plain not knowing what the hell he was doing.

CHAPTER NINETEEN

Sunday Evening—June 7th

Maude and James left the Endecott manor in the middle of the afternoon. Sunday supper, therefore, was left to Judson—which, of course, was nothing to compare with the previous sumptuous feasts of the previous night. Judson's preparations had been more than adequate. The food had been tasty but far too plenteous for the group's diminished appetites. The gradual passing of time since that awful moment at the pool had done little to relieve the somber mood of the remaining guests—all of whom were seated around Jeff's dining room table and were sipping after-dinner coffees.

The dining room table had been de-leafed, and thus, its shorter proportions afforded closer intimacy for Jeff, Ethel, Lena, Kevin and Sybil. The empty place next to Lena was for Cornelius, who still had not made his appearance. Someone remarked that Cornelius was going to be starved by breakfast time if he didn't show up soon. Jeff suggested that Cornelius be left undisturbed, as from their brief encounter before dinner, it was quite obvious that his friend was exhausted and in need of some rest.

"He's a great guy—a great friend, I'd say, wouldn't you folks?" Jeff was obviously tossing out a rhetorical question. "Two in the morning, or somewhere around that time when I called him, and he never went back to bed. Plane was an hour late, and then, when he finally gets here, he doesn't even take off his coat and relax before he puts his seventy-seven years knee-deep into helping the local boys find out who killed Tony. Sure hope I'm as zippy as Corny when I'm that old."

"I'll settle for sixty-one," Sybil deadpanned.

"You know," Ethel said, her lips barely moving, "I feel like there's fifty suspicious eyes peering down my throat every time I even cough. That's right! I mean it! Why'd Ethel say this? Why'd she ask that? I think we're all so dreadfully suspicious of each other we can't carry on a decent conversation around here anymore."

"Ethel dear, I agree with you," Lena said "I most decidedly do, if that's what you're after. I'm damned suspicious about nearly everyone who was here last night, and I don't mind saying so. That make you feel any better, honey?"

"My point, Lena, is I don't think it helps a bit for all of us to be so suspicious of one another." Ethel's voice had softened. "If someone here last night had anything to do with Tony's death, then the police will find out soon enough."

"What makes you think they'll find out?" Kevin asked.

Sybil looked sharply at her husband. "Don't *you*, dear?"

"What have they discovered so far? For God's sakes, I've been asking this right along."

"They'll find out, Kev," Jeffrey snapped.

Everyone turned their heads towards their host who was concentrating on the coffee he was stirring with the wrong end of a spoon.

"They'll find out. I don't know what they've run into so far, but I'm confident this thing's in good hands. Box has a good reputation. He's thorough. You can tell that by watching him. What Box misses, Corny won't. I'm glad I called him, and as I said, to think he'd come on such short notice, I think is fantastic."

"I was hoping he'd tell us something here tonight.," Ethel said.

"Well, he may yet." Jeff emptied his cup and stood up. "As I remember, he's a short-napper. Lots of short naps but not too many long sleeps. I'll wager the minute the first brandy hits a glass, he won't be far away."

But Jeff was wrong. The group retired into the living room, where a few after-dinner drinks loosened up the conversation again and eventually precipitated a bridge game with Kevin joining the three women. Jeff excused himself and retired to his study.

Meanwhile, no amount of brandy drew Cornelius from his lair. This wasn't because he was sleeping, however. Sleep had been very kind to him for about thirty minutes, but he had been awake now for the better part of an hour. Something was crawling through his system—a feeling he didn't recognize. It had suppressed his hunger, and it had rendered him immobile in his bed. From his supine position, his head propped up on two pillows, and his hands clasped together and forming a pyramid on top of his chest, he was staring up blankly at the overhead lamp in the center of the room.

A perfect crime? Was there such a thing as a perfect crime? An unsolved crime, yes, certainly. But these were the result of inept investigations, not the result of perfect criminals. A perfect crime? A perfect criminal? No! Perfection doesn't exist in the good. And perfection doesn't exist in the bad, either. Ethel Endecott? Strange. And a man with a vial of poison. Why poison? Unless—Ah, yes— Motives—motives—they're always the hardest to understand—

Cornelius glanced at his watch. Eight o'clock. Gracious. He'd been dreaming long enough. He wanted to chat with Jeffrey, and he certainly couldn't do it from this bed. He sighed and forced his head off of the pillow. Soon, a cascade of warm water was rolling off his back. The shower felt good. That nap had done its job. It was good to be in the house of an old friend, even if it was an unexpected visit. Cornelius smiled contentedly and turned off the water.

———◆◆◆◆———

The clock on the mantle over the fireplace struck twelve. It was midnight, and the two men sitting in a corner of Jeffrey's study had been there conversing for three hours. They were thoroughly enjoying the experience of reliving the bygone days when mutual interests had brought them so close together. Wars seldom die for such men. Tonight was no exception. They didn't hear the clock as it struck its midnight toll.

However, the conversation hadn't started reminiscently. When Cornelius had discovered his friend in his study shortly after nine, Jeff had asked how things were going with obvious curiosity.

Cornelius had tried to bring Jeff up to date. No, he couldn't put his finger on anything positive yet. Maybe a few negatives. But no positives. Ethel, for example—The evidence on her was false. Contrived, maybe. Contrived by Ethel? He didn't know. But, for that matter, it could have been contrived by anyone—anyone who wanted to implicate Ethel. Ethel, Cornelius felt, was a significant factor in this case, but he wanted to assure Jeffrey that, at the moment, he wasn't sure he knew why. Oh yes, there were a couple of positives. The blow on the head—Ice from the punch bowl maybe. Jeff had seemed surprised, so Cornelius had pointed out that ice was nothing particularly new as a murder weapon and then went on to explain how he had arrived at this theory.

"Only theory, Jeffrey. In fact, this whole case is highly theoretical at the moment."

Cornelius had reached into his pocket and pulled out a piece of paper. It was the piece of note paper Reston had discovered in a kitchen wastebasket. On it was

Tony Bleckmore's name and what appeared to be a telephone number. It was in Judson's handwriting.

Cornelius had smiled. "Oh, here's another piece of evidence, Jeffrey. Does this relate to you in any way?"

Jeff had taken the note and studied it briefly.

"Oh, sure, Corny. Judson gave this to me. A call came in for Tony from this number. Rammutti. I don't know the guy."

"You gave the note to Mr. Bleckmore?"

"Yes, I did. As I recall, I gave him the note here in my study. Yeah, I believe it was right here."

"Do you happen to remember the time, maybe?"

"Around noon, I think."

"Any idea if Mr. Bleckmore returned the call?"

"I don't even know if he even tried. I left him here in the study. Why do you ask? Is it important?"

"Probably not."

Cornelius had taken the note Jeff returned to him and stuffed it back into his pocket. He had then leaned back in his chair and indicated that, based on what he had discovered so far, Jeffrey was pretty much up to date.

Their conversation gradually drifted away from the murder, and soon they were reminiscing in earnest about the days gone by. Thus it went until the fireplace clock struck again and reminded Jeff, as clocks will sometimes do, that he was tired. No, not tired. Exhausted. Jeff explained that after he had left Corny at the house, he had returned to the airport and waited for Tony's sister to arrive. He had gotten her settled at a Holiday Inn and then had spent the afternoon helping her get in touch with the people necessary to handle Tony's funeral and financial affairs. A tiring experience. Cornelius sympathized with him and suggested that it might be good for both of them to turn in. However, he needed a favor first, Cornelius said. He wanted to visit a few of the missing guests at their homes tomorrow—starting, maybe, with a stop-off at the sheriff's office in the morning. He wondered—should he use a taxi or—

"No problem," Jeff stated emphatically. "I'll have Judson spend the day with you. He's a good driver. Doesn't look like one, I'll admit," Jeff chuckled, "but he'll surprise you—very alert."

"But you need him here."

"No! Judson's yours, Corny. The Tones, Ethel and Lena are all leaving in the morning. I can go it alone around here quite well. When you get home tomorrow night, we'll go out for dinner. How's that?"

The two men, who by now were on their feet, said good night to each other and went their separate ways—Jeff to his room, which was soon bathed with the evening's darkness—and Cornelius to the back screened-in verandah. By prearrangement, he was to meet Kevin Tone.

<hr />

Cornelius was uncomfortable. The man sitting across from him, his features barely visible in the tree shrouded moonlight, was interrogating him in a decidedly unfriendly manner. Also Cornelius was still having trouble understanding the urgency of a private chat at this late hour. He hadn't understood the reason why when Tone had requested the meeting earlier, and he understood less now. Mr. Tone was obviously impatient about the progress being made in solving the case. But the longer Cornelius listened to the diversity of questions being put to him, the stronger his impression was that, de facto, he was being pumped.

Cornelius replied in non-sequiturs or artful double-talk until, finally, his interrogator seemed to run out of gas. Kevin's shoulders sagged. He leaned back in his chair and glowered at the silhouetted image of Cornelius's face. The silence of the midnight air filled the space between the two men. Clearly, each was determined to outwait the other.

Kevin gave in first.

"You play your cards very close to your vest, Mr. Pire. You've been here for nearly a day now. Judging from your preeminent reputation, I anticipated that your prowling would have led you to more preliminary conclusions than you're revealing."

"You are correct, of course, Mr. Tone. I have not revealed everything—especially the one overwhelming feeling I have at the moment which is—" Pire smiled mischievously—"that you are suppressing a strong compulsion to tell me something."

Kevin leaned over, rested his arms on his legs and wrapped himself in thought.

"All right. I don't know how you figured that out, but you're right. I wasn't going to say anything, but now I guess I'd better."

Kevin looked up and eyed his companion through the murky moonlight.

"By now, I'm sure you've heard that a certain unknown chap by the name of Alfie has been footloose in the community."

Cornelius indicated that, yes, he had.

Kevin then proceeded to tell Cornelius a little of what he knew about this man Alfie. It seems that this mystery man was a regular customer of his wife's—as of course was Tony Bleckmore. Well, what he was getting at was that his wife, Sybil, after having dealt with both men for some time, had reason to believe that there was no love lost between them. Kevin then vaguely referred to the prevalent rumor afloat that someone had tried to kill Tony in his condo a few days before Jeff's weekend party. Kevin keyed in on Collin Strabo's professional opinion about the burn marks on Bleckmore's neck. Finally, in a brief summation of his thoughts on this matter, Kevin stated that he and a number of the other guests felt strongly that this fellow Alfie, whoever he is, ought to be ferreted out and questioned most vigorously about Bleckmore's murder.

Tone peered intently into the shadows, patiently waiting for a response from the vague shape sitting across from him. If he could have seen Pire's face clearly, Tone would have been decidedly disconcerted. As it was, he was not able to perceive the relaxed body, the folded hands, the slightly tilted head or the closed eyes of a man who was either enjoying a catnap or was deep in thought.

Kevin coughed. "Mr. Pire, I hope I have not been boring you with all this."

"I am wondering, Mr. Tone, why you have chosen to reveal your knowledge of this matter to me."

"I am not aware that I have revealed very much, Mr. Pire. I really don't have much to reveal."

"On the contrary, sir, I believe you have revealed a great deal."

"I have?"

"That you are nervous about your place in the scheme of things, maybe."

"Touché, Mr. Pire. Your antenna is even better than I imagined. I *am* nervous."

"Perhaps it would help both of us if you cared to tell me why, Mr. Tone."

"It's not a very complicated answer. Some of my friends have intimated rather strongly that my movements last night were, at certain critical moments, not very accountable. I believe, from what I've heard, that somehow Lt. Box has acquired the same presumption. Well, I'll admit that I was not highly visible at the time someone killed Tony. Yes, I'll admit that. I was restless, and I don't know why. Also, I guess I was a bit stressed up by matters relating to Jeff's coming Senatorial campaign, and I chose those unfortunate minutes when Tony met his maker to let the solitude of Jeff's Gardens mollify my disquietude. If you heard I didn't like Bleckmore, it's true. I detested the man. But I didn't see Tony in my wanderings last night, and I certainly didn't kill him. That's the plain and simple truth of it, Mr. Pire. One of the guests here last night may have killed Bleckmore. I don't know. But I do know that it could also have been an outside job and the first place to look, for my money, would be at the man we know as Alfie."

Cornelius waited until he was certain that Kevin had finished and then rose to his feet.

"Thank you, Mr. Tone, for assuring me of your innocence. I will pass this on to the Lieutenant. Every suspect he can cross off his list will undoubtedly expedite the apprehension of the guilty party."

"You are sounding a bit sarcastic, Mr. Pire. I hope you haven't read me wrong. I was merely attempting to be helpful. This case is dragging, and I—"

"Mr. Tone—if I may interrupt—This case is, I believe, only some twenty-four hours old, maybe. Some murderers have been known to take thirty years to apprehend. It is you and I, I suspect, who are dragging. Perhaps we should locate our beds and rest our cells until tomorrow. Tomorrow, sir, is a delightful day."

"It is? How do you know that?"

"I decide it that way. Always have. And so far, I've never been wrong."

Cornelius struggled with his tired feet, following Kevin to the the verandah door. Suddenly, Cornelius's eyes narrowed. His focus sharpened. For the first time, he had a feeling rolling around somewhere inside him that this case will be broken. Yes, and quite a bit sooner than in thirty years.

CHAPTER TWENTY

Monday Morning—June 8th

"That's about it, Corny. Jake and I have some damn strong suspicions, but nothing we can go to court with yet. So far, we've stumbled up one blind alley after another."

Bill Box was sitting behind his desk at his county office. A cigarette was glowing between his teeth. Jake Reston was sitting with his arms wrapped around the back of a wooden straight chair. Cornelius Pire was straddling a chair and was leaning forward, both knees pressed hard against the desk. He was straining to catch Box's every word.

"I think you know more than you think, Lieutenant. Patience. That's the key here, maybe."

Cornelius had been listening attentively to Box's review of the case for some fifteen minutes. He had not interrupted but had merely nodded his head in apparent agreement from time to time.

"What d'you mean by that?" Box asked

"I mean that perhaps you have acquired the possession of facts about Mr. Bleckmore's untimely death which, with patience and time, will fall into their proper place."

Cornelius's ruddy complexion and twinkling eyes were beginning to have a warming affect on the Box disposition. He put his feet up on his desk and laughed.

"You amaze me, Corny. You look and act like we've not only licked this case but have won a lottery somewhere to boot."

"The morning is the top of the day, Lieutenant. Best time to let the cells talk."

Cornelius pulled out his small leather notebook containing the picture of Tony Bleckmore and some miscellaneous notes he had made while visiting with Box during their poolside visit.

"I put down some items regarding times, which in retrospect—well, I am wondering if I might have made a mistake, maybe. Would you be so kind to check me?"

Box spread out his own notes on the desk in front of him.

"Shoot."

"You say one of the guests, a Mr. Kennelly, estimated that dinner was over at eight-thirty?"

"Yep."

"And that shortly thereafter, the guests went up to Mr. Endecott's recreation room?"

Box nodded.

"And that sometime between eight-fifty and nine-twenty, Mr. Kennelly estimates they were all killing time, maybe, waiting for Jeffrey to show them his movie?"

"Agree."

Cornelius looked up from his notes.

"As I understand it, sometime near the end of this game, Mr. Bleckmore entered the room from the terrace, passed directly through the room without stopping and then closed the hallway door behind him?"

Cornelius eased back in his chair.

"Corny, you've got it as I've got it."

Cornelius stared at Box for a few moments and then leaned forward again.

"All right, Lieutenant. This means the group started looking for Mr. Bleckmore sometime after nine-fifteen and the body was discovered in the pool at exactly nine-thirty-seven?"

"No, according to Kennelly, nine-thirty-seven is when the guests arrived at the pool en masse. The body was discovered about five minutes earlier. Judson claims Mr. Tone got there just ahead of him. Mr. Tone will not confirm this."

Cornelius took no time to correct his notes.

"And the coroner's report places the time of death sometime between eight-fifty-five and nine-fifteen?"

"That's right. Would you like to see the report?"

Cornelius shook his head. "I was hoping somewhere I was wrong, maybe."

"It sure as hell doesn't add up. I know," Box said.

"Why would Mr. Bleckmore come up to the house sometime before or after nine o'clock—obviously not feeling tip-top—and then rush to the bottom of that pool not more than fifteen minutes later—maybe less?" Cornelius scratched the back of his head.

"I'd guess you'd say he was on a pretty tight schedule," Reston offered in a dry monotone.

Cornelius smiled. "Yes, as you say, pretty tight. One might think Mr. Bleckmore was in a hurry to die. A nubby little mystery, eh?"

Box's phone rang. He asked to be excused for a minute on another matter, and so Cornelius quickly moved into the next room. He sat down on a wooden bench up against a wall and stared at his notebook. Tony's picture fell into his lap. He glanced at the picture and then back to his notes again. Finally, he closed his notebook, leaned his back against the wall and glanced casually at Tony's picture again. Slowly, he became absorbed in what he was looking at. He remained transfixed for some time. Then, he jumped up and moved over to a table by a window on the other side of the room. He laid the snapshot on the table, reached in his pocket and pulled out a packet of paper matches. He tore off one match and laid it carefully on the picture. Cornelius then leaned over the table, one hand on each side of the picture, and stared down at Tony Bleckmore.

It's possible. Sacramento! Maybe!

Cornelius's lips were set. His expression was suddenly grim. He moved to the doorway of Box's office and waved to the Lieutenant who was still on the phone.

"I'll be in touch. Thank you so much."

And then, Cornelius was out the door. He got in the car and was so preoccupied that Judson had to ask twice where Cornelius wanted to go next.

"What? Oh, sorry, Judson. Aa—well, let me see—Can you find the Strabo's residence, maybe?"

Cornelius leaned back, put his head against the back of the seat and closed his eyes.

"Sacramento!" A soft whisper.

"What did you say, sir?'

"Say? Oh nothing. Just an old man muttering to himself, I guess. Sorry."

Judson headed the car towards the city.

The Tones' car was parked in front of the Endecott home where Kevin had left it the day before. The Tone's two pieces of luggage had been carefully placed in the back seat of their car. Sybil had run back into the house for something she had forgotten. Kevin and Jeff were standing under a pair of umbrellas as, for the first time in many days, a mid-morning drizzle was falling.

"You and Syb were great to stay on an extra day, you know. Sure do appreciate what you folks have done to make life tolerable around here."

"Nonsense. You were good to agree to our staying. Syb and I enjoyed ourselves, if that's possible under the circumstances."

"Well, I suppose it's been said a thousand times since yesterday, things are in a hell of a mess. Never in my wildest moments, did I dream—"

"What the hell, Jeff, I think the only sensible thing we can do, you and I, and everyone else for that matter, is to forget this whole damn thing and try and get back to normal."

"You've forgotten one little detail, pal. There's still a murderer loose. There's still—"

"I haven't forgotten, but—"

"And until the authorities indicate otherwise, in the public's eye, it still could be one of us. You know—if they don't get this thing cleared up pretty soon, the lot of us will be damned forever."

"Oh, Jeff—Jeff—" Kevin was obviously alarmed. "I don't think that is true—not at all. Besides, don't you have confidence in Cornelius? I thought you were cocksure your friend will sniff this thing out—and fast."

"Yeah, he will. I sure hope so."

Jeffrey dropped his umbrella, looked up at the dark clouds overhead and let the light rain splash on his face.

"Yeah, I sure hope so. But ya know, Kev, last night, Corny sounded like the pickings so far have been kind of thin."

"Well, I think I'm beginning to learn a little more about the police, Jeff. Cops talk but only to cops, and that includes a cop's best friend."

"Corny's different. He'd have said something to me last night if he'd had anything on his mind."

"Could be. But I wouldn't worry too much about public opinion—especially not on this senate thing. Time heals, you know, and we've got plenty of that before you have to start campaigning. Besides—Well, I haven't wanted to say this before, but I think—Jeff I think we should consider Bleckmore's death a blessing in disguise. Really, I—"

"Kev! For Christ's sake! You know what you're saying?"

"Jeff, I—"

"Tony's body is hardly cold yet, and you're telling me you feel like celebrating?"

"I—I didn't mean it like it sounds. I only meant—"

"What *did* you mean, for Christ sake?" Jeff was eyeing Kevin coldly.

"All right. You're asking me. I'll tell you. I think your chances of becoming a United States Senator are a thousand times better now than they were yesterday morning."

"Because Tony's dead?"

"Because Tony's dead! This is not a feeling, Jeff. It's closer to being a fact."

"Well, if what you're telling me is true, then you can take the Senate and ram it."

Jeff moved away from Kevin. His voice was quivering.

Kevin followed him.

"Ah, Jeff, come on."

"If I have to swallow that kind of cold-blooded crap of yours, Kev, then I'm not interested in the Senate. That's all. I'm not interested."

"Jeff, I'm sorry."

Kevin put his hand out and grabbed Jeff's arm.

"Let's cool down. We'll discuss this thing in a few days. We'll have our murderer by then. You know damn well we will. Then we can get back on track."

Kevin glanced up towards the Endecott house as Sybil started down the front steps. He looked back at Jeff and smiled. "Sorry I offended you, friend. Really, I am."

Jeff withdrew his arm from Kevin's grasp and turned towards the clicking heels of Sybil.

"I'm sorry, boys. I just can't find that little green purse I was carrying last night. I must have misplaced it somewhere."

Sybil walked over to Jeff and took both of his hands.

"You'll call, if you find it, won't you Jeffrey? I'll send someone out to pick it up."

"Will do, Syb."

"Darling, I can't say we had a nice time, and I know you can't either. But Kevin and I have commented to one another several times the last couple of days what a stalwart brick you've been. We know how close you felt to Tony and all, and I'm sure in our own little selfish ways, we've had no real appreciation of how difficult it's been for you."

Jeffrey took a hold of Sybil's elbow and guided her towards the car.

"Come on, let me help you in or your husband's going to leave without you."

Jeff closed Sybil's door and waved perfunctorily as the Tone's Cadillac faded from sight down the long tree-lined, winding drive.

Jeff thought again of Lena, as he was walking up the steps to his front door. Her last words to him, as she had driven off earlier, were all of a sudden haunting him.

"So this is how it feels to be a divorced widow. You know, Jeff, I don't feel any different than I did yesterday."

Lena's smirk had turned into a genuine smile as she extended her hand out the window and waved at Jeff.

Funny. He hadn't thought anything about her remark at the time. But now, in retrospect, Jeff was struck suddenly by the notion that Lena had probably meant precisely what she had said.

━━━●•◄╉►•●━━━

Marva opened the front door of her home and squealed.

"Mr. Pire! Oh my goodness! It is Mr. Pire, isn't it? It's been such a long time!"

She opened the screen door for him, grasped his hand and gushed, "Oh my, I'm such a mess. I hope you don't mind. Please come in."

"A thousand apologies, Ma'am. If the hour is too early, just a gesture and I'll return later, maybe."

"No, no, please do come in."

Cornelius shuffled through the doorway and cast an appreciative glance at a room full of lovely antiques.

"What a beautiful surprise to see you, Mr. Pire—especially at this hour of the morning. Won't you sit down?"

Cornelius sat down and quickly agreed that, indeed, he would love some good, hot, strong coffee—but no, nothing else. Coffee would be just fine, thank you. When the coffee returned a few minutes later, Cornelius was equally quick to extol the virtues and esthetic values of the room they were sitting in. The obvious sincerity of his appreciation impressed Marva, and so for a half an hour she thoroughly enjoyed discussing one of her favorite hobbies, antiques, with her quaint guest. But obviously, Mr. Pire had more serious reasons for coming by than to chat about antiques Marva finally observed. Cornelius smiled shyly and indicated that well, yes, the matter of that vial of poison had struck him rather curiously, and as a matter of fact, this was on his mind maybe.

Of course. Of course. Marva leaned towards Cornelius and let him know how pleased she was that he had brought this matter up. It would give her a chance to explain. She began by saying that although she loved her husband dearly, she certainly didn't understand him at times, and his behavior at the Endecott's was a perfect example. *Not* that he had anything to do with Tony's death, mind you. She *knew* he didn't. But she *was* glad Cornelius had brought up the matter of that poison, because she didn't like the thought that possible suspicions might be cast on her misunderstood husband. There was a perfectly logical explanation for that poison being tucked away in his valise, and Collin would be more than happy to explain it to anyone who would listen. Goodness knows, she still couldn't understand why Collin hadn't said something about it at Jeffrey's.

Judging from the occasional affirmative nod of Cornelius's head, Marva felt reassured that he was finding her explanations entirely rational. She relaxed, leaned back and crossed her legs.

"But Ma'am, this doesn't quite explain you and your husband's rather abrupt departure from the premises during the early morning hours the other night. Do you think so?"

Marva paled. "Oh, Mr. Pire, I *didn't* know why my husband was so agitated, or why he behaved so strangely that night. But I do now. He hasn't told me. But tiny bits and pieces—Yes, I think I know. But really, you should talk to Collin about it, not me. I'll call him home."

"Oh, no, ma'am. I wouldn't think of it. Your husband's a busy man. I was wondering perhaps—maybe—if in your own words—"

Marva was already on her way to the phone.

"I think Collin would prefer to use his own words, *really*. He's only fifteen minutes away—just long enough for you and I to talk a little more about antiques."

An hour later, Cornelius was on his way out of the Strabo house. He paused at the front door, turned and shook Collin's hand solemnly. He thanked Marva profusely for her hospitality and then quickly headed towards the roadside curb and Judson, who was sitting patiently behind the wheel of the Endecott car.

"Judson, judging from your relaxed manner, you must be a man possessed with infinite patience. Please forgive me. I was far longer than I anticipated. Do you think you can locate one of those public telephones somewhere?"

"There's a phone in the pocket behind the front seat, sir."

"Amazing. The next thing they'll be installing in these vehicles is a television. Dear me. I hope not."

Judson stopped the car. Cornelius got out and climbed into the back seat. He took a rumpled piece of paper out of his pocket and then pulled the telephone out of its zippered enclosure. The number he dialed was quickly answered.

"May I speak to a Mr. Rex Rammutti, please. Thank you. Mr. Rammutti?—This is Cornelius Pire. I'm associated with the police officials who are investigating the Bleckmore homicide—Aa, yes, that is correct. And I am wondering if you would mind extending to me the courtesy of answering one little question—What?—Oh yes, thank you. Well, I believe you made a telephone call to Mr. Bleckmore last Saturday sometime around noon. Is that correct?— Yes, well perhaps you could tell me if Mr. Bleckmore returned your call.—He what?—Oh, yes, I see—You are very kind. I thank you for your help. So sorry to have troubled you."

Pire replaced the receiver back on its hook and sat staring thoughtfully out a side window into space. Finally, he reached into his pocket and pulled out another rumpled piece of paper. He glanced at it for a moment, then reached for the phone and dialed another number.

"Aaa—May I speak to Mr. Romanareo, please. Cornelius Pire speaking."

CHAPTER TWENTY-ONE

Monday Noon—June 8th

Judson had gotten out of the car and was stretching his legs a few feet away. As he did so, he studied the man sitting in the back seat with a phone to his ear.

It sure was hard sometimes to realize that this funny little fellow was a policeman. When he was close by and you were talking to him—then you knew he was a policemen—Lordie-Moses, you did. Those eyes—you can feel 'em—they give you the geebees—but, get safely away from him, like right now—Judson shook his head.

From here, that ain't no cop. That's just a plain—Oops, he's through talking. Can't be dreaming like this or, sure as cars have wheels, he'll throw me in jail.

Judson quickly climbed back into the car.

"Where's there a good place to have lunch, Mr. Judson?"

"Sir?"

"Where would you take Mr. Endecott for lunch about now?"

"He usually likes the Colony or the Recess."

"Are you hungry?"

"Sir?"

"So am I. Let's go to the colony, and we'll slack off a bit, eh?"

"Sir, I—"

"Judson! Do you know where the Colony is?" Cornelius's beady eyes were boring into the side of Judson's head.

"Yes, sir!"

"Then drive there, please. Park the car. And let me treat you to lunch. I'll never remove myself from your debt for all this chauffeuring, but it will be a step."

Judson looked over at his passenger and grinned. He opened his mouth to say something. But nothing came out. So he closed his mouth and headed for the Colony.

Ethel's three pieces of matching luggage were sitting in the central foyer near the front door of the Endecott home. Near them stood Jeff Endecott, arms folded across his chest, watching his ex-wife descend the circular staircase. She had a small cosmetic case in one hand. Her purse was in the other. As Ethel reached the last step on the stairway, she paused, smiled demurely, and then slowly, silently, sank to a sitting position on the second step, her eyes riveted on the object of all her hopes.

Jeff shifted from one foot to the other, submitting to the momentary silence with an inner embarrassment his sheepish smile scarcely concealed. But he made no effort to break the silence.

Ethel had her arms in her lap. She was leaning forward with her hands clasped together and her head tilted slightly to one side.

"I've enjoyed being here with you this weekend, Jeff. I know this is an absolutely hideous thing to say or even think, what with the terrible tragedy the other night and all, but I just had to say it to you before I leave."

Jeff walked over to Ethel and pulled her to her feet. He held her gently by the shoulders at arm's length.

"Ethel, you're a great gal. You know how much it has meant to me to have you here this weekend. You've been a great help."

"I wish you meant that."

"Ethel, love, I do mean it. I—"

"No. No, I mean I wish you really thought I was great." Ethel's eyes were dangerously moist.

"I've never changed my feeling for you. You know that, Ethel. Our divorce was for the best. We agreed on that long ago."

"*You* agreed."

"Now, honey, there's no sense in going through all that again. It's worked out for the best. Now, hasn't it.? You'll agree to that."

Ethel slipped inside Jeff's outstretched arms and put her head on his shoulder.

"Oh, Jeffrey, darling—I'm flaunting myself. I'll hate myself for this tomorrow."

For a few moments, neither moved. Finally, Ethel tilted her head back. Her moist eyes focused on Jeff's.

"I'm sorry. Please forgive me. I'd better go."

Jeff pulled out his handkerchief and repaired her eyes. He then picked up her cosmetic case and walked over to the door. Ethel picked up her purse and slowly followed him. He leaned over with his empty hand to pick up one of her two large bags. Then, suddenly, he stopped, straightened up and turned to Ethel.

"You know, I've got to be downtown today. Tony's sister needs some help and a few other things. But if you want to wait here, we can take Corny out for dinner when I get back."

Two broad smiles appeared from out of nowhere on the faces of the two people facing each other. Neither smile moved or spoke until, again, Ethel broke the silence.

"You mean it?"

"I always mean it."

Ethel threw her arms around Jeff and gave him a kiss. Then she took her cosmetic bag from him and headed back towards the stairs.

"You go ahead, darling. I'll be here when you get back," she called over her shoulder.

If Ethel had glanced back or paused to think as she was climbing the stairway, she would have known that Jeff had hurriedly followed his thoughts out the front door. She had long ago learned, however, that sometimes it's best to look straight ahead.

.

———◆◆◆◆◆———

"Mr. Kennelly, you are so kind to agree to a few minutes with me on such short notice. I assure you I won't impose on your busy schedule but for one or two questions."

"Sit down, Pire. I told the police out at Endecott's I'd do what I can to help and it still goes."

"Excellent."

"And don' worry about my time. My business is well staffed. I prefer to think that some day I'll be in the way around here, and they'll leave me no choice but to sit back and catch the dividends."

Sam Kennelly was not normally even mildly effusive. He was being exceptionally cordial at the moment to a man with whom he'd had only a few words. He was curious as to what this hawk-shaw was up to, and being nice to a breed of cats he didn't particularly cotton to was probably the easiest way to get some information. Trouble was—he'd undoubtedly have to answer some idiotic questions before he could learn anything.

Cornelius was unusually serious. His eyes had lost their customary twinkle.

"Mr. Kennelly, you have an avid interest, I'm told, in the time of the day."

"I usually know what time it is, if that's what you mean."

"Lieutenant Box showed me the sequence of events of last Saturday night as you recalled them to him."

"Yes." Sam's relaxed manner was already disappearing and being replaced by a wary sense of uneasiness.

"I am wondering, maybe—those times—" Cornelius pulled out his notebook and handed it to Sam—"I have them here. Please—I am wondering—these times are in your opinion accurate, maybe?"

Kennelly shoved the notebook back to Cornelius without looking at it.

"I told the Lieutenant that they're all estimates—all, that is, except that nine-twenty-seven time at the pool. That's on-the-button because I remember standing there looking at my watch and shaking it to make sure it was running. The rest—I don't know—they're all right, I guess. We were all pretty upset Saturday night, and I was no exception. I told Box, as best I could remember, when certain things happened."

"There are some who have wondered if you might not have recalled these times to suit your own purpose, maybe."

"What?" Sam stood up. "What do you mean? Are you implying I'm not telling the truth?"

"No offense, sir. I personally do not share this concern. It is, however, important for me to know how reliable you think the information is you have given to the police."

"Damn it! I don't understand your questions. I told you, Pire, it's as reliable as I can remember it."

"Undoubtedly, Mr. Kennelly, my questions are poorly put and without substance. I apologize. May I try one more question? Then, I'll leave."

Sam barely nodded.

"Someone suggested to me last night, Mr. Kennelly, that you and Mr. Bleckmore were not on the best of terms. I am wondering, maybe, if you would care to comment about a man who, I believe, was your business partner?"

"No, I wouldn't," Sam snorted.

"Then, I have no more questions," Cornelius said softly.

"I despised the bum, if that's what you're looking for. But so what! This don't exactly make me one of a kind. There's dozens more like me, and a few of them were at Endecott's last night in case you don't know."

"You're telling me things I had no idea," Cornelius murmured.

"You know, or you wouldn't be asking me. I haven't the foggiest what you don't know or what you're here to find out—but it's probably whether I killed Bleckmore or not. That what you're after?"

Cornelius smiled and said nothing.

"Ha—You won't admit it, will you?"

"Mr. Kennelly, I don't believe I have ever known a tippler who emptied his bottle and then fell into the arms of Morpheus right after slaying a dragon. Have you?"

Sam groaned.

"My God, you know about that too. I remember Jeff talking about you once. You don't miss a trick, do you. Yes, Pire, I got bombed last night. For the first and last time in my life, I got bombed. Mark it down. First and last."

"An effective but unpleasant way to forget what you do not want to remember, maybe."

"I got bombed, Pire, because I think I know who killed Bleckmore. That lousy bourbon was only temporary relief, cause I can still remember."

Sam sat down.

"And don't ask me who, cause I won't tell you, Pire. And if anyone else asks me,

I'll tell them I plain-ass don't know. Okay?"

Cornelius rose to his feet, thanked Sam profusely for his inestimable help and took his leave.

Grimly, Sam picked up his phone and dialed a familiar number.

"Anne—You alone?—Yeah, I'm at the office. You send that guy Pire over here?—Well, if anyone else calls you and asks where I am, tell 'em I'm in Europe—Yeah, Europe—Why? Cause, damn it all, Anne, I don't want to talk to any more cops, and I don't want you to either—Well, I'm not going to argue about it on the phone with you, Anne. Just do what I said."

Sam reached for a handkerchief and wiped off his perspiring brow. He held the receiver a few inches from his ear until he was reasonably sure his wife had stopped talking. Then, he quietly placed the receiver back on its hook. He smiled and reflected lugubriously.

Sure be hell going home tonight, but not as bad as having another lousy cop come snooping around.

CHAPTER TWENTY-TWO

Monday Afternoon—June 8th

As Sam was completing his contentious phone call to his wife, Cornelius was seated next to Judson in the passenger seat of Jeffrey's Eldorado. They were parked in front of Sam's office building. The Cadillac's engine was running, but Judson had left the gear shift lever in "park" in deference to Cornelius's suggestion that they not move until they had a better idea as to where it was they were going.

"One of my great frustrations in my younger days, Judson, was that I could never expeditiously locate a piece of paper when I needed it, especially if it was crumpled up and hiding in one of my pockets."

Cornelius's hands were prowling as he talked, relentlessly frisking himself in search of a scrap of paper Box had handed to him earlier in the day.

"At one time, I strongly considered having all of my pockets sewn up but one, thereby significantly reducing the scope of my problem. However, my dear departed wife's wisdom quickly convinced me of the folly of that approach. I think her words were, 'What you don't lose to the winds, my dear, won't be worth looking for if you only have one pocket'. So—like everything else, Judson, I decided to solve my problem with nothing but bulldogged determination."

Cornelius turned to Judson and triumphantly waved a piece of paper in his hand.

"Eureka! I have won again.!"

Cornelius unraveled the crumpled up piece of paper and studied it for a moment.

"This is a map drawn up by Lieutenant Box. It is designed to help us locate our next destination."

Cornelius shook his head as he inspected the crude hand-drawn map.

"As a cartographer, I'm afraid the Lieutenant would starve, maybe. Here, Judson, I will turn this over to you. Its interpretation requires a more experienced pair of eyes than mine."

Cornelius handed the map to Judson.

"That black square is supposed to be at the end of a cul-de-sac where a gentleman by the name of Romanareo lives. Do you think you can find it?"

After only a cursory glance at the paper, a rare smile from Judson.

"Ah, that must mean I just asked a foolish question. All right, sir, let's see what you can do. Oh—but wait, Judson. I have another favor first. Do you think we could pass by a confectionery before we drive to Mr. Romanareo's?"

"Confectionery?" Judson frowned.

"Chocolates, Judson—a store that sells five pound boxes of creamy sweets."

Judson put the car in gear and pulled out into the street.

"Begging your pardon, sir, I wish I could eat like you do."

"Oh—The chocolates are not for me, Judson. They will be a gift and will, I hope, help us to obtain a confession. "Judson looked askance at his companion and unconsciously wrinkled his nose. It was a passing reflex action which helped him to tolerate the fancies of people whose actions he was sure he didn't understand.

Thirty minutes later, the two men were approaching the sought after cul-de-sac. A ribbon-bound box of Fannie May chocolates was lying between them on the front seat.

Cornelius took stock of the white framed house, sitting behind a broad expanse of lawn and a white picket fence, and murmured quietly to himself, *Hello! Enchanting!*

At precisely the same time Cornelius was preparing to open the same swinging gate Lieutenant Box had passed through some twenty-eight hours earlier, two unseen people in the immediate vicinity were making love in a manner unfathomable to most westerners.

One was a lovely young oriental woman with raven black flowing hair and flawless café-au-lait skin. She was sitting cross legged on a pale straw mat on the grassy bank of a foot wide rivulet whose origin was hidden by a nearby thicket of scrubby trees and whose destination was a small bog garden lying below the couple some fifty yards away.

The woman's pink kimono was lying at her side. She was sitting erect. Her head was held high. Her tiny sculpted breasts were pointing in the same direction as her outstretched hands, which were resting gently on the similarly outstretched hands of her male partner.

The man was sandy haired and looked like a youthful Greek God — until, that is, one took a closer look at the depth of focus of a pair of pale blue eyes. Those eyes, closely perused, obliterated the rest of the man's face and made him seem almost ageless. Also cross legged, he was sitting on the other side of the rivulet and was gazing intently into the misty green eyes of his wife. A leather tunic and a pair of loose fitting breeches were carefully folded and lying at his side. Like the woman, he had nothing on, and like the woman, the intensity with which his shining eyes were locked onto his partner's was evidence of the concentrated game of love the two were playing.

The man was seemingly impassive to the lusty flush of his own large erection. But his wife could see his lips tighten ever so little and knew that, this time, she was winning. Though usually she succumbed to the implacable control of this iron-willed man, this time he would be the first to yield to uncontrollable desire and erupt volcanically by leaping across the rivulet. Instinctively, she readied herself for his pounce and the subsequent ecstasy, wherein they would eventually lose themselves completely in violent orgasms. The euphoria of a rare victory would make today doubly sweet for the lady.

The couple's enchantment was as soundless as their milieu. No wind was rustling the leaves of the surrounding trees. The rivulet was tiptoeing by, courteously trying not to interfere with the two finely tuned minds playing against each other overhead. The lady's face was beginning to relax ever so slightly into the trace of a gentle smile. She could see it in her husband's face. She knew she had won. She knew beyond a doubt that it would be only a few more moments and one of the sweetest forms of coital success would be hers. It was testimony to the incredible willpower of the lady that she could anticipate victory without allowing her concentration to wane.

How in the twinkling of an eye things can sometimes inauspiciously change. One moment! One moment these two lovers were on the verge of unparalleled rapture. And then—the next moment, in one magical movement of arms, bodies and legs, they were fully dressed. A high-pitched sonic beep, barely audible to the average ear, had sounded from within the foliage of an adjacent group of rhododendron scrubs and had galvanized the couple into reactions incomparably swift and decisive. The swinging gate had actuated the sonic beep.

Not long after the gate had lazily swung closed behind him Cornelius glanced up. He was slowly trudging his way up the pathway to Romanareo's front door and was surprised to find a man waiting on the front steps to greet him.

In spite of the alacrity with which Alfie had moved from the garden, he seemed to be barely breathing. He was leaning against a porch pillar and was smiling down at the white haired wizened gnome approaching him. Alfie tripped lightly down the steps and stuck out his hand.

"Cornelius Pire, is it now."

Cornelius accepted the proffered hand.

"Corny. Much less wear and tear on both of us, if you don't mind."

Cornelius checked his watch.

"Unforgivable. I'm over an hour early, maybe. It's a wonder you didn't mistake me for a street peddler."

"You are early. But you're no peddler, friend. Your step gives you away."

Cornelius stepped back and studied the man looming before him.

"Well now, my step. That's a curious observation I've never heard before. Excluding the awareness you had of my pending arrival, how did my step announce me?"

Alfie grinned. "Cock-of-the-walks advertise themselves with their feet. Simple answer."

"Cock-of-the-walk." Cornelius beamed. "A superb compliment, maybe. But I shall have to look to effecting a more modest shuffle lest—" Cornelius glanced skyward—"Lest I upset dear Emily. Modesty in all things was her credo, and alas, that included her poor husband."

Cornelius eyed Alfie sharply.

"Incidentally, sir, I assume that I *am* in the presence of the Roman?"

A loud chortle from Alfie.

"I am Alfie, Corny—the same handle you gave me on the phone."
He placed his hand on Cornelius's shoulder.

"Would you like to come into my parlor or would you prefer the solitude of my gardens?"

Cornelius shrugged his shoulders and held out both hands palms up, leaving the choice up to Alfie.

Gently, Alfie took Cornelius by the arm and pointed him down a path leading to the back of his house. Side by side, they strolled silently, until they came to a depressed area containing a spacious bog garden. Royal, Ostrich and Chain ferns weaved themselves in and around a variety of lilies and trilliums. Rising out of the center of this picturesque bog was a formation of large sandstone rocks. A narrow walking bridge over the gently flowing water led to the rock cluster. Cornelius paused and held his breath as he absorbed the enchantment of nature surrounding him.

"Lovely! I thought Jeffrey's gardens ne plus ultra. Yours are even more so, maybe."

Alfie grinned and pointed to the rocks.

"Good spot to sit, Corny, if you don't mind a wooden bench to sit on and a rock to lean your back against."

The two men passed over the bridge and sat down across from one another on a pair of twin benches. Alfie savored an inner glow as he watched Cornelius stare in wonder. *This is good. Control. But for how long? Yes, for how long?*

"The Devil!" Cornelius rapped the palm of one hand lightly on his temple and shook his head. "You have cast a spell on me, Alfie, and—" Cornelius smiled slyly—"You are enjoying it, maybe."

Cornelius suddenly remembered the package he had been carrying under one arm and quickly leaned forward and handed the gift wrapped box to Alfie.

"I almost forgot. A present for you. Please accept."

"I feel the prick of a bribe in my hands," Alfie said as he laid the box in his lap.

"Absolutely!" Cornelius grinned. "It is a bribe. But it is not from Pire."

"Oh?"

"Compliments of the Lieutenant. He would like you to confess and has commissioned me to represent him."

"Confess? To what?"

"Oh? But I thought you knew."

Alfie smacked his lips appreciatively. "Sweets. Their aroma is too much for the box to contain."

He made no attempt to unwrap the package. Instead, he placed it by his side on the bench.

"I shall pass this along to my wife. I am incorruptible, Corny. Even so—You can tell the Lieutenant that Alfie confesses."

Corny's eyes sparkled. "But you have not indicated the nature of your confession, maybe."

"You can tell the Lieutenant that if the chocolates please Sing Sang, Alfie will be very specific."

"Sing Sang?"

"My wife. Would you like to meet her?"

Cornelius held up his hand.

"Please—Perhaps after we visit."

Cornelius removed his jacket, carefully folded it and placed it by his side.

"Your abrupt confession leaves us time to talk about more pleasant things, maybe."

"Pire." Alfie breathed the name thoughtfully. "Would you believe that the name has bounced off my ears more than once in my wanderings?"

Cornelius's cheeks glowed with the smug self-satisfaction of a man who loves a compliment, especially one which he knows is deserved.

"Yes. And likewise, I am familiar with the Roman. We have a mutual acquaintance in Hong Kong by the name of I.M. Tolerable."

Alfie frowned. "A fishy character. The Roman never trusted Tolerable."

"But—" Cornelius leaned forward and cracked a wry smile—"That gentleman's a tolerable judge of character, maybe. It was his opinion that the Roman was the matchless artist."

"Probably because he dug the Roman's Bluegrass piano," Alfie replied flippantly.

"I still find it regrettable that someone as perceptive as Mr. Tolerable prioritized the Roman ahead of me as an artist. Sad. Yes, it is sad, maybe, that the Roman and Pire never had the opportunity to match wits."

Alfie glided to his feet and began to stroll back and forth with the lazy gait of a cheetah stretching it graceful limbs.

"I suppose you got this guy Pire winning such a contest?"

Cornelius paused before answering.

"I think the Roman and I would somehow have managed an assignation and two gin sours together to celebrate a tie."

"Hey, I'll tell you a secret, Corny. I don't think I ever realized how damn good the Roman was until he retired and moved anonymously into a groggy back woods hamlet about a year ago and discovered that from day one the shamus had their prying eyes on him."

"Eyes that were not *successfully* following him, maybe," Cornelius murmured.

"It is impossible to follow someone who wishes otherwise. That your point, Corny?"

"I am saying," Cornelius replied, his eyes twinkling as they followed Alfie lithely pacing back and forth, "that if the Lieutenant had followed, rather than merely observed, he might have known who it was that paid Mr. Bleckmore a visit a week ago."

Alfie stopped, placed a foot up on the bench next to Cornelius, and rested an elbow on his knee.

"Makes sense, Corny—provided, of course, any such visit ever was made. I guess you'd agree to that."

Cornelius cocked one eye and glanced around at the pastoral scene they were a part of.

"Alfie, do you suppose your lilies would be offended if I savor just one smoke?"

Alfie laughed. "Probably. But do it anyway, Corny. What can they say?"

Cornelius picked up his coat and reached into a pocket.

"I have my doctor's permission for just one of these cigarillos a day. I trust you won't tell the gentleman that this is already my third."

Both men were silent while Cornelius extracted a miniature cigar from its pack, placed it carefully between his lips and then held a match to it. As the smoke wafted in the breezeless air, Cornelius allowed his eyes to refocus on Alfie.

"What I don't understand, sir, is why a prodigy such as the Roman would be interested in annoying a relatively small fish like Bleckmore."

Alfie guffawed and sat down.

"Hey, Corny—Man, you've got this Roman fellow being quite a rascal. I'm wondering , you know, what's prodding all this curiosity. Obviously, we're beginning to get down to the nuts and bolts of why you're here."

"Jeffrey Endecott mentioned the Bleckmore condo visit to me and said that his source of information was Mr. Bleckmore himself."

Cornelius leaned back and stared wistfully at his feet.

"One of my friend Jeffrey's attributes, as far back as I can recall, is that he never lies."

"Don't suppose your friend Endecott could hang that same tag on Bleckmore though, do you Corny?"

"No," Cornelius replied, a studious frown masking an inner smile. "I don't expect so—unless Mr. Bleckmore was wearing a fresh rope burn around his neck, maybe."

Alfie studied his visitor for several moments. Finally, he leaned over and placed a hand on the old man's shoulder.

"I have a suggestion, Corny. Let me send for a couple of noggins of a rare Marachuchi Saki, warmed to exactly one hundred and eighteen degrees. We'll sip them and allow their trickle to help us get to know each other better. In the meantime, while we wait briefly for the saki, if we can manage to still our vibrations into absolute silence, I can guarantee you that these lilies will whisper and help us to stomach a bit more what we love to hate."

Cornelius let his eyes acquiesce.

Alfie leaped to his feet and clapped his hands together twice. He then returned to his seat. Partially closing his eyes, he sat transfixed and allowed the exquisite perfume, graceful forms and subdued coloring of the Comanche water lilies to talk to him with their mysterious wonder.

Cornelius, slightly hunched over with his hands clasped between his knees, followed suit. He was not, however, similarly mesmerized. His mind was busy rationalizing the intuitive decision he had made earlier—that the surest approach to the core of the Roman was one of compliance.

Besides, this was not an unpleasant way to get one's batteries recharged. BUT, he better stay on his toes or the next thing this crafty pro would do would be to lure him into listening to some of that devilish Bluegrass.

Suddenly, Cornelius was aware of a third presence in their midst. He glanced up. Startled, he looked into the crystalline eyes of the tiniest lady he'd seen in a long long time. She was holding a tray on which were two noggins, a pitcher and two white linen napkins. Standing at her side was Alfie. Where in the devil had she come from? As he rose to his feet, a frustrated Cornelius was silently chiding himself for not being more alert.

"Meet my wife, Corny. Compared to her, I am a mere roustabout. This Saki she's prepared is a treat. Sing Sang, meet Mr. Pire. As I told you, he would be a worthy opponent for anyone we know."

"Madam."

Cornelius felt strange as he looked down and bowed to the diminutive kimono-clad form in front of him. Rarely did the stature of anyone in his presence permit him to look down.

Sing Sang's facial expression remained vacant as she bowed her head. And then, before Cornelius could further address her, she was gone. Cornelius shook his head and refocused on Alfie who was handing him one of the two noggins. Alfie kept one for himself and sat down.

"A charming lady," Cornelius said, as he likewise returned to his bench. She vanishes almost as magically as she appears. Can you call her back?"

"She won't come."

"No, you say?" Cornelius's jaw dropped.

"She won't allow herself ever to interfere in my business. It's part of her religion."

"Some other time, maybe?"

Alfie cracked a broad smile as he sipped his Saki.

"She could teach you a lot, Corny."

"I'm too old, maybe."

"That's the first phony thing you've said since you arrived here. We stop learning when we die. I'm sure you learned that long before I did."

Cornelius took a long sip from his noggin, and then let his eyes lock onto Alfie's.

"You are helping me to remember, maybe, that I am at the home of the Roman, and so far, I have learned nothing. You only suggest that this has nothing to do with my age."

Alfie's eyes sparkled. "So—You want me to tell you that the Roman paid Bleckmore a visit at his home."

Cornelius placed his empty noggin back on the tray.

"Alfie, you should tell the Roman, maybe, that Cornelius Pire *is* an old man who tires very easily. You should tell him that Pire doesn't want to waste what few working hours he has left in this old hulk attempting to unravel the mysteries of an *inside* job if, de facto, it was an *outside* professional that done Mr. Bleckmore in."

Cornelius paused and let the palms up gesture of his hands, the unassuming tilt of his head and the twinkling in his eyes radiate the amicable mettle of a man anxious to play ball.

"I have a proposition for you to pass along to the Roman. Tell him, please, that if he will admit to me culpability in Bleckmore's homicide, I will abort my mission of searching for the killer under the pretext of an old man's fatigue. I will say nothing further about this case to one and all. I'm afraid I have no stomach anymore to match wits in the working arena with a consummate professional— especially one who would have been a formidable adversary when my staying power was boundless. If, on the other hand, I am assured that the Roman is innocent in this regard, then I shall continue fishing until Bleckmore's amateur executioner is ferreted out."

Alfie threw back his head and roared with laughter.

Cornelius frowned. "You do not believe me, maybe?"

"Wow! Corny, you got to slow down. You're going too fast for me. I thought you said you're a tired old man?"

"Yes. But in ways, you and I are the same age, maybe. It's mostly up here," Corny added, pointing to his head. "I'm suggesting a little honor among peers—to slow down the vanishing cells and the passing of time."

Alfie rose to his feet and bottomed up the rest of his Saki. He licked his chops as he considered the pale blue laser eyes sitting in front of him.

"Corny, I got a question for you. You wired?"

"Wired?

Cornelius thought for a moment.

"I am familiar with the expression. It refers to a lazy contrivance invented to supplant the gray cells, maybe. You want to know if I am recording or transmitting. Well, sir, I told you. I am an old man. I would rather have a murderer go unapprehended than to entrap him through the use of such chicanery. I was never, as you say, wired yesterday. And, I am not wired today."

"Good play!" Alfie grinned.

"I have convinced you, maybe?" Cornelius asked skeptically.

"Yes. You're surprised?"

"Yes."

"You shouldn't be. You think I could get away with lying to you, Corny?"

"I don't believe so, no."

"Well, it works both ways with the two of us."

"Ah yes—All in the eyes. We see alike," Cornelius murmured.

"We talk in confidence, then?"

"Absolutely!"

"Okay. Okay. Sorry, friend. I can't offer you a breather. The Roman wasn't the dandy who bumped off Bleckmore. Otherwise, though, you're on the money. I hear tell The Roman does know what the inside of Bleckmore's joint looks like. I understand he's even familiar with the Bleckmore mug. And—having gone this far—I might just as well share the spicy rest with you."

Alfie paused, leaned over, picked up his empty noggin and studied it abstractly for a few moments. Turning to Cornelius, he asked him if he'd like more Saki. Cornelius declined. Alfie then sat down, eased one foot up onto the bench and clasped his hands around his knee.

"Let's start with that rope burn you mentioned. The word is that the Roman paid Bleckmore a visit late at night, stayed about ten minutes and left the big man standing on a block of ice with an overhead noose dangling around his neck. Now Corny, the rest is guesswork the way I understand it. It's fair to assume, I think, that sooner or later that treacherous block of ice melted. When that happened, as you can imagine, his Majesty's bulk probably tightened up that noose real good. That would explain the rope burn, more or less, don't you think?"

"But not Bleckmore's continued breathing, maybe."

"Yeah, of course not. The obvious mystery. Why didn't Bleckmore croak? Well, let's see—The story is that the Roman learned some of the tricks of his trade from a one time Mongolian master by the name of

Juno. Juno could make ropes talk. It was said that his artistry was an upshot of the days of yore when torture in that country was a means of first resort. Juno could take anything from goat's hair to fine strands of cat gut and alter their tensile strength by minute degrees just by the way he would let the blade of a sharp shiv play on the fibers. The Roman has often told me that patience at a master's feet will always be rewarded in surprising ways. So, that's the answer. I don't suppose it was too difficult for The Roman to alter the breaking point of a four-ply nylon line such that it would break just before snapping the bull-neck of a two hundred and seventy pound whopper. You ask *why* this little play. Well, I guess the short answer is that the Roman was giving into an urge to scare the shit out of Bleckmore. The longer answer involves a juicy secret I'll share with you—that is, if you're still interested.

Cornelius was hanging on every word. The twinkling eyes had faded. The smile was gone. He was trying to fit every phrase, every intonation, into the puzzlement rattling around in his brain. He pondered before replying. When his voice softly broke the silence, it was as one who was confident that he was speaking the truth but was in wonderment as to what this truth meant.

"One who kills for a living enjoys instilling fear in others, maybe— the unrepressed residue of a profession."

"Enjoy?" Alfie snickered. "Corny, you're either pulling my leg or you never knew Bleckmore—or, if you're dishing out some free goose manure, you're sitting at the wrong table. No pure artists I know enjoy their work. And they sure as hell don't get a hard on scaring people. They usually do what they do because they're damn good at it and the pay's right."

Alfie stood up straight and stretched his back.

"My little secret—I can't tell you what it is half as well as I can show you."

Cornelius struggled to his feet and let his hands massage his fanny.

"My padding down here is not enough for benches. It's good your secret asks us to move. I'm ready. Whatever we see, wherever we go, tell The Roman, please, he can trust me."

With a follow-me tilt to his head, Alfie led the way back across the narrow wooden bridge and onto the vast expanse of the undulating lawn. Side by side, they silently made their way to the rear patio entrance of Alfie's house. They traversed a large sitting room, walked down a narrow corridor and entered a solarium brightly lighted by the sun's rays which entered the room through three large circular sky lights.

Alfie pointed to several overstuffed chairs facing the glass windows which framed three sides of the room. Barely visible behind the green swells of Alfie's backyard were the tawny rocks rising out of the bog garden.

"Sink into one of those, Corny, and give your tush a treat."

"My curiosity is blocking out the pain down there," Cornelius said with a chuckle.

He eased himself into the folds of one of the chairs.

"Curiosity. You wonder about my little secret. Why did The Roman want to try and scare some sanity into a turd like Bleckmore? I won't keep you waiting. Actually, a lady was behind the whole idea. Oh, in case you've already picked up on that classy dame who has been selling me some of my paintings, my secret doesn't involve Mrs. Tone. I'll admit she didn't exactly cool the Roman off on Bleckmore, but no, it was another snazzy doll I'm related to that pulled The Roman's trigger. You wanta meet her?"

Cornelius nodded.

Alfie walked a few steps over to a closed door and chortled.

"Here she is, Corny. My surprise! Standing, I'll bet, right behind this door with her hands on her hips and wondering when'n hell I'm gonna open this thing up."

Quickly, Alfie took a hold of the handle and flung open the door. He stepped aside and revealed Magdelena Bleckmore framed in the doorway, hands akimbo, as advertised, and with a saucy smile on her fuchsia lips.

"Mr. Pire. You darling little man. We meet again."

Lena sauntered provocatively into the room.

Cornelius rose to his feet and bowed.

"Mrs. Bleckmore. Again, the sight of you has allowed me the momentary recovery of part of my youth, maybe."

Lena turned to Alfie.

"You see, Bro dear, I told you what you had to look forward to. By the time you're Mr. Pire's age, look how glib and absolutely beguiling you'll be."

One of Cornelius's eyebrows raised slightly.

"Madam, I believe the term 'Bro' refers to one's sibling, maybe."

"Like—my kid brother, Mr. Pire—although you'll have to admit, I look much younger than he does."

"And infinitely more beautiful, maybe," Cornelius added as he turned to Alfie. "You are right, sir. I am surprised. I was expecting your wife or one of her sisters."

"You were?"

"Yes. I understand from Lieutenant Box that they are professionally on a par with The Roman."

"I told you already, Corny. They stay out of The Roman's business. My sister doesn't."

"I pry," Lena said, smirking, "but all I really ever find out about my brother is that, contrary to his advertisements, he does not spend time in Europe and Asia brokering Abstract paintings."

Lena sat down demurely on the edge of a large leather covered ottoman and probed in her purse for a cigarette.

"Long ago, I learned that anything my Bro reveals about himself to me is precisely what he does not do. What is real about him I have divined by knowing that he is loaded, guileful and therefore probably illegal."

Alfie put a match to the Virginia Slims Lena had in her hand.

"I moved to this country and into this castle a year ago in order to be near my only living blood relation, Corny. I have to put up with her sassy tongue once in a while, but it's a small price to pay if you're a brave man, wouldn't you say?"

Cornelius pulled a small pad and pencil out of his coat pocket and made a brief note before putting them away. He glanced at Alfie.

"You are curious as to what I just jotted down. It is one of *my* secrets, Alfie. My secret of success. Whenever I fall under the influence of obsessive people who are capable of depriving me of my reason, I write down on a scrap of paper the letters 'N.B.'—Nota Bene. Note well. Observe, it reminds me, lest these people lull me to sleep."

"Ha! Another good play, Corny. Grease your opponents with words and sow seeds of over-confidence. But it won't do you much good. I've introduced you to my sister. Now, you'll have to figure out how she fits into the scheme of things. I'll tell you this much, though. That ex-husband of hers wouldn't let go—wouldn't leave her alone. And it was getting worse—much worse. So she decided that if someone tickled his gizzard good—real good—it might drive some sense into him. Who knows, it might have."

"If someone hadn't hit him over the head, maybe," Cornelius countered softly, his eyes regarding Lena with a lingering glance.

"Yes, too bad we couldn't find out if the experiment worked, eh Corny? Sad.

Now, we'll never know."

"It's obvious that The Roman couldn't have been the perpetrator of the act that would have negated his own experiment," Cornelius said lightly.

"Yes. We have settled that, haven't we."

"But so far, not Mrs. Bleckmore, maybe."

Lena shifted her tightly clasped legs in Cornelius's direction.

"Oh, my dear Mr. Pire. You must get to know me better. I couldn't kill a monster even if he were a tiny little fly. I'm sure you can tell this about me just by looking."

Cornelius smiled sadly. "Just by looking, Madam, I can only see what others want me to see. It is only when the gray cells are dancing in tune with these perceptions that the eyes begin to talk."

Lena opened her mouth to reply, but only astonished silence ensued. Alfie grinned at his sister, obviously enjoying seeing her in a rare moment of tongue-tied frustration.

Suddenly, Cornelius felt a wave of weariness engulf him. He glanced at his watch. Zounds! He'd been here nearly two hours. Judson. Poor Judson. He'd told the man thirty minutes at the most. Judson would never forgive him. Oh but—yes, he would. Judson was a good man. He would understand. Especially, if he was assured that this visit had been a productive one. Well, it *had* been a productive one. Yes indeed. He'd learned a great deal this afternoon. A great deal. He'd learned, heaven forbid, that one of the world's highest paid assassins was a man Pire could be comfortable getting to know better. Over thirty years, at least, separating their ages. Universes apart in morals, ethics and legal perspectives. Yet, in honor, integrity, some practical and abstract curiosities, they were, maybe, kindred spirits operating from the same pod. There was something about Alfie which hit Cornelius right. Something about the man Cornelius trusted. And people who Cornelius trusted, he invariable liked. Alfie had said that he hadn't killed Bleckmore. Alas, Cornelius believed him. It would have been so much simpler the other way. He could have taken his tired bones home. As it was, he would now fulfill the pledge he had made to his dear friend

Jeffrey and continue his search for Bleckmore's murderer. If it wasn't The Roman, then certainly, it was someone in attendance at Jeffrey's party. And—Cornelius managed a smile through his weariness—that someone, Cornelius knew, he was getting much closer to.

Ah yes. He was in the near proximity to one of the suspects right now, wasn't he. Lena's perfume was tantalizing Cornelius's nostrils. It jarred him out of his brief reverie. His eyes passed over an exquisite ivory chess set reposing on a small oval table in the corner of the room. He rose to his feet and moved a few steps over to where Lena was sitting. Gallantly, he kissed the back of her hand and allowed that he was delighted to have met Alfie's *younger* sister. Cornelius basked in her smile for a moment. Then, he remarked that his greatest joy would be to ultimately discover that she and her friends were all innocent of any complicity in her ex-husband's death. But alas, he hastened to add, he was afraid that this pleasant denouement was not in the cards.

Cornelius did not further elaborate but, instead, turned to Alfie. He shook his hand and complimented him on his chess set. It was a game he was familiar with, he said. Perhaps the Gods would one day bring the two of them together over some chess men for a further test of wills.

Alfie explained that he was moving back to Japan within a few weeks so Sing Sang and her sisters could be more comfortable in their native habitat. And not even the come-on of a game of chess with Pire could change that. Alfie added that it was just as well he was leaving this country. Seemed like he was getting too popular around here for his own good.

At the front door, Cornelius handed Alfie his card and suggested that patience was the answer, maybe. Two retired wizards should never let geography stand in the way of the ultimate vanquishment one over the other. To triumph and let live, Cornelius observed with a smile, that is part of the glory of the next day.

Cornelius bowed, passed through the front door being held open for him and headed for the white picket fence.

"Ah Judson, you're still here," he said aloud.

Cornelius was talking to no one in particular, including himself, as he approached the swinging gate, because before the words had left his mouth, his mind was already absorbed in the mystery he had come to solve.

Judson glanced at Cornelius apprehensively as they were heading into the country and away from Alfie's home. It wasn't that Cornelius hadn't told him where to drive to next, so much. It wasn't that Cornelius had told him rather abruptly that he wished to drive slowly. Rather, it was the hard set to Cornelius's mouth that bothered Judson. Not like him. The fact that his friendly little man was suddenly both grim and quiet was not like Mr. Pire at all.

So, Judson pointed the car towards home, drove slowly as requested and frowned. *Queer ducks, these policemen. Never can tell what they're thinking—especially when they look at you—or when they say nothing—just sit and say nothing. Huh—maybe it's you that's done something wrong. Must be that. But—wonder what it was?*

A few more miles down the road, Judson expressed his concern.

"Wrong? You're a most amiable and obliging companion. It's my thoughts which have been wrong, Judson, and I am busy straightening them out. Please forgive me."

This concluded their conversation for the afternoon, except for a brief request from Cornelius asking Judson to please stop at the Sheriff's office.

Cornelius disappeared into the County Seat, as he had done earlier in the morning. When he emerged some thirty minutes later, the Lieutenant was with him. After Bill Box closed the car door behind Cornelius, Cornelius lowered the window glass and leaned out the open window.

"Lieutenant, may I be so rude as to suggest that just for the moment at least our little chat remain between the two of us?"

Box bent down and smiled at Judson.

"Mr. Pire says you're a good man, Judson. I'd say that is some kind of a compliment, coming from him. Tell your distinguished passenger, I agree."

A few moments later, Judson pointed their car down a long straight narrow macadam tree-lined country highway. Jeff Endecott's home was only ten minutes away. Cornelius tried to relax by resting his head against the back of the seat.

It had been many years since he had put two strenuous days like this back-to-back. When they got to Jeffrey's, he would have to lie down for a few minutes or dining out for dinner, which Jeffrey had suggested at breakfast, would be out of the question. First, however, before any nap, he had one more item he needed to check out. It simply had to be. One more item, and if he found what he was looking for, his grim picture would be nearly complete. He'd find it. Yes, he would. Then, he'd tie up the rest of the case with Box tomorrow. That Box— he was a good policeman. A good man. Yes, he was. And incidentally, so was Cornelius Pire—even after all of these years.

Cornelius brought himself back to reality with a start.

Never cook the chicken until you've caught it!

He turned his head, looked out the side window and smiled sheepishly.

Cornelius opened Endecott's front door and walked in. He was somewhat surprised to discover Mrs. Endecott seated in the living room. He greeted her cordially, but did not comment on her apparent change in plans. Instead, he inquired as to Jeffrey's whereabouts. Ethel indicated that Jeff had been gone all day but was planning on taking them out for dinner. She added that she and Jeffrey certainly hoped that Cornelius was planning on going with them. Cornelius's eyes twinkled in reaction to her careful choice of words. He then allowed as to how eagerly he was looking forward to the event. But first—well, would she tell Jeffrey, when he got home, that he was catching a short nap and would be ready at seven. Ethel returned her attention to her book, and Cornelius slowly climbed the stairs, his pace accelerating with each step.

At the top of the stairway, he pulled out his small leather notebook and walked over to a table lamp in the upper foyer. He shoved his notes into the glare of the light bulb and studied a small diagram he had made showing the location of each room on the upper floor level, including the identification of bedrooms used by the guests over the weekend. Quickly, Cornelius entered each room and expertly combed the closets for the object of his search. Cornelius's mind was concentrating intently on design and color. His eyes were piercing into the depths and corners of each closet he entered.

Yes, Cornelius knew what he was looking for. But he didn't find it in any of the closets. Unbelievably, it was casually draped over the back of a soft chair in the third room he entered.

Cornelius returned the notebook to his coat pocket, and then walked out of the room. He was carrying a green and white checked sport jacket over his arm. Carefully, he closed the door of the room he'd just been in and then wearily trudged down the hall. He studied the coat as he walked. A brighter green than he had figured, It would be difficult to conceal, maybe. Conceal? Cornelius smiled maliciously. Ha! What he should do is to wear it. But then, of course, he was much too small a man for that.

Cornelius chuckled at his own sense of humor and headed for a nap.

CHAPTER TWENTY-THREE

Monday Night—June 8th

"And you, sir?"

"I'll have a gin sour, if you please, waiter."

"Corny's been drinking the same thing for forty years."

"Gin sour? I've never heard of it. Is that true, Corny?"

"Yes, and every year each one costs me twenty-five cents more."

"Eth, I've been listening to this moaning off and on since World War II. The reason Corny keeps paying more is he's the only one in the world who drinks that crazy drink."

"My friend, if you would savor one of these just once, you would no longer make fun of me."

Jeff, Ethel and Cornelius were all in a festive mood. The Moonlight Grove helped. It was an exquisite restaurant with a romantic atmosphere and food any gourmet would label as matchless in both service and in taste. The three were seated at a small table in a cozy, dimly lighted corner of one of the restaurant's smaller rooms and were. happily aware that for the first time in years they were alone together.

"Slow down, Corny. You won't make dessert, ol' buddy."

Cornelius's third drink, coupled with Jeff's awareness that Cornelius's limit was usually one or two of anything during an entire evening, prompted the friendly warning.

Cornelius picked up his glass and cupped it in his two hands.

"Jeffrey and Ethel, I probably won't see you two again for a long time. Each year, we all get older, you know—and so—why not celebrate any way we can tonight—No?"

He raised his glass to his two friends and then took a large swallow.

"If I get slightly bottled tonight, you two will take care of me, maybe, eh?"

Jeff chuckled. "I don't recall *ever* seeing you bottled, as you say, but I imagine we can get you home."

Again, Cornelius raised his glass to his lips.

"Skoal!" Corny closed his eyes as if he were savoring a particularly pleasurable memory. They remained closed for several moments then suddenly popped partially open.

"Bye the bye, Jeffrey. I almost forgot to ask you. Do you think we could have your weekend guests out for dinner tomorrow night?"

Jeff put his own drink down and eyed Cornelius dubiously.

"Come again?"

Cornelius repeated his question.

"I thought that's what you said."

Ethel laughed. "Corny, you have the most delightful sense of humor."

Corneliuis smiled shyly and looked away.

"The whole crew? Tomorrow night? I hope Ethel's right. You are joking?"

"On the contrary, I am being quite serious, maybe. I realize the imposition it would be on you, Jeffrey, but I would like to help. Please allow the expense to be on me, if it could be arranged."

"Whatever you do is certainly no imposition on me, Corny. You've done me a giant favor by coming out here. I hope you know that."

"You asked me to come out and help, and that's what I'd like to do. I was thinking that if it was possible to get your friends together, I'd attempt to fulfill my commitment to you tomorrow night."

Ethel glanced over at Jeffrey and felt a chill run up and down her spine.

My, my, Ethel dear, you're beginning to feel nervous all over again.

She forced a smile. "Corny, are you trying to tell us something?"

"Not tonight, maybe."

"Oh? Why not tonight?"

"Tomorrow night, Ma'am. Tomorrow night. By then—after dinner, let us say—I think I will be ready to tell you who killed your good friend, Mr. Bleckmore. And it occurred to me that perhaps your guests would want to hear this first hand, seeing as they were a part of the drama. If you desire, I will reveal the guilty party to all."

Ethel paled. "You mean, Corny, that you would expose one of our friends right in front of all of us—right in Jeff's home? Isn't that a little barbaric?"

"Yes. Like the crime, very barbaric."

"Corny, you really know who did this thing?" Jeff asked.

"By tomorrow night, maybe, I'll know."

"And you want me to get *everyone* out for dinner?"

"It isn't necessary. Just an idea, Jeffrey."

"Can't do it. Not a Chinaman's chance of getting them all on such short notice."

Cornelius nodded his head.

"But you want me to try? You're serious about this?"

"I'm serious, but will understand if you'd rather not."

"Okay. Guess I'd better get humping. I'll see what I can do. Eth, why don't you ask Corny to dance? As I remember, the girls used to think he was pretty smooth."

Jeff excused himself and headed for the nearest phone booth. And Cornelius gallantly was at Ethel's side before she had time to react to Jeffrey's suggestion.

A slow waltz eventually changed to a fox trot and then to some syncopated beat which Ethel knew was way over their heads. But the music really made no difference. Ethel was uncomfortable for other reasons, and she wasn't sure precisely why. Cornelius's smile—it looked different. Friendly? Paternalistic? Laughing at her? Condescending? What was it? She couldn't tell. Suddenly, she felt she didn't know the little man she was dancing with. She was relieved to see Jeffrey returning to the table.

"Sorry it took so long, folks, but it's done. They'll all be there, including the most important people of all: Maude and James."

"I don't believe it," Ethel exclaimed. "You're a magician."

Jeff looked over at Cornelius, who was sipping a fresh drink. "Not really, Eth. It wasn't any magnetism of mine. All I did was use Corny's name, refer to his invitation, and I got back every time a nervous, 'We'll be there', from the other end of the line."

"Excellent, Jeffrey. You'll do me one more favor? Allow me to go to your favorite butcher and purchase the meat."

"My God, Corny, tell us—Who do you think killed Tony?"

"You're right, Jeffrey. Tonight, I think. Tomorrow, I will know, maybe."

"Think—Know—Come on, Corny—Who? Who you pointing at?"

"Not tonight, Jeffrey. You and Ethel would have a hard time keeping a secret."

"You've always trusted me before, Corny."

"There's an old saying that to trust a temptress is to pay the devil." Cornelius seemed to be gazing at the empty glass in his hand with half closed bleary eyes.

Jeffrey's eyes were boring in on Cornelius. Ethel was looking at Jeffrey. This pantomime seemed to last for an eternity. Finally, Jeffrey broke the silence with a barely audible whisper.

"Temptress? Who's the temptress, Corny? You don't think—"

Jeffrey couldn't continue. He cast a furtive glance at Ethel.

Cornelius wrinkled his nose.

"Ah, the waiter—He has our soup. Yes, Puree de Marrons. The aroma says our chef has it just right."

Three hours later, after a period of muted soup savoring, some delectable food and excellent wines, Jeffrey and Ethel helped a quite helpless Cornelius into the back seat of Jeffrey's car. Slowly, as the Endecott manor approached, a pleasant evening came to an end.

Jeffrey guided Cornelius across the threshold of his bedroom, watched the door close behind this genie of a man, and then turned back down the long dark hall. At the other end, stood the silent, motionless silhouette of Jeffrey's ex-wife. He walked up to her, lightly placed his hands on her shoulders, and gently touched his lips to hers. A moment more, and then he walked to the door of his room far down the hall. He entered the room and noiselessly closed the door behind him. For many minutes, Ethel stood where Jeffrey had left her, a quiet figure reflecting the light from a single lamp which burned at one end of the hall. Finally, her shoulders sagged. She too moved slowly, very slowly, to her room a few doors away.

CHAPTER TWENTY-FOUR

Tuesday—June 9th

Lieutenant Box parked on the circular drive and stepped out of his car. He pulled his raincoat tightly about him and hurried up the steps to the front door of the Endecott home. He rang the bell and then turned around and looked up at the murky sky.

Cold and dreary—just like my bod. Weather's sure changed. Thought some rain would be a welcome relief to all that hot weather. But the novelty's already worn off. Wonder when that shine'll be back.

Box was surprised to find Ethel and Jeff opening the door almost before the chimes stopped sounding. They indicated that they were on their way to the city for Bleckmore's funeral. Judson was around, Jeff said, and, amazingly enough, Corny was up. Box was told to make himself at home—and that he and Ethel would be back sometime around noon.

As soon as the door closed, Box, by prearrangement, headed for the living room. He and Cornelius ignored formalities when they met. They greeted each other by nodding their heads, then headed for the stairway. Box took the steps two at a time.

Cornelius followed but at a more modest pace.

They entered Cornelius's bedroom and closed the door. Cornelius walked over to one end of the room and pointed to a hot-air register located a few inches up from the base of the wall. This was the common wall with the bedroom which had been previously occupied by Tony Bleckmore, Cornelius explained. The register had its counterpart in the same location in the next room. Cornelius had checked it out yesterday, he said, and found that the register was in a position which could afford a pretty clear view of the room. As far as he could tell, there appeared to be a clear passage between the two register openings.

Box placed the small duffel bag he had brought with him on the floor near the register. He took off his coat and threw it on a chair. Then, rolling up his sleeves, he sat down on the floor and opened the bag. Cornelius joined him, and for the next hour and a half, the two men worked to fit a small periscopic viewer into the gap between the two register openings. The adaptation of the viewer to the two openings proved relatively easy. The problem area lay in the obvious requirement that the scope had to be capable of being pivoted around noiselessly. They finally hit on the idea of cushioning the inner sanctum between the two walls with an abundance of foam padding.

Box then put his eye to the viewer and watched as Cornelius paraded around the Bleckmore bedroom. When Cornelius returned to his room, he reported that he had heard or seen nothing suspicious in Bleckmore's room, even when he had looked directly at the room's register.

A few minutes later, Box was back in the rain. He'd be back around nine that night he had mumbled to Cornelius as they were passing through the lower foyer. Cornelius had nodded his head in agreement. Then, as silently as they had met two hours earlier, the two men had parted.

Box started his car, put his hands on top of the steering wheel and glanced back at the Endecott home through the rear view mirror. He smiled and shook his head.

Crazy! Yeah, real crazy—but this little guy's idea might be fun—or more to the point—grim. Yesterday, he'd bet Pire a buck he was wrong, And what had that cocksure midget done?

Box's smile turned into an audible chuckle as he recalled the little man pulling a dollar from his pocket and handing it to him.

"Give me back two, Lieutenant, if I'm right." Pire had then changed the subject.

Box gunned his car around the circular drive and decided as he was doing so that he had probably made a lousy bet with the white haired guy from Boston.

———◆·◆◆◆·———

Jeff had suggested seven in the evening and, as the hour might be late, bring an overnight bag. As if by magic, at the stroke of seven, four cars appeared at the Endecott front door. And out stepped seven worried, serious counterparts of the same festive group who had arrived three days before. Lena was dressed in black—the same dress she had worn to Tony's funeral. Sybil had met Kevin at his office, from where they had proceeded directly to Jeff's—both in suits of somber gray. Collin's switch to a pale blue sport coat didn't relieve his weariness from a long hard day at the office, so Marva was behind the wheel of their car when they arrived, wearing a slinky red dress. Sam and Anne pulled up last, cranky in brown tweeds, in Anne's Ford. The better half of Kennelly's two automobiles was resting in a repair shop for a stupid reason Sam damn well didn't want to talk about, but knew he'd have to. He'd already decided that, if pushed, he'd lie a little rather than admit to having backed out of his garage before opening the door.

Drinks were nursed in the drawing room, where Cornelius, Jeff and Ethel were waiting when the rest of the group arrived. Ethel became the focal point for some good-natured kidding about her "new" address. She took this in stride for some time before revealing that she was returning to her own home in the morning.

The conversation soon got off Ethel and switched from one aimless thing to another. Tongues were willing, but spirits were not. And not even Jeffrey's expertise as a host could enliven this uptight group of familiar faces who were trying very hard at the moment to politely indicate that they were delighted to be in each others company once again.

Cornelius huddled in a corner of the room talking quietly to Lena about the romantic beauty of Southern Mexico. The rest of the room was filled with nebulous sounds concerning what part of the world the superior places to eat were located. Dinner seemed to be on nearly everyone's mind—probably because it represented another prerequisite to be dispensed with before their intense curiosities could be and would be finally satisfied.

The porterhouse steaks were superb. Maude and James had done justice to the fine cuts of beef Cornelius had purchased. Cornelius grimaced like an embarrassed schoolboy as the compliments rolled in. Jeff was particularly eloquent on the subject. He was not only impressed with the meat but also let everyone know that he considered Corny's treat the ultimate expression of how far a friend can go beyond the call of duty.

Box arrived promptly at nine. Judson was serving coffee, and Box was invited to join the group.

"Kind of you. Thanks." Box pulled up a chair at one corner of the table. "I can't stay long. That everlasting boss of mine wants me back at headquarters."

"At this hour?" Sam checked his watch. "You work all night too, Box?"

"Sometimes, I guess I do. People don't break the law from eight to five as often as they do after hours, it seems."

"Lieutenant, we were going to move into the drawing room, but we can stay here," Jeff said. "I understand either you or Corny have something you want to tell us."

Box started to reply, but Cornelius overrode him.

"I told Jeffrey last night that I believe I—that is—" Cornelius pointed to Box and himself—"*we* know who killed Mr. Bleckmore. I told Jeffrey that we believe this person to be a member of the group sitting here around this table tonight. I also told him, that out of courtesy to him and the fact that he invited me here, I would confide the information we have with him first. This I did not do tonight, because the Lieutenant called me late this afternoon and indicated that he thought we ought to delay reviewing this matter with you tonight until tomorrow morning. Accordingly, we are suggesting that at nine a.m., maybe, we should get together here."

"What's the reason for the delay, Lieutenant?" Kevin's question snapped sharply through the room.

Box pulled out a Marlboro and methodically put a match to it before answering.

"We received a visit late this afternoon from Mrs. Rosssetti, Mr. Bleckmore's sister. She stated that after her brother's funeral this morning, she received information from a close business associate of Mr. Bleckmore's that the clue to Mr. Bleckmore's death might be found in locating, what she referred to as, an extremely controversial article he always carried on his person. Mrs. Rossetti did not care to divulge what this article was but indicated that it was not a part of his personal possessions which were turned over to her. She requested permission to examine the room he was occupying while staying here. We offered to bring her out here tonight, but she declined in favor of early tomorrow morning."

Collin scowled at the Lieutenant through his large horn-rimmed spectacles.

"You think anything Mrs. Rossetti might find here will alter your opinions on this case, Lieutenant?"

"No, I don't, and neither does Mr. Pire. In the first place, we feel that we've combed this whole place pretty thoroughly. We also feel that any new evidence will merely substantiate the evidence we already have. But to be aware of a loose end and not wait for it to be tied up, we feel would be—a—a—"

"Presumptuous." Cornelius smiled modestly as he helped Box with the elusive word.

"Well, Anne, I don't think we should spend another night in this house. We came out here in good faith and—"

"Neither do I, Sam," Lena added quickly.

"I think this is typical of the way you've been handling things, Lieutenant," Collin added. "It's quite obvious that the nerves of many in our group are at the breaking point, and you want us to wait still another day?"

"I agree with Sam and Collin. I think we're all being taken advantage of." Anne was speaking softly, but she had the floor. "If someone here killed Tony, as you say, then I think he or she should be exposed and brought to justice. The rest of us have suffered long enough."

Cornelius stood up.

"Ladies and gentlemen—please—please. If anyone here is offended by any indiscretion, Lieutenant Box and I offer you our apologies. If the thought of another evening together is repugnant to your natures, then by all means go your separate ways tonight. This should be. We were merely trying to be accommodating, maybe."

Kevin was on his feet and had Sybil by the hand.

"Syb and I are going into the drawing room, where we're going to grab a snootful of Jeff's cognac."

Kevin turned to Jeff.

"We'll be here tonight and tomorrow morning."

"Good ol' Kev. Always the stout fellow." The somewhat sardonic voice belonged to Ethel who was busy pouring herself some more coffee.

Collin smiled sadly and shook his head.

"I think this whole group's in need of therapy. I'd probably be accused of neglecting my duty if I left you all to yourselves. Come on, Marva. We'd better stay too."

Marva quickly joined her husband, and together they left the room.

"Well, if that headshrinker's going to analyze us for nothing, I suppose we might as well change our minds too. What d'you say, Anne."

Anne grabbed her husband's hand in affirmation.

"Besides," Sam sighed to his wife as they followed the Strabos out of the room, "who wants to hear what these gumshoes have come up with second hand?"

Ethel's eyes followed Sam and Anne out the room. She then looked at Lena.

"Sam's right, I suppose. A few hours more here isn't going to hurt any of us. Lena, why don't we make it unanimous?"

With Lena's reluctant assent, the room quickly emptied, leaving Jeff with Cornelius and Box.

"Anything else I can do for you fellows?" Jeff was standing between the other two men.

"No thanks, sir. I've got to run. As I say, that guy who gets reelected every four years thinks he owns my body and part of my mind. And, so far, there's nothing I can do about it."

Box put out his cigarette.

"I'll let myself out. See you gentlemen tomorrow. Oh, I almost forgot. Can I bring that Rossetti woman in here at the crack tomorrow. She's catching a mid-morning plane, I believe."

"Sure thing. Anytime. I'll leave the front door unlocked."

Jeff put his arm around Cornelius and together they headed for the drawing room. They heard the front door slam closed as Box let himself out.

Or—Did Box let himself out? A man was standing in the dimly lighted foyer next to the door which had just been closed and was glancing around furtively. A few seconds later, this same man sped up the circular staircase and down the long bedroom hallway. The door to Cornelius's bedroom opened and closed very quietly. The lights in the room were extinguished, and Bill Box, penlight in hand, settled down on the floor next to the register. He made himself comfortable as possible. It might be a long night.

———◦•◦••◦•———

Cornelius checked his watch. He rubbed his eyes and brought the watch up close to his face. Two-forty-five. He must have nodded off for a moment. No more of this! He glanced over at the dark form on the floor next to him. He poked its shoulder and a head rose slightly revealing the barely perceptible register opening.

"Want me to spell you, Lieutenant?

Box shook his head.

"Sorry. I must have nodded off for a minute or two. Let me know when you want me to take over."

A half hour later, Box rolled over. His eyes found the dark form of Cornelius lying on the carpet nearby.

"Not fair keeping a tough ol' critter like you up so late, sir."

"The evening's still young, Lieutenant. Don't give up."

Box rolled out of the way, and Cornelius moved over in front of the register opening. Box struggled to his feet and walked slowly back and forth on the carpeted floor, working the kinks out of his legs. A few minutes later, he settled down on the floor again and stretched out, his arms under his head. He stared blankly at the ceiling.

He had been listening to the hallway grandfather clock strike out the quarter hour for how long now? He couldn't remember. Just hours and hours, that's all he knew for sure. Hours and hours. What'd they call them? Westminister Chimes or something like that. Whatever—Those chimes reminded him of his own existence. Same thing. Over and over. Starting with a phone call. Always a phone call. Ending up, sometimes, with a packaged job. Mostly, though, ending up with damn little of nothing. A challenging life. Yeah, it was that. And God knows, he fulfilled a real need. But—well, just like those damn chimes—the same thing over and over—over and over—over and over.

Box turned his head to one side and studied Cornelius. That twinkle in his eye—How old did Corny say he was? Seventy seven? Maybe if he sparkled a little like Corny, he wouldn't get old so fast. Better look closer in the mirror more often and see if he could pick up one of those twinkles. Good idea. A man with a twinkle probably doesn't get in the dumps no matter what he's doing.

Box noticed Cornelius's back suddenly stiffen. He propped his head up on one elbow and stared hard at Cornelius. Cornelius raised one hand ever so slightly up in the air. Box moved up close to Cornelius—then didn't move—hardly breathed.

"Lieutenant!" Cornelius's whisper cut into Box's left ear. "Take a look in the viewer and observe, maybe, the murderer of Tony Bleckmore."

For several minutes, Box's head didn't move from the viewer. Finally, he stood up. Cornelius was already on his feet, leaning against the edge of his bed. Box walked over and switched on the lights. Without a word, he removed the viewer and replaced the register cover. He placed his tools and the viewer in the duffel bag and then walked over to Cornelius.

"I'll be here in the morning with Reston bright and early. I think, however, you should handle this thing—any way you'd like to—that is, if you don't mind."

Cornelius dropped his chin. His eyes moved to the floor.

Box stuck out his hand.

"See you in the morning."

Suitcase in hand, Box then walked out the bedroom door and closed it behind him. It was four a.m.

Cornelius took off his clothes, and carefully placed them where they would be easily accessible in a few hours. He put on his pajamas and got into the large comfortable bed. He turned off the light and let his head sink into the soft pillow. He closed his eyes. But Cornelius didn't sleep. He too started counting the chimes until, finally, it was seven a.m.

CHAPTER TWENTY-FIVE

Wednesday Morning—Jume 10th

Cornelius Pire closed the study door behind him and walked out into the hall. He took a few steps down the hall and reached the glass doors leading to one of the outdoor balconies. He checked his watch.

Eight-thirty. Not hungry—and haven't had breakfast yet.

Cornelius opened one of the double doors and walked out onto the balcony. A white wrought iron chair at one end of the balcony glistened with the early morning dew. He pulled out his handkerchief and carefully wiped the dew off the chair and then sat down.

He felt a hundred years old. Not tired. Just old. It would be good to get home.

He reached in his pocket and pulled out the afternoon plane ticket for Boston, which Jeff had just handed to him a few moments ago in his study.

Non-stop to Boston, and then about an hour later, home. When he reached his little white Cape Cod, he'd just pull back the sheets, climb in and then sleep—sleep, maybe, for three or four days. Although he didn't feel physically tired exactly, somewhere inside he must be exhausted. Maybe it was more in his head than anywhere else. It had been a long three days—or had it been four days. He couldn't remember.

He tried to recall what day it was, and finally, after getting his feet up on the balcony railing and allowing his head to tilt back gently onto the white brick of the house, it came back to him. It couldn't be anything other than Wednesday morning. Three days it was then. It seemed longer.

Cornelius looked up at the wispy white cirrus clouds, so high up in the heavens that he could hardly see them.

No rain today, surely. A day just like the one when he had arrived here. A good day for flying home, maybe.

Cornelius could hear voices down below. He peeked over the railing but could see no one outside.

Probably the voices of Jeffrey's friends gathered in the recreation room. Those voices—Ah yes, they were probably waiting for him. He still had a job to do, didn't he.

He smiled bitterly as he visualized the sight of eight people sitting down there, nervously twitching their fingers, wanting to leave and return to their normal occupations, but too obsessively curious to do so.

Was it curiosity that kept them glued to their seats? Or was it the compulsive hope and desire for personal exoneration? Or some instinctive form of sadism? Cornelius admitted to himself that he did not know. He had observed group behavior like this many times in the past, but he had never understood the mysterious magnet that drew these people together.

He checked his watch again.

Eight-forty-five. Box would be here by now. Better get moving.

Cornelius pushed himself up to his feet, yawned once, straightened his shoulders and then strode briskly back into the house.

Bill Box and Jake Reston were standing quietly just inside the lower foyer's front door. Cornelius paused at the bottom of the stairway. His eyes found Box. The two men nodded to each other. Cornelius then continued on his way towards the sound of the conversation emanating from the recreation room. He opened the door.

"Good morning. I'm sorry. I must be late. My watch sometimes loses, I'm afraid."

Cornelius found an empty chair by a window

"No, it's we that are early," Ethel said impassively.

"Early and anxious to leave, Pire," Sam Kennelly added curtly.

Collin cleared his throat and then paused a moment to get Cornelius's attention.

"Yes, Mr. Pire, this group seems sufficiently nervous this morning to listen to you with rapt attention, including, I hasten to add, myself. We have been wondering, last night and again just now, what the import of your remarks to us this morning will be. More specifically, the question on our minds seems to be, can those of us in this room be considered vindicated of any complicity in Mr. Bleckmore's murder by what you might decide to say to us this morning?"

Everyone's eyes were glued on Pire.

"My dear Dr. Strabo, the answer to your question is most emphatically, no. I have no authority whatsoever to either indict or absolve you or anyone else of a crime committed here or anywhere. Only the courts have this authority. But let us proceed to the matter at hand."

Cornelius shifted to a more comfortable position in his chair.

"As you say—all of you are most anxious to leave. You have my sympathy here, maybe, and so if you'll permit me, I'll attempt to be quite direct."

Cornelius opened up his notebook and laid it in his lap.

"As you know, I live in a small city near Boston, where early Sunday morning, I received a phone call from an old associate and a dear friend of mine—your host, Jeffrey Endecott. Jeffrey asked me to come out here and assist in whatever way I could to uncover the murderer of your associate, Mr. Bleckmore. Jeffrey was recalling, with his phone call, my days as a private investigator. And—what man can ignore the compliment of a dear friend? So I came. I told Jeffrey, when I arrived, that I would do what I could, that I would keep him advised, and that if I reached any positive conclusions as to who killed Mr. Bleckmore, Jeffrey would be the first person I would share my conclusions with—outside, of course, the police officials. Jeffrey was very appreciative of my coming and indicated that the local Sheriff's office had agreed to cooperate with me in every way."

"Cooperate is exactly what Lieutenant Box and his staff have done, and as a result we, the police and myself, reached the conclusion yesterday that we knew beyond any shadow of a doubt who Mr. Bleckmore's murderer was. You notice, I say 'knew'. We were sure we *knew*, but we also had doubts that our knowledge could be substantiated with any reasonable degree of proof. This being the case, we decided to let the chips fall where they may. We decided to share our knowledge with all of you. So—according to my commitment to Jeffrey, I spent nearly forty-five minutes with him in his study this morning. I told him who I thought killed Mr. Bleckmore. He expressed complete amazement at much of what I told him—much as you undoubtedly will do in a few moments, when I tell you. When I finished my conversation with Jeffrey, he agreed that I should not hesitate to tell the same story to you people, and suggested that I start without him, as he had some business to attend to in Lancaster."

"I imagine, maybe, that you are all hoping, as was Jeffrey, that I will tell you that the murderer was someone—some outside party whom you've never heard of before. The thought that the murderer could possibly be a friend, a person you have known for years, someone in attendance at your party Saturday night—this thought is repugnant to you. Incredulous. It simply cannot be, you say. And yet, that gnawing doubt, it brings you here this morning, maybe. Every fiber of your beings—they need to know who. Yes, no doubt, you are hoping that we will tell you that an outsider *is* the guilty party. I must say—this possibility has been examined thoroughly by us and rejected."

"And so—I tell you sadly—Your fears are justified. It is, I think, a member of your group who killed Mr. Bleckmore. It is sad, but it is true. As I say, the proof is not irrefutable—except to me, maybe."

Ethel's two hands went quickly to her purse. Her right arm was trembling, and her eyes were beginning to well up with tears. Cornelius shifted his position and confronted Ethel. His eyes were glowing with kindness.

"Ethel Endecott, you think it is you who I am going to point my finger at, but my dear lady, no, you are wrong. You did not kill Mr. Bleckmore. The whole idea that you did is impossible."

Cornelius stood up and faced the rest of the anxious group.

"You see, ladies and gentlemen, Mrs. Endecott has known for some time that she was a prime suspect in this case, and although she has also known herself to be innocent of any involvement in the crime, her natural apprehension of a possible miscarriage of justice has made it difficult for her to control her emotions."

Cornelius shifted his attention back to Ethel.

"You have my sympathy, Ma'am, and my apologies, but for reasons, I can perhaps explain to you later, if you like, I could not reveal to you sooner than this morning that the clues involving you in this crime were indisputably false. It became quite obvious that either you were deliberately trying to mislead us, or else some other party was trying to associate you with the crime by attempting to plant incriminating evidence against you."

Cornelius walked over a few steps, leaned over and took Ethel's hands in his.

"May I say, dear lady, that as some other aspects of the puzzle began to fall into place, the possibility of your involvement diminished. We are now certain that you are innocent."

"Thank you, Corny."

Ethel leaned back in her chair, too weak to say more.

Cornelius's smile instantly vanished as he turned and faced Lena.

"Ah, Mrs. Bleckmore—You too are concerned. The man who was once your husband is dead, and it is well known, I'm afraid, how much you disliked him—no, even hated—that is the word I believe I heard you once mention during our brief acquaintance. You are a charming lady, I think, partly because you are quite attractive physically, but also—certainly also—because you are so delightfully frank in expressing yourself. But it is this reflection on your part of what you have said to me in private that concerns you now.

You, likewise, know that you did not harm your ex-husband, but are afraid that we will confuse your hatred for him with some kind of incriminating evidence."

Again, Cornelius grinned.

"But you are fortunate—ah, fortunate indeed, Mrs.Bleckmore, that the gray cells investigating this crime see through your hatred and find no evidence which can associate you with the murder—except that, as in the case of Mrs. Endecott, a woman could have physically committed the crime. No, in only three days, it is easy to see that the greatest proof of your innocence, beyond a lack of evidence, lies in your volatile nature. In my experience, it is never the volatile nature that commits the carefully premeditated crime. Mr. Bleckmore died, we are certain, a very premeditated death. May I say to you, Mrs. Bleckmore, calm your fears. Return to normal. You did not kill Mr. Bleckmore."

"What a dish of crap, Mr. Pire. But aren't you a sweetie. And oh, how I believe what you are saying. Every precious little word."

Cornelius glanced at the Strabos, who were sitting together on the couch in the center of the room. Then, he turned away from them and faced the window through which the Endecott gardens lay shimmering in the early morning sun.

"You know, Dr. and Mrs. Strabo, I hope you will permit me a small suggestion. I would think, maybe, that if you ever become associated with another group of people where animosity is in the air, it would be well if you left one of the world's more lethal poisons at the pharmacy—or at least well hidden from public discovery. It would be also to your advantage to behave quite differently than you did during the early morning hours this recent Sunday."

Cornelius swung around and faced the Strabos.

"Lieutenant Box is, I think, a very competent police officer. You are lucky to have him in these parts. But, if I may say, you made it extremely difficult for him to be objective in his investigations by your rather strange behavior. I say strange. I do not say illegal, because it is obvious that you were not disobeying any laws. The police had no legal right to detain you. And although you are licensed to handle unusual drugs, bringing methylbenzethonium chloride to a party involving old friends—Well, you turn on the searchlights that can blind with their glare, my friends. Indeed, if it were not for the ring of truth to your conversations with me at your home yesterday, I would say that your actions this past weekend would have been examined much more thoroughly. I might also add that the police consider you to be innocent because another is quite obviously, to us, guilty."

Cornelius high-pitched voice was hard. His piercing gaze in the Strabo's direction was unrelenting.

"May I say to you two that there appears to be no logical way you could be involved in Mr. Bleckmore's death, but that your actions hampered us in arriving at this conclusion."

Collin let his chin drop to his chest, closed his eyes and rested his folded hands in his lap. Marva's attention was riveted on the hallway door, which had noiselessly opened and allowed two uniformed policemen to enter the room. They were standing quietly by the door. Marva squeezed her husband's arm, looked at him sharply, then realized that her squeeze had been unnecessary. His nearly closed eyes were intensely alert.

A momentary silence captured the room.

Cornelius returned to his chair and sat on its arm such that he was facing Sam and Anne.

"Mr. Kennelly—"

Pire's voice had dropped to almost a whisper.

"It is your penchant for preciseness, particularly in the chronicling of time, that struck at the heart of this case. You like to know exactly where and when you are during each hour of every day. It is a well-known idiosyncrasy of yours, maybe. Your friends say about you that you are a walking watch-watcher. And so—you told us quite freely the timed sequence of the events of last Saturday evening as you recalled them. Estimates, you kept repeating—but the rapidity and unhesitating manner of your recall caused us some doubts. I say doubts, Mr. Kennelly, because your estimates of time left us with a mysterious contradiction."

Cornelius rose to his feet, pivoted around and studied the rest of the group.

"What Mr. Kennelly indicated to us by his recollection of time was quite provocative. Stated simply, we were faced with the fact that Mr. Bleckmore was seen in the recreation room, where everyone else was in attendance, at a time when, according to the coroner's report, Mr. Bleckmore was dead, maybe. Our first reaction was that perhaps the coroner's estimated time of death needed a looser tolerance attached to it. This reasoning permitted us to assume that Mr. Bleckmore, after passing through the recreation room, had to move with considerable alacrity in order to end up at the bottom of Jeffrey Endecott's pool at nine-thirty seven, the time when, you say, he was discovered. We were told that Mr. Bleckmore was normally not an impulsive or fast-moving man.

And so, Mr. Kennelly, we had still another reaction to your information."

Sam's facial expression was becoming progressively grimmer as he listened intently to Pire. He had a gold-plated Cross pen in his hands and was twirling it around and around in his fingers, a nervous habit analogous to his wife's habit of resorting to knitting needles when she got angry.

"We concluded, Mr. Kennelly, that possibly you were presenting us with false evidence, in order to deliberately mislead the police."

Sam was on his feet.

"Pire, that's a slanderous accusation!"

"Please, Mr. Kennelly—Please, sit down. I agree—if it *were* an accusation. But if you'll permit me, it was only offered to you this morning as an observation. The possibility that you were not being objective with us gradually diminished in our minds as we became more intelligent about this case. And indeed, it was not long before we concluded that actually, within this contradiction, this mysterious stopping of your clock, so to speak, lay the actual, very plausible explanation of how Mr. Bleckmore was killed Saturday evening."

"You recall, Mr. Kennelly, that last Monday afternoon, you were kind enough to spend a few minutes with me. By then, the possible picture of the murderer was on my canvas. You could not see this picture, of course, but your answers to one or two questions further substantiated in my mind that the picture on my canvas was correct.

"It was not you, Mr. Kennelly, who killed Mr. Bleckmore. But it was you, who with your excellent memory, helped put us on the right track of the person who did."

Sam eased himself back into his chair.

"Damned if you aren't a contradictory cuss, Pire. The next thing I suppose you'll surprise us with is that you think Annie had something to do with this bloody affair."

Sam reached over and took his wife's hand in his.

Cornelius smiled.

"No, Mr. Kennelly, we believe Mrs Kennelly is as remote from any attachment to this crime as you are."

Cornelius surveyed the group in front of him.

"Would you like me to proceed, maybe?"

"Please do, seeing as Sybil and I seem to be—"

Kevin Tone coughed several times in an ill-disguised attempt to conceal a tremulous voice.

"As we seem to be the only ones left."

"Ah yes, Mr. Tone. There is the sound of our last worried man this morning. Mr. Tone more than once shared concerns with the Lieutenant and myself about the lack of progress being made in solving this case and about areas he thought we ought to be investigating more thoroughly. Gradually, it became apparent, however, that the real concern eating away at Mr. Tone was his deep-seated impression that we suspected him."

"You see, ladies and gentlemen, Mr. Tone knew that the police had discovered a packet of paper matches, representing a private club Mr. Tone belongs to, on the table near where Mr. Bleckmore had been sitting when he was struck on the head, with what was probably a large piece of ice. Mr. Tone customarily has a packet of these matches on his person, and so he was considerably alarmed when the police revealed to him that two burnt matches were found lying next to the chair in which Mr. Bleckmore had been sitting just sitting just before he died."

Cornelius turned to the group.

"What Mr. Tone did not know was that we concluded that these two matches were dropped near Mr. Bleckmore's chair by the same person who tried to incriminate Mrs. Endecott. You see, under microscopic examination, these two burnt paper matches were proven to be from the packet found on the table, but were torn out by a person holding the match in his left hand and the packet in his right. If you'll notice, the next time Mr. Tone lights a cigarette, he does just the reverse in the custom of a normal *right-handed* man."

"Mr. Tone was one of the first to conclude that the contradiction in the accounting of time just prior to Mr. Bleckmore's death was striking at the heart of this case and strongly urged me to pursue this line of reasoning."

Cornelius walked over to Kevin and placed his hand on Kevin's shoulder.

"Mr. Tone's grave concern about his own position in this matter was motivating him to be very critical of others, maybe. Like many of you here this morning, he had reason to want Mr. Bleckmore out of the way and realized that his feelings in this respect were not exactly obscure."

"Actually, sir, I don't believe you were ever a suspect in this case. If you were," Cornelius smiled, "then the fact, maybe, that you were not endowed with left-handed characteristics helped considerably."

Sybil's head had dropped. Tears were welling up in her eyes and she was attempting to stem the flow with the handkerchief she had clutched tightly in one hand. Kevin suddenly became aware of his wife's distress and snuggled up closer to her on the settee they were sharing. He put his arm around Sybil and looked up sharply at Cornelius who was staring abstractly at the ceiling.

"I hope your exoneration, Mr. Pire, was intended to include my wife."

Cornelius came to with a start. He immediately moved over to Sybil, leaned over and took her hand in his.

"A thousand pardons, Mrs. Tone. I momentarily lapsed into an autistic bit of grim unreality, maybe." Cornelius smiled kindly. "Two Tones exactly the same. Please forgive me."

Cornelius turned and walked aimlessly away. The room suddenly became a pantomime of eight silent people sitting and staring blankly at the floor and one white- haired hunched over man, his hands clasped tightly behind his back, staring at nothing out a window.

Suddenly, Ethel leaped to her feet, her ashen, distorted face making her almost unrecognizable.

"Oh no!" she shrieked "Oh, my God no!"

She was facing the door.

"No—no—please, my darling, it couldn't have been you."

She turned and started at Cornelius. One of her hands was covering her mouth. The other was clutching her stomach.

"Ethel, dear—Are you all right?"

"She's okay. Just leave her alone. Guess we're all upset. We still don't—"

A sharp, muffled explosion turned everyone's rapt attention towards the hallway door.

"What was that?"

"Sounded like a gun."

"Oh, please—No, no, no—"

"Ethel's hysterical. Someone help her."

"Mr. Pire, for God's sakes, what's going on here?"

"Yeah, damn it, you still haven't told us *who* killed Bleckmore."

Cornelius moved away from the group besieging him. Suddenly, he looked years older—a wizened, stoop-shouldered, sad old man. He put his hands up, palms out towards the group and spoke in a trembling voice.

"Be patient, please. Be patient. You'll learn soon enough I'm afraid."

The hallway door burst open and Box entered. He moved quickly to Cornelius and whispered in his ear. Box and Pire started for the door. Halfway, Cornelius stopped and turned slowly to the group.

"Excuse me, my friends. I must go upstairs. Lieutenant Box has just informed me that the man we think killed Mr. Bleckmore has turned a gun on himself. The Lieutenant tells me that Jeffrey Endecott, my dear friend Jeffrey, is dead."

Lieutenant Box took Cornelius by the arm and led him from the room. Cornelius was blinded by his own tears.

CHAPTER TWENTY-SIX

Wednesday Evening—June 10th

"What I don't understand, Mr. Pire, is two things."

The man questioning Cornelius was Kevin Tone. It was Wednesday evening, and a familiar group had gathered in the Tone home for dinner and conversation. Lena had flown off mysteriously to an unknown destination for some sun and rest. But Ethel Endecott was there. So were the Strabos and the Kennellys. And Cornelius. The funeral—Jeff's funeral—was to be Friday morning, and Cornelius had immediately decided to stay over.

Before leaving the Endecott home earlier in the day, Kevin had come up to Cornelius, compassionately put his arm around this sunken, dispirited man and invited him to stay at the Tone home until Cornelius wished to return home.

Cornelius had agreed. He must now delay his flight home. He was very grateful for Kevin's offer. And yes, this would be nice. Kevin had picked up Cornelius's luggage and had placed it, along with Cornelius, in his car. Meanwhile, Sybil had been asking the others whether or not a quiet dinner at the Tone home that evening would appeal.

The group's acceptance of Sybil's invitation was unanimous, except for Lena, who refused in deference to previously made plans.

Sybil had served a light dinner. A shrimp bisque, tiny tenderloin tip sandwiches and some light cool wine had more than satisfied the sparse appetites of the group now sitting on the Tone patio enjoying some after-dinner coffee in the cool pleasant summer evening breeze.

The color had once again returned to Cornelius's cheeks. His eyes were still without their customary twinkle, but his back was straight, and if his spirits were weary and downcast, he was doing an effective job of concealment. He was sipping cognac instead of coffee, and now, somewhat rejuvenated, he was facing his host. Kevin was repeating his question.

"What I am saying, Mr Pire, is—none of us understand what real motive Jeffrey had for killing Tony. Nor do we understand why Jeff sent for you—of all people—to come out here and unravel this mystery we've all been a part of. All of us would be interested in your comments, if you feel free to speak."

"Yes, of course. The mystery. I will give you opinions only, maybe, Mr. Tone."

Cornelius held up the goblet of cognac he had in his hand.

"Like this delectable brandy I am drinking, it is not a *fact* that it is delectable, but merely an *opinion*—my opinion, yes. That my friend's name is Jeffrey—this is a fact. What his thoughts were I can only give you my professional opinion. If this is satisfactory—"

Cornelius glanced around the room. All were nodding their heads.

"Let me then answer your second question first. Jeffrey Endecott was a very intelligent man. This *left-handed* gentleman—" Cornelius smiled sadly at Kevin—"he knew he had committed a technically perfect crime. He was, therefore, quite certain that the perpetrator would remain undiscovered and no one would be held legally accountable for his crime. He also knew that just as there would be no accountability, there would be no absolutions either. Without any absolutions, everyone at the scene of the crime might well remain tarnished forever in the public's eye. It was, of course, important to

Jeffrey to have his image as white as possible, particularly in light of his senatorial ambitions. And what better image insurance could he possibly secure than the investigatory services of—"Cornelius blushed—"if you'll excuse the expression, maybe—of a superb detective and a lifelong friend. Perhaps Jeffrey assumed that this old crony was, indeed, now ancient and feeble enough to be confused by a few misplaced clues such that he would turn the floodlights on someone other than himself. Who knows for certain? But I am saying to you tonight that bringing me here was a risk Jeffrey was willing to take. His strategy backfired on him, because he was naively unaware that the absence of perfection in the world applies to crimes also. There is no equation between an unsolved crime and a so-called perfect crime. If Jeffrey had understood in advance that the equation is, rather, between the competence of the investigator and the cunning of the criminal, he would be alive today."

"As to your first question, Mr. Tone—Motive? What motivates man to do anything? We do not fully understand the subtleties involved in this question in spite of our high-blown theories. We can only guess. Mrs. Bleckmore told me that her ex-husband was a highly possessive man who liked to dominate the lives of those about him. It is Dr. Strabo's opinion that Mr. Bleckmore's bulldogged nature was having a progressively domineering influence over Jeffrey's extra-curricular life, and that, as a result, Jeffrey was having an increasingly difficult time being his own person. This is one of the many things Dr. Strabo discussed on the record with me when I visited him at his home. Dr. Strabo was very quick to perceive in the relationship which existed between Mr. Bleckmore and Jeffrey a strong compelling motive for the murder. Dr. Strabo's reaction to this perception of evil in a very close friend was to reject what he saw and temporarily lose the full use of his finely tuned mind.

I am told that the lure of lovely ladies was the bond of mutual interest which kept the two men together. Mrs. Endecott has indicated that she thinks this bond remained strong only because Mr. Bleckmore was a man highly possessed. It seems logical to assume then that Jeffrey wanted to break this bond but was reluctant to try— possibly because he was fearful that his unpredictable and stubborn friend might, as a result, turn on Jeffrey and make malicious use of their past to embarrass him. When Jeffrey decided to seek the relatively saintly life of a United States Senator, this kind of fear might easily have become very compelling, especially if he had decided that all other options had vanished."

"Why do I think Jeffrey committed murder? As I already told you, I don't *know*. I can only surmise. This you can do better than I if you will sit back and look objectively at the two men you knew so well."

"Mr. Pire—" Sybil Tone paused long enough to make sure she had the floor. "We knew Jeffrey very well for many years. We can do what you say, and perhaps we will better understand what caused Jeffrey's mind to twist such that he would kill a fellow man and particularly a fellow man who had been his friend. But need I remind you, sir, that before we indulge in an odious mental exercise of this kind, it would be nice if you explained to us why you are reasonably certain that Jeffrey was guilty of anything other than his dreadful suicide."

"Yes, yes, of course, you are right. You need to know. I have been dallying too long, maybe."

Cornelius settled back in his cushioned patio chair and savored a sip or two more of his cognac.

"I will attempt to be brief and will start at the beginning of this sad ending. The question at such a beginning usually is—what is the obvious solution to the mystery? The obvious solution in this case was that Mrs. Endecott murdered Mr. Bleckmore. The reason was obvious, because the evidence seemed obvious. A strong motive. Fingerprints on a controversial cocktail glass. Mrs. Endecott's hairbrush with a suspicious looking dent on its surface, and her heel print in the sandy crevice between patio blocks under the chair the victim had been sitting in. All of these things were obvious and at first blush clearly indicated that our murderer was already identified."

"However, it wasn't long before we discovered that our obvious solution was not a solution at all, but rather a strong indication that someone else was the person we were looking for. The clues were false. The heel had been imprinted with hand pressure. And the brush and cocktail glass were entirely misleading as evidence."

"What were the alternatives? There were no alternatives. Just bits and pieces of conversations from a number of you people and tiny— very tiny—scraps of evidence."

Cornelius smiled.

"Evidence? The wrong word, maybe. What we had wasn't actually evidence at all. Just a couple of vague unrelated clues. An outdated life preserver tucked away in the laundry room. One Judson had never seen before. A hand-written note for Mr. Bleckmore asking him to return a phone call to a Mr. Rammutti. A snapshot of Mr. Bleckmore that looked strangely familiar. A pair of partially burnt paper matches you've already heard me mention. And—" Cornelius glanced at Collin Strabo and smiled sadly—"a vial of deadly poison, well-known commercially as a surgical disinfectant, belonging to a man who was behaving quite abnormally."

"These, my friends, were our clues. And then—there were the little bits and pieces—all unrelated. A written invitation to an Endecott party. Apparently unprecedented. And—as Mrs. Strabo would wonder aloud—'Six weeks ahead of time?' Not abnormal, but, according to some of you, a little out of style for Jeffrey. Liquor and setups on a table near a ship's bell. Someone told me, I believe it was Judson, that Jeffrey usually had his liquor served from a rolling chrome-and-glass bar table which was missing Saturday."

"No, there seemed to be no hard evidence, and the bits and pieces we found were certainly not going anywhere. By Sunday evening, I had decided that the techniques applied to this crime had been carefully worked out in advance—that we were, maybe, confronted with a technically perfect crime. So Monday, the gears were shifted."

"Motives. Who might have wanted to kill Mr. Bleckmore? As a starter we had: Ethel Endecott, Lena Bleckmore, Kevin Tone, Sam Kennelly, and Collin Strabo. All of these people had a strong dislike of Mr. Bleckmore. But it didn't appear that their dislikes were compelling enough to precipitate murder."

"Then, the first real clue. Include the female spouses with these names, and the aforementioned list included *all* of the guests. Was this coincidental that all of the guests had deliberately been brought together, with written invitations sent out six weeks ahead of time, because all on this list had a strong dislike for Mr. Bleckmore? An interesting question. It became particularly interesting to me, after I heard Mrs. Bleckmore say that her ex-husband had been called out to the Endecott home a day early by Jeffrey. Was this possibly to make absolutely certain that Mr. Bleckmore would be there for the weekend?"

"And then I recalled the telephone call Mr. Bleckmore had received Saturday noon. Judson had answered the phone and had given the written message to Jeffrey, as Mr. Bleckmore had not yet risen. Had Mr. Bleckmore returned the phone call? A subsequent check revealed he had not. The call was one Mr. Bleckmore would have considered quite important. Thus, if Jeffrey had failed to give the message to Mr. Bleckmore, was there a reason? Was the reason, perhaps, because Jeffrey was concerned that Mr. Bleckmore might be called away? No motives yet, my friends, but by Monday morning, the gray cells had us pointed in an unusual direction."

"But then—I protested my thoughts and roared at myself. No—no—no—this is crazy! This cannot be! I am looking at the wrong man."

"A long treasured friendship, you see, had managed for the first time to affect Pire's cells."

"For a while, our main interest in this case centered around the after-dinner activities Mr. Tone was so preoccupied with. Mr. Kennelly put the recreation room diversiosn as taking place between the hours of eight-fifty and nine-twenty. Other guests agreed, with varying degrees of certainty, that you were in and out of Jeffrey's recreation room for approximately twenty minutes. This placed Mr. Bleckmore passing through this room at about nine-ten. The coroner's report places his time of death at no later than nine-fifteen. The mystery, which became an obsessive one with me, was how could Mr. Bleckmore end up where he did in such a brief period of time? When seen in the recreation room, he was apparently headed for the nearby rest room. Any leisurely walk back to the pool, by whatever route, takes at least five minutes according to Jake Reston. The timing of Mr. Bleckmore's mysterious movements during this critical period seemed to me to be somewhat unreal. It didn't feel right, but the complete answer was still hiding from me."

"Until, that is—Until a phone call interrupted a conversation I was having with Lieutenant Box in his office Monday morning. I retired to his outer office in order to afford him some privacy, and occupied my thoughts by staring at my notes and at a snapshot Lieutenant Box had given me of Mr. Bleckmore. Something about that picture had been bothering me ever since the Lieutenant had given it to me the day before. There was an odd familiarity about it, which I couldn't put my finger on. Then, suddenly, I was shocked by what this familiarity might be. I laid the picture on a table in the sunlight, picked up a pack of matches from the table and carefully placed a single match stick on Mr. Bleckmore's face in such a manner as to blank out most of his mustache. And there, staring up at me was Jeffrey Endecott. It was faint, mind you—only a vague likeness—but, Lord above, though I didn't want to, I could see my friend. I pulled the picture out of the sunlight and into the shadow of the room, and the likeness slightly increased. The repulsive idea I had been previously nursing had suddenly come to life. Jeffrey, maybe, was at the root of what we were looking for."

"But why Jeffrey? Incredible! I would go no further with this thing, unless I could find a motive which would explain why Jeffrey would be involved in such a dreadful business. I sincerely hoped I would fail. But finding the motive, when one knew where to look and what questions to ask, proved relatively easy."

"Dr. Strabo was the first to supply the answer by describing the uncompromising position Jeffrey had worked his way into with a man whose company he both enjoyed but, at the same time, absolutely needed to break away from in order to start a new life style—hopefully as a United States Senator."

Cornelius turned to Sam Kennelly.

"I am guessing, but during my very brief conversation with you, sir, there was an overtone of concern in your eyes that told me that you had, maybe, suspicions running along the same line."

The barest hint of a smile from Sam.

"You're right, Pire, I knew for sure who did it, but I had the wrong man. Good thing I'm not one of you cops, I guess."

Cornelius's eyes sparkled as he replied. "Ah, yes, you were wrong, but then so was I about you, Mr. Kennelly. A rare boner for each of us, I'm sure."

He shifted his attention to Kevin.

"I believe your words to me, Mr. Tone, were something to the effect that Tony Bleckmore was not about to let Jeffrey Endecott go?"

"If you say I said it, then I'm sure I did. Looking back, yes, I think this was true. Say, before I forget to ask, whatever happened to Tony's sister? Did she show Wednesday morning?"

"Ah yes, Mrs. Rossetti. You want me to finish my story. I am driving the car too slow, maybe."

"By Monday night, Pire knew, not only who killed Mr. Bleckmore, but also how it was done. Mind you, I only had scraps of proof—nothing that would hold up in a court of law—but I was as certain of my conclusions as a prosecutor would be standing in front of a jury with an incriminating weapon in his hands."

"Monday night, I did what no man of my years should ever do and particularly not this old-timer. I went with my dear friend, whose veneer I was cracking, and drowned my sorrow with too much gin. Incidentally, a few of you might be interested in knowing that, as a precautionary measure, I preceded this lamentable Monday night toot with an afternoon visit with a Mr. Romanareo, whose first name may, for some of you, have a familiar ring to it. He calls himself Alfie. I will not comment on this visit except to say that I came away convinced that this gentleman was not in any way involved in Mr. Bleckmore's death."

"After visiting with Mr. Romanareo, I dropped by and told my story to Lieutenant Box. We were both unsure where to proceed next. I told him of the pending dinner engagement with Jeffrey, and you, Mrs. Endecott, and revealed to him my plan to set out the bait. Unless Jeffrey took the bait, I told the Lieutenant, I would be unwilling to proceed further and would return home. I needed to be that sure."

"Lieutenant Box agreed to help me, and accordingly, we fabricated the story concerning Mr. Bleckmore's sister and her anonymous phone call. We were fairly confident that Jeffrey did not suspect our hoax, as I had previously led him to believe that my suspicions were centered on Mrs. Bleckmore or you, Mrs. Endecott."

"At three-forty-five Wednesday morning, the Lieutenant and I observed, using a device carefully positioned between an adjoining pair of hot air registers, Jeffrey enter Mr. Bleckmore's room. He spent approximately seven minutes exhaustively searching through every nook and cranny in that room. Five hours later, I walked into his study and told him, step by step, how I *think* he planned and killed his good friend, Tony Bleckmore."

Cornelius's voice dropped to a whisper. He was struggling to hold onto his emotions.

"Jeffrey looked at me without wavering. He never took his eyes off me for a moment. He asked me not a single question. He never moved as he sat behind that enormous desk of his."

"He had invited me to sit down, but I chose to remain standing. When I finished talking, I waited for his reply. It was almost immediately obvious that I would hear nothing from Jeffrey. So, I turned around and moved away. At the door, I faced him again and told him that his friends were downstairs waiting for me, and that I intended to tell them they were all considered innocent in the Bleckmore affair. I added that I would leave it up to their own imagination as to who the guilty party was. I told him that I did not intend to bring up the name of Jeffrey Endecott in this regard. Jeffrey's eyes were still locked on mine as I swung around and left the room, closing the door behind me. Ah yes—forever, maybe."

The night air had become somewhat chilly. The group on Tone's patio had moved inside. Cornelius asked permission to retire to his room. He was very tired, he said, and probably would sleep until noon—that is, if his host didn't mind. The group thanked him profusely for his patient explanations and wished him good night. Cornelius shuffled to the front hall with Kevin at his side. Cornelius paused at the first step of the stairway and turned to Kevin.

"I never told your friends what really happened, did I. I am curious why they didn't ask. I suppose they assumed that this old man has been through enough for one day. Well, it's true. I have. But if I don't finish the story today, someone will surely ask me tomorrow. And tomorrow—well, tomorrow, I'd like to forget about today."

"Tell them, if they ask that Jeffrey, in all probability, used a piece of ice on Mr. Bleckmore's head, shortly after the last guests left the pool area Saturday evening, and then let the wedding present I had given to him years before help with the rest. Tell them also, that it wasn't Mr. Bleckmore, but Jeffrey Endecott, maybe, who walked through the deliberately darkened recreation room, after most of the guests had been diverted by more spirits from Jeffrey's cellar. Jeffrey was probably wearing an old fashioned racing type life preserver in order to simulate Mr. Bleckmore's bulk. Tell your friends that he was also wearing a green and white checked dress jacket identical to the one frequently worn, and worn that night, by Mr. Bleckmore. Tell them, please, that in the shadows of the room, Jeffrey and Mr. Bleckmore would look very much alike—especially if Jeffrey had happened to paste on a Bleckmore style mustache."

"It might have happened some other way, Mr. Tone. But I don't think it did—not at all. And apparently, my good friend, Jeffrey, finally concluded the same thing."

Kevin put out his hand.

"Goodnight, Mr. Pire. And thank you."

"Goodnight, Mr. Tone."

The two men shook hands and parted. Kevin returned to the group in the adjoining room. Cornelius started upstairs, then stopped, turned around and descended. He opened the front door and quietly slipped outside. It was cool. No, to Cornelius, it was cold. But never mind. He turned up his collar, stuck his hands in his pockets and trudged down the Tone's front walk until he came to the sidewalk. Then, he turned and walked down the sidewalk through the dark, deep shadows of a seemingly endless row of giant oaks.

The sidewalk finally found a small park, and the little white-haired man found a bench. Cornelius sat down, leaned back and rested.

Who knows what thoughts passed through his mind as the moments slowly became minutes and the minutes—Well, it didn't matter how long. If he had thought an anxious friend was nearby at the moment, he'd have probably looked up, smiled and said, "Tired? Oh yes, I'm tired—but I've got plenty of time to rest, thank you."

The End

Printed in the United States
33856LVS00005B/124-156

9 781413 767629